# The year is 1937

Dust Bowl refugees toil for twenty cents an hour. Soup lines stretch for blocks. Hoboes ride the rails from coast to coast. But the nation is battling the specter of Depression.

Roosevelt's New Deal has employed millions, who are building highways, planting forests and decorating city halls. Ordinary citizens are tightening their belts, sharing what little they have and keeping their spirits high.

Americans are forgetting their troubles watching curly-top Shirley Temple, fast-paced screwball comedies and elegant Fred Astaire and Ginger Rogers. They're crooning along with Bing Crosby and tuning in to the president's fireside chats. And they're falling in love to the genius of Benny Goodman.

It is a time of hardship, a test of the country's fortitude and resolve.

It is a time of heroes, of visionary leadership and countless acts of generosity and courage.

It is the time of Angela Hogan and Jack Clancy.

Dear Reader,

We hope you are enjoying A Century of American Romance, a nostalgic look at the lives and loves of American men and women from the turn of the century to the dawn of the year 2000. These stories give us all a chance to relive the memories of a time gone by and sneak a peek at romance in an exciting future.

We've traveled from the 1899 immigrant experience to 1906 San Francisco's tumultuous quake to the muddy trenches of France's Western Front in World War I to the carefree, decadent Roaring Twenties. Now Anne Stuart takes us to the thirties—an era of lost fortune, indomitable spirit and record-setting aviation.

In the months ahead, watch for all the titles—one each month—in A Century of American Romance, including two upcoming books by Barbara Bretton.

We hope you continue to enjoy these special stories of nostalgia and romance, written by some of your favorite novelists. As always, we welcome your comments. Please take the time to write to us.

Here's hoping that A Century of American Romance will become part of your most cherished memories....

Sincerely,

Debra Matteucci
Senior Editor and Editorial Coordinator

# ANNE
# STUART

## 1930s
## ANGELS
## WINGS

# *Harlequin Books*

TORONTO • NEW YORK • LONDON
AMSTERDAM • PARIS • SYDNEY • HAMBURG
STOCKHOLM • ATHENS • TOKYO • MILAN

To Stuart Todd (1971-1990),
beloved nephew,
who's flying with the angels now

Published October 1990

ISBN 0-373-16361-4

# Chapter One

Angela Hogan tipped back in her squeaky office chair, propped her open-toed spectator pumps on the littered desk and surveyed her options. She lit a cigarette, taking in a deep drag, and stared out past the open door to the cavernous airplane hangar beyond. Hogan's Air Freight Service looked efficient, prosperous, the planes shiny, well cared for as they waited their turn to soar out into the bright Illinois sky just outside of Chicago.

And that was the problem, Angela thought. They shouldn't be sitting idle on such a wonderful day. They should be out earning her a dubious living. It was Saturday, a perfect late-spring day in 1937, a day made for flying lessons if nothing else. Only Sparks had been out that day, testing the small Lockheed Vega, checking its paces, and he'd taken no paying customer with him. She didn't know where he was now, but it didn't matter. There were no cash customers on such a perfect flying day.

Her other pilot, Robert Bellamy, was probably sleeping off a hangover. And she was all gussied up to do what she hated most. To charm money from what was left of her mother's family, just enough to keep things in the black for another month.

If she had her choice, she'd be wearing trousers and a tailored shirt instead of her sister Constance's version of a

Vionnet day dress. She'd be wearing lace-up brogues instead of these idiotic shoes. Her chestnut hair would be tied back from her angular face, instead of sweeping around it in a seductive pageboy. She'd look like what she was, a pilot, a girl who cared about nothing but flying, her business and her beautiful half sister, not necessarily in that order. Instead she looked like what she was born, a young woman from the heart of Chicago society, the product of a misalliance between one of 1909's top debutantes and her Irish chauffeur.

Angela's grandmother, the indomitable Harriette Lindsey Maynard, was powerful enough that young Julia's fall from grace was quickly glossed over, particularly since it was preceded by a hasty marriage and followed by Frank Hogan discovering airplanes and becoming scarce indeed. Divorce was out of the question for a Maynard, but frail Julia died young, leaving Frank free to follow his passion for flying, not to mention his passion for a certain blond waitress in Evanston. It didn't leave him free to take his young daughter with him, but by the time Angela was eighteen, her overwhelming grandmother had died, the crash had taken the bulk of the Maynard family fortune and everyone was too concerned with their own financial disaster to spare a thought for one young lady.

She'd had two splendid years away from designer dresses and white gloves and pearls. Away from debutante parties and speakeasies and pressure to make a good marriage. She spent those two years living in a rooming house in east Evanston with her father for the first time, learning to fly.

It hadn't taken her long to realize that was what she'd been born to do. From the moment she'd sat in the cockpit of her father's spiffy little Avro Avian, she felt as if she'd come home. She'd earned her pilot's license in record time, chafing at every delay, and from then on she'd spent every available moment in the sky.

When she wasn't obsessed with flying, she'd been devoted to her little half sister, Connie, and even managed to enjoy her stepmother Goldie's company. She'd been too absorbed in her own life to realize exactly what Frank was doing during his flights to Canada and back. Exactly what he was carrying and what he was skimming off the top.

His employers, however, had no such problem. They knew Frank was selling a goodly portion of the Canadian whiskey they brought in to a few customers of his own, and they had no qualms about making their displeasure known. Al Capone wasn't famed for his forbearance, and when Angela had just turned twenty-one years old, the rooming house exploded in a ball of fire, killing Frank and Goldie and old Mrs. McCarthy, their landlady.

Angela had been flying at the time; Connie had been in school. In the morning they'd been a happy, if somewhat motley family. By the afternoon they were two orphans with no home, no money, nothing but an old airplane hangar on a private airfield, two slightly battered planes and the uncertain fear that gangland recrimination might not end there.

Angela's tears had dried the moment she understood the situation. The police made it very clear—Frank Hogan's feckless ways had gotten them into this mess, endangering his children, killing his wife and another innocent woman. Therefore he wasn't worth mourning. What mattered now was for Angela to make some sort of life for herself and her teenage sister.

She'd managed to section off a part of the cavernous hangar and to beg and borrow enough furniture to provide a makeshift home for Connie while she waited to see whether mob honor had been satisfied or if one morning the entire airplane hangar was going to explode.

Her small, postcrash inheritance lasted them exactly fourteen months, long enough for Connie, now calling herself Constance, to graduate from high school, long enough for Angela to win a few air races, earn a little bit of money giving lessons, carrying freight.

But Angela couldn't earn enough, not at first. People were reluctant to hire a woman, a young one at that. They were frightened enough of airplanes, not to mention the utter panic of entrusting their lives to a female not much past twenty-one. So Angela had made her first trip back into Chicago, to her Great-uncle Richard, who'd always had a fondness for her.

His gift had enabled her to become the first woman to fly nonstop from Chicago to Denver, not to mention pay their overdue bills and keep Constance in nail polish. The newspaper coverage, calling Angela the newest darling of the air, brought in more business, enough to keep them going awhile longer.

It had gone on like that, Angela thought, for far too long, each time finding another relative with an interest in air travel and a not completely decimated income. She'd hoped she'd been past all that. For a while it seemed as if a happy ending was hers when Hal Ramsey had flown into her life.

He'd been everything she'd ever wanted. One of the world's great pilots, he'd made her puny little records seem laughable. He'd forgotten more about flying than she would ever know, and he'd taken Hogan Air Freight in hand and brought in more business than they could handle. They'd bought two more planes, hired Thomas Crowley, better known as Sparks, as a third pilot, and become practically solvent. And Hal, dear man, had loved her, wanted to marry her and never pushed her further than she was ready to go.

She wished he had pushed her. Maybe now she'd have something to show for those years besides a mountain of debts, a mechanic who didn't know a twin-engine from a biplane, one pilot whose eyesight wasn't all that it should be and another who was an out and out drunk and a thief.

But she kept postponing things, and two weeks before the wedding Hal had died trying to break the record flight from Newfoundland to Havana, Cuba. And breaking her heart at the same time.

So she was back to begging money from her family. She had enough to make ends meet, particularly since she was about to fire both Bellamy and the half-baked mechanic he'd recommended. Constance had taken a job at the local Woolworths, though all her money seemed to be eaten up by the local movie house and her inexhaustible lust for cosmetics, but even with the planes idle far too much of the time, the money still managed to stretch far enough, at least for now.

Not, however, to pay the expenses of a record-breaking flight from Newfoundland to Havana. And that was exactly what Angela intended to do.

She knew just how to approach her Cousin Clement. He was a decent businessman—he had to be, in the dark days of the Depression, in order to keep any of his money. He was looking ahead toward the darkening clouds of warfare that hung over Europe and thinking of the future. And he knew as well as she did that the future of warfare, and the world, was in the air.

The one drawback was that Clement considered her merely ornamental. If she'd been a boy, all the money left to the far-flung Maynard family would have been at her command. As a female, she had to work doubly hard to prove her abilities. Thank heavens for her idol and inspiration, Amelia Earhart. The more publicity Amelia, or AE as she preferred to be known, got, the better Angela's own position was. And with AE's upcoming round-the-world flight, Clement would want to get on the bandwagon in some way or other. Angela had every intention of helping him do just that.

If only Sparks wasn't lying to her about his eyesight. If only she had another pilot she could count on. If only she wasn't fighting tooth and nail for every single contract with her biggest competitor, Transamerica Freight. Not that Charlie Olker had ever actually flown across America. That beer-bellied old creep had probably forgotten how to fly, probably forgotten everything but how to steal business from her. He used his past as a pilot in the Great War to good advantage. Everyone loved a hero, and even some of those who knew she was a better pilot still wanted to help out a veteran, even if it meant paying Olker's inflated prices and risking his badly-maintained planes.

He hadn't had a crash yet, but that time would come, and Angela didn't know whether she'd be glad or sorry. No pilot ever wished a crash on another one, but Olker's sheer, blind luck drove her crazy.

Damn, she didn't want to face Clement. She wanted to yank off the silver charm bracelet her mother had left her, dump her high heels on the cement floor and go flying. She wanted to be free, soaring high above life and its petty problems. She didn't want to have to charm and weasel money out of someone, and she most definitely didn't want to have to do what she was about to do.

She heard the slight shuffle of Bellamy's footsteps and mentally braced herself, taking a final drag off her Lucky Strike and leaning forward to stub it out in the pink ashtray Constance had given her for her birthday.

"Got another one of those?" Robert Bellamy lounged in the doorway, his self-assured smile fixed on his handsome face.

"No," she said, meeting his gaze with a stern one of her own. In the two years he'd worked for her, Bellamy still hadn't realized that she was immune to his somewhat shopworn charm. He was a very handsome man, she had to grant him that, and not much older than she was. Someone had once made the great mistake of telling him he looked like Robert Taylor, and he made a determined effort to present his pretty profile whenever the opportunity arose. His fondness for liquor had started during Prohibition, but unlike most of the heavy drinkers of that era, legalizing it only made it easier, not less enticing. The signs of debauchery hadn't set in, apart from a faint puffiness around his eyes, but he didn't have long to wait.

"What'd you want to see me about, boss?" he asked, his ingratiating smile never wavering.

She wished she had another cigarette, but she didn't dare light one, afraid he'd notice that her hands were trembling. Up in the air she was completely fearless—down here she was feeling cowed and miserable.

Not that she'd ever show it. "Robert," she said, clearly and distinctly. "You're fired."

He blinked, then straightened. "What did you say?"

"You heard me. You're fired. You and that so-called mechanic you brought along. Effective immediately. Get your flight bag and get out."

Robert Bellamy could look very ugly indeed. For a moment his expression soured, and then he pulled himself together with all the aplomb of a practiced liar. "You want to tell me why?"

"Gladly." She gave in and lit another cigarette, figuring he was probably so hung over he wouldn't notice her hands trembling. "You're drunk half the time. You fly drunk, you don't maintain basic safety standards and you and Martin have been skimming money from some of the accounts. Martin has been reselling my fuel and pocketing the money. You've been helping him do it. I can't prove it, so I can't call the police as I'd love to do. But I'll take my chances if you don't get out of my sight within the next hour."

"Think you're pretty smart, don't you?" he snarled. "This is a sucker's proposition, lady. You're on a crash course with failure, and nothing Martin or I did will make any difference. It'll just come a little faster this way.''

''I'm not going to fail,'' she said calmly. ''Why don't you see if Charlie Olker will give you a job? You two seem to be his kind of employees.''

Robert Bellamy grinned then, an ugly expression. ''Doll,'' he said, ''who do you think sent us here in the first place?''

CLEMENT WAS JUST AS GLAD to have her call and cancel, Angela thought wearily, alone in the darkened office. He knew as well as she did what she wanted from him, and Clement hadn't remained a wealthy man in a time when one-third of the nation was on the dole without being particularly loath to part with his money. There was a note of triumph in his voice when he told her he was heading out to California and wouldn't be back for a month.

All right, she'd thought. She could live with that. She hadn't survived as long as she had by negative thinking. She'd go ahead with her plans, assuming she'd be able to talk her tight-fisted cousin out of the money. As long as his wife didn't hear about it, she was pretty sure she could.

The radio was on in the background. Some in-house orchestra was playing Gershwin, something upbeat and jazzy. Constance probably hadn't returned home yet—she usually went out to the double feature on Saturday night, and there was a new Joan Crawford movie out. Angela never could understand Constance's fondness for Joan Crawford and noble suffering, but she'd accepted it. Katharine Hepburn was more her style, though heaven knows it seemed like years since she'd been to a movie.

She hadn't dared leave the hangar until she was certain Bellamy and his pal had left. She'd been so tense, so angry since her confrontation that she'd done nothing but sit in her chair and smoke, crumpling up the empty pack and starting in on another. Her throat was raw, her eyes stung and her nerves were shredded. And much as she needed it, she was in no mood for night flying.

What she needed to do was get out of these stupid clothes and find Sparks. Tell him what had happened, ask his opinion. Sparks was someone you could count on for a shoulder to cry on, for good advice, for a slap on the back or a hug when you needed it. Though chances are he'd want to go after Bellamy. He'd never liked the other pilot, had even warned her against him, but at the time she thought she'd had no choice in the matter.

He probably knew what she'd had to do. And he would never say I told you so, God bless him. If she knew him as well as she thought she did, and after five years she figured that she did, he'd be over at Tony's Bar and Grille, the best Italian restaurant and pilot's bar in the entire universe. She'd find him, weep into her beer a little bit and let him cheer her up. And between the two of them they'd figure out what their next step was.

"You there, Angela?" Sparks's rough Irish voice echoed through the hangar.

"In here," she called, switching on the goosenecked desk lamp and pushing her hair out of her eyes. If it wasn't such an effective tool for charming money out of her cousins, she'd hack it all off. She had a hard enough time fitting it under a leather flight helmet, and even tying it back wasn't good enough.

Sparks loomed up in the darkness, his rough face creased in a smile, his blue eyes sparkling beneath his bushy eyebrows. "Rough day, honey?"

"You bet. I fired those two bums."

"It's about time."

"They were on the take from Olker."

"I know."

"You knew?" she shrieked, finding a piece of string on the floor and wrapping it around her thick hair. "Why didn't you tell me?"

"Would you have believed me?"

"I always believe you, Sparks," she said.

"Then why didn't you listen when I told you not to hire that trash?"

"Just because I believe you doesn't mean I listen to you," she said ruefully.

He shook his head, used to her by now. "Got any more of that coffee?"

Angela glanced over toward the aluminum pot still simmering on the beat-up hot plate. "Have you ever known me not to?" she countered, pulling herself out of the chair and stretching her cramped body. "I'll pour you a cup."

"Make it two. There's someone I want you to meet."

She stopped in the act of reaching for the chipped ceramic mugs. "Who?"

"A new pilot. You know as well as I do we can't keep this business going with just the two of us. You have to spend too much time drumming up business and dealing with the paper work as it is, and there's a limit to how much flying I can safely do. Let's face it, we need another man."

"We need another pilot," she corrected. "The question is, how are we going to pay for it?"

"I've got that all worked out. He's got a plane of his own, in the shop somewhere down in South America. He'll work for expenses and a percentage, and as soon as he can get his plane up here, he'll work part-time for storage. You can't say no to an offer like that."

"How good is he?" She had the unpleasant feeling Sparks wasn't telling her everything. She'd always trusted him, implicitly, but this time he was holding something back.

"The best there is," Sparks said simply.

She set the cup back down and turned to face him. "You'd be the one to know," she said. "Where is this paragon right now?"

"Doing what you'd be doing. What any decent pilot would be doing. He's checking over the planes."

It took all Angela's self-control not to protest. Clearly Sparks was both proud and nervous, like a mother hen with a prized baby chick, and for his sake, and the sake of common sense, she didn't say a word. He was right—any decent pilot would be checking out the equipment before committing himself to a job. If the maintenance was sloppy, the hangar a mess, it would translate into a safety factor sooner than anyone cared to think about it.

Despite Martin's shoddy work, she knew she had a setup worth being proud of. She stifled her instinctive resentment at the thought of some hotshot pilot passing judgment. Sparks was right—she needed help, particularly if she were going to follow through with her dream of making the Newfoundland to Havana run.

But she was damned if she was going to be coerced into hiring someone who thought he was God's gift to airplanes. And she wasn't going to be impressed by anyone, anyone at all, unless it was her decision.

"The setup's okay." The voice was grudging from the man who appeared in the office door without warning. He filled the space, and one look told her she didn't like him.

"Glad you approve," she said wryly, giving him her coolest once-over, looking for faults.

There were more than she cared to count. For one thing, he was too tall to fit in the crowded cockpits of most airplanes. For another, he was too handsome—she never did trust a handsome man, and Bellamy had just proven her prejudices justified. Not that the man standing there was a pretty boy. He was a little too rugged looking, a little too tough to make it in Hollywood these days. His hair was almost black, slicked back from a widow's peak over strong brows and a pair of wicked dark eyes. His mouth was full and sensual, his jaw firm, the cleft in his chin almost ridiculously masculine. And damn him, he was looking her up and down with the same cool appraisal that she was giving him.

"I didn't say there wasn't room for improvement," he added, not moving from his spot in the doorway. He was dressed in khaki pants and an old leather flight jacket, as if he didn't give a damn about modern sartorial requirements. He glanced toward the anxious Sparks. "This the boss lady?"

Before Sparks could speak, she stepped forward briskly and held out her hand, firm and businesslike. "I'm the boss lady. Angela Hogan, to be exact. If I decide to hire you, you'd be taking orders from me."

He stared at her outstretched hand for a moment, then lifted his eyes to her face. "If I decide to take the job," he drawled, "I'd take orders from nobody."

"Children, children," Sparks admonished, stepping between them. "That's no way to start out a working relationship. Listen, Angela, you need Jack. You need his skills as a pilot, you need his ability to bring in business. And Jack, you need Angela. You need a steady job, you need planes to fly and you need a space to keep your plane while you work on her. It's a match made in heaven."

"I'm not too sure of that," Angela muttered. On top of everything else, Sparks's Jack looked annoyingly familiar. She'd seen that face before, that arrogant, too-handsome face, and it wasn't on a movie screen. There was something about him she didn't like.

"No, Sparks is right," the man said. "We could help each other out. It's up to you, lady. I'm better than you could hope to get in the normal run of things. You want me or not?"

*Oh, no, Jack whoever you are,* she said to herself. *I don't want you at all.* "Yes," she said, to her own amazement. "On a trial basis."

"Sounds good to me. I'll let you know if I don't think it'll work out," he said carelessly. "When do I start?"

She stifled her irritation at his high-handedness. Her instincts, usually reliable, were telling her to put him to work. For now. "Monday," she said. "We don't have anything set for tomorrow."

"It's supposed to be a beautiful day. No lessons lined up?"

She glared at him. "No lessons lined up," she agreed through her teeth.

"I'll see what I can do about that. Come on, Sparks. Let's go find something to drink. It's too late for coffee." He started out the door without even a farewell.

"One moment," Angela said in her sternest voice, half expecting him to ignore her.

He didn't, however, turning back to stare at her out of those bold dark eyes. "Yeah?"

"Have you got any other name besides Jack? I like to keep good records."

His mouth curved in a self-mocking grin. "Clancy," he said. "You just hired yourself Jack Clancy." And without another word he was gone.

# Chapter Two

The bungalow was dark and quiet when Angela let herself in that night. She'd been lucky to find the small house within a ten-minute drive from the hangar. Even if the aging Packard she inherited from her grandmother decided to give up the ghost, she could always walk, and shank's mare definitely had its advantages during these warm spring days. Once she got to work, she was either trapped inside her windowless office or tucked inside the comfortable little cockpit of her favorite Lockheed Vega, neither spot terribly good for stretching her legs.

"Constance?" she called as she unlocked the flimsy front door and stepped inside. No answer, but then she hadn't expected one. On a Saturday night her gorgeous younger sister wouldn't be home by nine-thirty. If she wasn't at the movies, she'd be out with any of the scores of handsome young men who swarmed after her like bees around honey. Constance had learned early how to play them against each other, keeping everyone happy and enjoying herself tremendously.

Moving through the shabby, one-story house, she reached behind her for the row of tiny, cloth-covered buttons that ran down her back. Constance's one practical gift was a talent for dressmaking, and she insisted on getting the details right. The Vionnet day dress would have been a lot easier to manage if she'd just put a zipper under the arm, like most of Angela's ready-to-wear dresses had. But no, she had to cover seventeen buttons with silk, and Angela had to risk dislocating her arm to get herself out of the silly dress.

She dumped it on Constance's unmade bed, sank down on her own neatly made cot and began to peel off her stockings. No runs, thank heavens. Silk stockings cost a fortune, and this particular pair hadn't earned its keep yet. All they'd merited was an overlong look from Jack Clancy's dark eyes.

Jack Clancy, she thought, standing up and shimmying out of the girdle she certainly didn't need. Of all the men to turn up at her penny-ante operation, why did it have to be him! He made Hal Ramsey's solid reputation fade into obscurity. Clancy was the first man to fly nonstop from Hawaii to Oakland, the first man to fly from Capetown to England, holder of more records than Angela could even begin to remember. He was absolutely fearless, a man to reckon with, the sort of pilot Angela had always instinctively avoided. The kind of man whose face turned up in the gossip section of the paper as often as the news section. Along with his taste for record-making flights, he'd had a definite affinity for beautiful women and high living, and the newspapers had always found him a fascinating counterpart to Charles Lindbergh's straight-arrow reputation. If only Lucky Lindy had shown up at her hangar that night, she thought, smiling at the absurd thought. Though having Jack Clancy appear out of the night was almost as unbelievable.

She didn't need daredevils in her business; she didn't need flying aces, barnstormers, war heroes. She needed someone who knew how to get a heavily loaded plane from point A to point B in a minimum of time with the minimum of fuss, someone who could teach a clumsy novice how to handle the intricacies of single-engine Vega, someone who could do his job and keep his nose clean.

Jack Clancy was a born troublemaker. He hadn't been around for the last few years, and Angela had almost forgotten his existence. Sparks said his plane was somewhere down in South America; maybe he'd been involved in the dangerous flying down in the Andes. Pilots were heading to all corners of the globe, constantly looking for new challenges, ignoring the more basic challenge of setting up reliable air transport here at home.

If Clancy was looking for adventure, she'd have to make very certain he didn't find it here in Evanston. She'd use him—she'd be a fool to turn down a pilot of his undeniable gifts because she didn't like his reputation. That reputation had never hinted at carelessness in the air, or there would have been no question. But he only took the informed, intelligent chances any pilot had to take. He just showed more reckless daring getting himself out of the messes anyone could get into.

The sooner he tired of her business and went looking for his own kind of trouble, the sooner she would be able to hire someone safe and dependable, someone like Sparks. And then maybe her topsy-turvy world would begin to right itself.

Angela unhooked her bra and dropped it onto the bed, pulling a plain white nightgown over her head and staring down at her own narrow cot. The one bedroom in the tiny bungalow didn't hold two full-size beds, and while she'd shared the double bed for years with Constance, she'd finally decided she needed to sleep through the night without getting kicked. Naturally Constance kept the double bed, Angela making do on a cot made for someone five inches shorter than Angela's angular five feet eight inches.

It had been a rotten, miserable day and a rotten, miserable night. Tomorrow things could only get better. What was the heroine of that wonderful book about the Civil War always saying? "I'll think about that tomorrow." Maybe she should reread *Gone With the Wind* and learn how Scarlett O'Hara managed to avoid facing her problems. For one short night, Angela wished she could learn that trick.

But she was no Scarlett, able to concentrate on herself. She was going to worry about Charlie Olker, worry about getting money out of Cousin Clement, worry about Jack Clancy. And if the latter invaded her dreams, they were going to be nightmares.

"SO WHAT DO YOU THINK?" Sparks demanded, draining half his beer with a hearty gulp.

Clancy took his time with his own mug, letting the noise and the sound of Tony's Bar and Grille wash over him. "About what?"

"About the king of England abdicating," Sparks said cynically. "Don't treat me like a sap. What do you think about the job? About Angela?"

Clancy shrugged. He'd known Sparks for close to fifteen years, knew him well enough to recognize that the big lug had a crush the size of the Hindenburg on his precious Angela. "Seems okay," he said. "It'll do for the time being. I'd work for Il Duce if it meant I'd get my plane up here sooner."

"What the hell does Angela have to do with Mussolini? She's a classy dame, Clancy, even if you're too blind to see it."

"Not my type, Sparks. I like 'em small and busty, with bleached blond hair and not too much intellect. And curves. I like curves." He took another sip. "You can keep your Angela Hogan."

"Not mine, Clancy." Sparks blew the remaining foam from the dregs of his beer. "Not mine."

"Look, I'm easy to please," Clancy said, changing the subject. In all the years he'd known Sparks, they'd never once talked about anything more personal than airplanes, though to Clancy's mind you couldn't get much more personal than that. He didn't want to start filling in for Dorothy Dix's advice to the lovelorn. "The setup's neat, clean. The planes seem in decent enough shape despite that jerk Miss Hogan had working for her. There's plenty of room for my little baby when she gets shipped up here. This place is fine, too. The room upstairs has its own outside entrance, its own bathroom, and the bed's big enough to share if I get in the mood. And the beer's cold, the food's hot, and they carry my brand of Scotch. What more could a man ask?"

Sparks grinned. "I thought this would be your kind of setup. And you'll like Angela, once you get used to her. Not your type at all, you're right. But she's jake, Clancy."

Clancy thought back to that hostile, snooty face. She was pretty enough, if you liked them aristocratic, skinny and cold. He liked her hair, what he could see of it, even if she pulled it back away from her face. And she had pretty eyes, despite their suspicious expression. Good breasts, too, beneath that ridiculous dress. No decent pilot ever wore a dress like that, he'd thought at the time. And he'd never seen a pilot with gams like hers.

"I'll take your word for it," he said lazily. "In the meantime, tell me where I can find someone a little more my style."

"What's your style?"

"Hell, you know," Clancy said lazily. "Someone with blond hair that came out of a bottle, real curves, someone who's got a chest that isn't stuffed with tissues. Someone who wouldn't tire your brain with stimulating conversation."

"I can think of several who fit that description, but you're not their kind of man," Sparks said morosely. "You're not rich enough."

"That's all right. I know how to get around gold diggers. I just flash 'em my pearly whites, tell them about what a war hero I was and offer to take 'em up in my plane."

"I suppose there's always Constance, Angela's half sister," Sparks suggested. "They're as different as night and day. Anyway, your plane's not here and Constance wouldn't be impressed with a pilot. Her sister's the next best thing to Amelia Earhart and Amy Johnson."

Clancy sat up a little straighter. "The hell you say."

"She is. Not that she'd give you a second look, you playboy. Besides, she's still in mourning for her fiancé."

"She's got a dead fiancé? No wonder she has that touch-me-not look."

"She's always had it."

"Then maybe the fiancé didn't mind dying."

"I'm talking about Hal Ramsey."

Clancy shrugged again. "You expect me to be humbled? Pilots die all the time—it's part of the business, and I'm not going to start getting sentimental at this time in my life. Ramsey was okay. So was Jeff Hawkins, Bart Livingston, Sam Waters, Izzy Maroni, Thomas Mitchell . . ."

"Sam died?" Sparks's voice was hoarse with sudden sorrow.

"Two years ago. I thought you'd heard."

"Where?"

"The Andes. Damned condor flew through the windshield of the plane he was navigating, broke his neck. It was over fast." He kept his voice cool and unemotional.

"What happened to the pilot?"

"He managed to land without any further trouble. Too late for Sam, though."

"Sorry, Clancy. I know you did your best."

Clancy met Sparks's sorrowing gaze and he managed a dry laugh. "I never could keep anything from you, could I? I guess that's when I decided that breaking records didn't really matter. All that mattered was flying. And that's what I intend to do from now on. No flights around the world, no races, no stunts. Just getting up in the air and not coming down until I damned well have to. And no more navigators.''

"I hope everyone doesn't feel that way about navigators.'' Sparks signaled for another beer.

"Eyes bothering you?'' Clancy was careful to keep his voice light.

"I never could fool you, either. It's not that bad yet,'' he said with a laugh, and Clancy knew he was lying. "But the time is coming, and I'd be a sucker not to know it. Hell, Clancy, I can't stay out of airplanes. I'd sooner go down in a blaze of glory than be grounded. You know that—you must feel the same way.''

"Don't worry, pal,'' Clancy said. "For you I'd even consider another navigator. In the meantime, let's talk about more important things. Like whether that waitress over there has a brassiere that isn't stuffed with tissue.''

It was early afternoon before Angela got back to the hangar. Church had taken a goodly portion of the morning, with a vivacious, slightly hung-over Constance at her side.

Angela had had a hangover herself, not from alcohol but from too many cigarettes and too little sleep. She was just as grateful for the silence, knowing that when Constance decided to break it, the chatter would be nonstop.

Sure enough, by the time they left the old Lutheran church on Market Street, her sister was jabbering up a storm. "You should have seen the clothes Joan Crawford wore! I swear, that Edith Head is an absolute genius. If I were a star I'd want her to design all my clothes. Not that Vionnet isn't wonderful, but a little staid, don't you think? More your style than mine.''

"I wouldn't exactly call my life staid," Angela said dryly.

"Not your whole life. Just your social life," Constance shot back, running a perfectly manicured hand through her marcelled blond hair. "Tell me honestly, how long has it been since you've been on a date? Been out to the movies? Gone dancing? You used to love to dance. And don't say no one's asked you. All you have to do is lift your little finger and a dozen men would fall at your feet."

"I wouldn't be able to dance if I had to step over them."

"Joke all you want to. You're not getting any younger, you know. You're pretty close to being an old maid already. If you aren't careful you'll turn around and find that life has passed you by."

"Life isn't going to pass you by, though, is it?" Angela countered, gazing at her half sister curiously. The dress she was wearing was another of her talented designer knock-offs, but for her own ripe figure she'd chosen a Valentina day dress, made of rayon, just a little tighter than it needed to be, a little shorter, a little brighter.

"Not if I can help it," Constance said. "You know, I thought I'd finish that evening frock for you. Maybe when Clement comes back to town you can wear it to entice some money out of him."

"How did you know Clement was out of town?" Angela asked.

Constance shrugged. "He called when you were at the hangar. Honestly, I don't know what you see in him. He's awfully old and boring."

"I don't see anything in him. For one thing, he's my cousin. For another, he's married."

Constance's wicked little grin had entranced more than one man. "There are ways around that."

"I don't think Clement's wife is planning on taking a train to Reno in the near future. Besides, I'm interested in his money, not his body."

"Sometimes you have to take one to get the other," Constance said breezily. "That's what marriage is all about."

"Which is why I probably will end up an old maid," Angela said gloomily. "I'm not willing to make that bargain. You don't have to, either, you know. Why don't you take some designing courses? You've got such talent. Wouldn't you like to be designing dresses for people? For Hollywood stars," she added, seeing Constance's moue of distaste.

"Heavens, no. I make clothes because I can't afford to have them made. If I had enough money I'd never touch a sewing machine again. Besides, I don't want to be a dressmaker to the stars. I have every intention of being a star."

Angela had heard this too many times over the last seven years to be surprised. "Well, then, why don't you get involved with the local theater? Take some acting courses?"

Constance bestowed a kindly look upon Angela, shaking her head at her sister's obvious naïveté. "I don't want to be an actress, Angela," she said simply. "I want to be a star."

There was nothing Angela could say to that, and it was too dreary a day to argue. Yesterday's perfect weather had given way to clouds and gloom, with the faint threat of rain lingering overhead. "All right, Joan Crawford," she said, ruffling her sister's perfect hair. "Dream on. I'm going in to work."

"But I need the car!" Constance carefully smoothed her hair back down. "Don't be such a killjoy, darling. I haven't had a chance to go anywhere in weeks! You can walk to the hangar."

Angela hadn't bothered to argue. She'd always had a hard time saying no to Constance, and today wasn't any different. Besides, the walk to the hangar was just what she needed. The peace and quiet of the deserted building was a haven she was looking forward to. Even Sparks seldom showed up on a Sunday when the weather wasn't fit for flying. She'd have the place to herself, and she could begin to figure out where in heaven's name she was going to find herself a decent mechanic.

The sliding metal door on the west side of the hangar was open, the padlock dangling uselessly. She stared at it thoughtfully for a moment. Someone had used a key, and the only person she'd entrusted one to was Sparks. But she knew without looking that it wasn't Sparks rattling around inside the hangar. For a moment she was sorely tempted to turn around and walk back home.

A light mist had begun to fall, a mist that could easily turn into a drenching rainstorm. And if she started out her working relationship with Jack Clancy by running away, it was going to set a precedent that would be hard to live down.

The delicious smell of coffee filled the air, mixing with the scent of gasoline and the fresh ozone of the spring rain. She didn't see Clancy anywhere, but that meant nothing. He had to be somewhere in the old building.

He was, all right. Sitting at her desk, booted feet propped up on the littered surface, drinking a mug of coffee. From her mug.

"I'm glad to see you've made yourself at home," she said when he looked up at her out of those lazy bedroom eyes.

"I thought you'd appreciate it," he said, making no effort to get up and move out of her seat. "You look more like a pilot today," he added, a note of approval in his voice. "You going up?"

"Not in this rain. I've got work to do."

"Chicken."

She slopped some of the coffee she'd been pouring. "You're calling me a chicken?" she demanded, whirling around. "Who the hell do you think you are?"

"Easy, Red," he said. "No need to fly into a fit. If a little rain scares you, far be it from me to tease you about it. Besides, your planes aren't fit to fly."

She didn't know what to start screaming about first. Taking a deep breath, she took the most important. "What do you mean, my planes aren't fit to fly?"

"Oh, they look pretty enough. And on first glance they seem in good shape. But the Avian's got a cracked fuel line. The Vega's altimeter is on the blink, and the Percival's got a wicked shimmy. I can take care of the fuel line, even replace the altimeter, but the Percival's beyond me. You need a mechanic, lady. And if you're going to make a go of this business, you need the best."

"How do you know about the planes?"

"Simple. I took them out. Not the Avian, of course. I checked them over first, like any wet-behind-the-ears pilot would do. The Vega's a sweet little thing, plenty of pep, and she handles well. Not bad for a single-engine. The Percival's sluggish and she handles like a barge, but maybe if someone could take care of the shimmy she might prove to be decent."

"You'd be flying the Percival," Angela snapped. "If you're not up to it, I can always find someone who's capable."

"Where?" he shot back. "You'd be damned lucky to get anyone to come here, what with Charlie Olker riding your tail. Don't look so outraged—Sparks and I are old friends. Of course he'd tell me what was going on. Listen, Red, let's get a few things clear. I said I'd work for you, and I will. And if a plane's capable of being flown, I'm the best there is to fly it. But I'm not going out with faulty equipment because you're too cheap to hire a decent mechanic."

"I'll hire the first good mechanic I can find. There happens to be a shortage of them, especially considering what Charlie Olker's willing to pay. And don't call me Red!"

"Why not?"

"My hair isn't red." It was a stupid conversation, when she'd rather talk about airplanes, but he had the annoying ability to distract her.

He cocked his head to one side. "I guess it isn't. Not really. Still, you've got the soul of a redhead, Angela Hogan. Fiery temper and all. You want a mechanic, we'll find you a mechanic."

"How do you plan to do that, Mr. Know-it-all?" She took a deep drink of her coffee and almost threw the rest of the mug at him. It was ten times stronger than she usually made it and infuriatingly better.

"You've only known me a few hours, Red," he said, dropping his boots off her desk and standing. She'd forgotten how tall he was, and it took all her fierce determination not to back up when he started toward her. "You'll find that there's no overestimating my capabilities. What I want, I get."

He was too close to her, she thought, struggling for breath. Too close, and he wasn't even in touching distance. "Good for you," she managed. "Get me a mechanic."

She didn't know what that look in his dark eyes signified. It looked a little like approval, a little like amusement. And uncomfortably tinged with a slumbrous, latent desire. And then it was gone.

"I'll find you a mechanic," he said. "But you'll have to do the getting." He took one step closer, and Angela had the odd feeling that her throat was going to close up. "Remember one thing, Red. You've got me. But on my terms." He stepped away. "I'll be working on the Avian." And he headed out into the hangar, whistling a jaunty little tune.

And Angela Hogan, noted for her cool head and iron self-control, slammed her office door after him, shattering the smoked-glass window.

## Chapter Three

"What happened to the door?" Sparks asked, ducking inside Angela's office, raindrops glistening on the top of his wiry blond hair.

Angela looked up and glared, her displeasure with Clancy spreading to all the males of the species. "What are you doing here? It's Sunday and we don't have any customers."

"I knew Clancy would be here, and I thought I'd show him around a bit."

"You don't have to show that man anything," she said bitterly, watching as Sparks helped himself to a cup of coffee. "He's made himself right at home. If I'd known I was going to get a nursemaid, I would have thought twice about hiring him."

"Sure, Angela," Sparks said easily, not fooled. He took a deep drink from the mug. "Your coffee's improved."

"Get out of here," she snarled. "I have work to do."

"Yes, ma'am." He backed away, grinning. "Want me to fix your door?"

"I want you to leave me alone."

"Yes, ma'am," he said again. "Great coffee."

She hurled her empty mug at him, not even wincing as it shattered on the cement floor outside her office. Sparks moved then, hastily, and Angela had the faint regret that there wasn't anything more she could throw and break. And that she didn't have Clancy as a target.

Leaning back, she turned on the cathedral-style radio, tuning past all the fire-and-brimstone preachers, past Father Charles Coughlin and his anti-F.D.R. tirades, past opera and comedy skits and family dramas, finally settling on something smooth and soothing, Benny Goodman's big band playing "Sing Sing Sing." She settled back with a frustrated sigh and began to concentrate on the stack of bills, not yet overdue, but close to it.

"You ready for dinner, Angie?" Sparks poked his head inside her office door hours later with the wary air of a man who rightfully believes he might have something thrown at him.

She stretched, looking around her. "Is it that late? Heavens, I'm tired. Do you think Rosa's made any lasagne tonight?"

Sensing all was well, Sparks straightened up and strode in, dropping down in the chair opposite her. "If she hasn't, all you have to do is ask. She'd do anything for you, and you know it."

"I didn't pay for little Tony to go to college."

"No, but you talked to the right people, helped get him in there and made arrangements for the scholarship. People like the Baldinos don't forget things like that."

"Little Tony earned that scholarship."

"Sure, but do you think he would have gotten it without your help?" Sparks shook his head. "What's wrong with taking credit for a good deed?"

Angela busied herself turning off the radio in the midst of Jack Benny. "I didn't do it for credit, Sparks. I just hate to see the waste of a good mind."

"Whereas I," Clancy said, lounging in the doorway, "hate to see the waste of a good woman. I can't decide, Red, whether I like you in pants or in a dress. Guess you haven't decided whether you want to be one of the boys or not."

She kept herself from breaking the knob off the radio and hurling it at him, managing a serene smile before she turned around. "I've decided," she said coolly. "You just aren't in any position to know what that decision is."

"Come on, now," Sparks said. "Why don't you two kiss and make up? We're all going over to Tony's for a nice spaghetti dinner and a couple of rounds of drinks. If you two keep arguing, I'm going to lose my appetite."

"You mean he's going?" Angela demanded.

Clancy grinned. "I live there."

"At Tony's? Where, under the bar?"

"You're getting me confused with your other pilot. Anyone with any sense would have known better than to hire a deadbeat like Robert Bellamy. And I bet you pride yourself on being a good judge of character."

Angela gritted her teeth. "I am. The fact of the matter is, I didn't have any choice at the time. Just as I don't have with you, Mr. Clancy. I simply have to grin and bear it."

He nodded. "Let's see a little more of that smile, Red."

"Tony's got a couple of rooms upstairs that he rents out," Sparks intervened quickly, before they could start in on each other again. "He was glad to let Jack have them."

"Great," Angela said. "Now I don't even have Tony's to go to."

"You gonna let me drive you away, Angel?" Clancy taunted lightly.

A tense silence filled the room. "Don't call me Red," she said. "And don't call me Angel."

"I'll admit, that one doesn't suit you in the slightest. But it tickles my sense of the absurd. Come on, *Miss* Hogan. Let's get out of here and figure out what we're going to do about a mechanic."

She could have refused. Told them Constance was due back, and that they always ate Sunday supper together. But Sparks would know it was a lie and he was already looking at her with too much concern beneath those bushy eyebrows. Besides, the sooner she managed to put Jack Clancy firmly in his place, the better.

"Okay," she said, pushing back a wisp of hair that had escaped from the rubber band she used to keep it out of her face. "As long as no one tries to pay for my dinner."

"Hell, no, Angel," Clancy drawled. "You can treat me."

TONY'S BAR AND GRILLE had to be Angela's most favorite place on earth. From the warm welcome of the Baldinos, to the easy-going camaraderie of the other patrons, two-thirds of whom were either pilots or somehow involved in aviation, from the smell of beer and whiskey and the strong, heavenly scents of garlic and tomatoes, to the smoke and noise and steady sound of music from Tony's prize possession, a brand-new jukebox, the whole place seemed more like home to her than any of the houses she'd ever lived in, both plain and fancy.

Even Clancy's presence couldn't diminish her pleasure. As she allowed herself to get cosseted by Mama Rosa, bussed by Tony and slapped on the back by half a dozen men, she felt the warm glow spread over her. By the time she got settled in her favorite booth, a foamy glass of beer in her hand, a plate of lasagne in front of her, she was feeling very mellow, indeed. Until she glanced over at the bar and saw Clancy deep in conversation with a thin, bespectacled man who'd never seen the inside of a cockpit.

She put her fork down, frowning.

"What's the matter, Angie?" Sparks asked over his own mug of beer, smart enough never to dare call her Angel.

"What's Clancy doing with Jefferson? He's Olker's man, or always has been. I don't like my pilots messing with him."

"He's left Olker, haven't you heard? He's working with a bank now. You know what a cheapskate Olker is. I guess he felt he's making so much money he doesn't need an accountant, and word has it that Jefferson's bearing a grudge. I'm guessing that Jack is just checking things out."

"I don't trust him."

"Listen, Angie, Clancy's one of the swellest guys I've ever known. If you'd just give him a chance..."

"I mean Jefferson," Angela said irritably. "I trust Clancy. As far as I need to, that is. I don't know if I trust anyone completely."

"What about me?"

She turned to look at him, at his crazy Irishman's face, the bushy eyebrows, warm blue eyes, cheerful mouth and burly, barrel-chested body. "I trust you, Sparks," she said softly, with real affection. "You're the brother I never had."

She was so absorbed with Clancy over at the bar that she almost missed the faint shadow that darkened Sparks's eyes for a moment. But when she looked closer it was gone, vanished, and she told herself she'd only imagined it.

When Clancy dropped down in the booth across from her, he was carrying his own half-empty beer and a plate of lasagne. He took another gulp of beer, wiped his mouth with the back of his hand and caught her fastidious gaze. "Got your mechanic," he said. And he dug into his lasagne.

JACK CLANCY WASN'T USED TO experiencing the intense, sophisticated pleasure of driving a woman crazy. But when it came to a stuck-up broad like Angela Hogan, he simply couldn't resist. He could feel her sharp blue eyes on him, watching as he calmly, slowly ate his lasagne, waiting to pounce on him with more questions. He had to be very careful not to wait too long before shoving another forkful of the delicious stuff in his mouth. He wasn't doing justice

to Rosa's wonderful cooking, but he'd make up for it later.
He'd already learned he could come down the back way and
raid Rosa's kitchen at all hours, with her maternal blessing.
For now he was content to wolf down the food and make
Angela Hogan wait for the news she so desperately needed
to hear.

He'd already figured out she was someone who prided
herself on her self-control. He'd also figured out some of the
best ways to make her lose it, and he couldn't resist experi-
menting. He wasn't going to enjoy his tenure at Hogan's Air
Freight, and he knew it. His boss lady had the ability to get
under his skin, instantly, just as he was trying to get under
hers. And it wasn't because she was a woman. He'd worked
for women before; some of the best pilots he'd ever met were
women. He just had a problem with Angela.

Maybe it was because he'd seen her in that damned sexy
dress first, got a view of her endless legs, her boyish body
with its understated curves. If he'd only seen her in flight
overalls, he probably would have never thought about what
lay behind the baggy cotton.

But now, every time he looked at her, he was remembering those legs of hers and thinking about what they'd feel
like, wrapped around him.

He started to choke on the last forkful of lasagne. He
quickly swallowed, washing it down with a huge gulp of
beer, and managed a deliberate belch for the lady's edifi-
cation.

He had to grant it to her—she didn't even flinch. Probably figured he was just living up to his reputation, he
thought, reaching for his pack of Luckies, politely offering
her one.

"Are you quite finished?" she asked in an icy voice, ignoring his gesture.

He took his time lighting the cigarette, glancing up at her
through the match flame. He shook it out, leaning back, his

gaze never leaving hers. "Finished," he said. "Unless you want to wait till I have dessert and coffee."

"I'll strangle you first," she said flatly. "What mechanic?"

"Yeah, Jack, what mechanic?" Sparks echoed. "I've been checking around for weeks, putting out the word, and I haven't heard a thing."

"I guess it's your legwork that's paid off, then," Clancy said. "Though it's not a direct offer, it's more along the lines of a possibility."

"I'll take anything I can get," Angela said. "Who, what, where?"

"Will Parsons."

"Who's he?" Angela questioned.

"I've heard of him," Sparks said slowly. "Wasn't he with Lockheed out in California?"

"For a while. He ran into a bit of trouble. I guess he's a drinker."

"I don't need another lush on the payroll," Angela snapped.

"You need what you can get. When Will's sober, he's supposed to be one of the best in the business—a genius with machinery. He knows the Wasp engine inside and out, practically designed them, and, lady, you have nothing but Wasp engines in varying states of disrepair. The least we can do is go see the man, see if he's in any shape worth salvaging."

Angela's face was a study in dismay. "What do you mean by that?"

"He hasn't been working the past few years. Been bumming around the country, riding the rails. He was last seen in a shanty town outside of Albany, New York. Or at least, that's what the word is."

"And I suppose you think I should fly to Albany, find the nearest hobo encampment and start looking for a mechanic to hire," Angela said, her voice rich with sarcasm.

"Nope." His eyes met Sparks's briefly, but his old friend wasn't giving anything away. "I think you should leave your crippled planes alone, take the train to Albany, and you'd damned well better have me along. From what I've heard of Will Parsons, he doesn't have too much truck with women. And I don't think a shanty town is any place for a woman alone, even one who thinks she's a man."

The noise of the bar surrounded them, with the underlying strains of Fats Waller in the background. Tony didn't believe in segregation—he had race music and hillbilly music on his jukebox, as well as the latest swing. Clancy could see Angela chew her pale lips, and he had the brief thought that she'd look good in lipstick. Something bright red, to contrast with her pale, almost translucent skin.

He waited for the explosions, the protests, the refusals, with almost happy anticipation.

"Sounds like a wise idea," she said slowly.

"What?"

"Angie!" Sparks protested at the same time.

"If I can take Clancy's word for it, none of the planes are in tip-top condition. Only the Percival's in running shape, and you're going to need that to fly the few jobs we have right now."

"But I could go with you," Sparks said. "Clancy can handle the few jobs we've got."

"Clancy doesn't know how we do things. You do," Angela pointed out calmly. "We can take the *Twentieth Century Limited* tomorrow afternoon. It costs more than the regular train, but it'll be worth it. Mr. Know-It-All has promised me a mechanic. It's up to him to put his money where his mouth is."

"Why can't he go alone?" Sparks demanded unhappily, and Clancy remembered with sudden regret that Sparks had a bad case on his boss lady.

"Because I don't trust him not to come back with some burned-out old rummy," she said frankly. "When, and if, he finds this man, it'll be up to me to decide whether I can hire him."

"Does this mean you're going to treat me to a bedroom?"

She smiled very sweetly. "Why not ask for a private car while you're at it? You get an upper berth, Clancy, and be thankful for that."

"Fine," he drawled. "I like being on top." He said it low enough that Sparks missed it beneath the hubbub of the bar, so that only Angela heard it and couldn't be quite sure she'd heard him correctly. The expression in her blue eyes was startled into sudden, heated awareness, and once more Clancy was reminded that his irritation with Miss Angela Hogan sprang from several sources, not the least of which was his unlikely attraction to her.

She wisely decided to ignore his comment. "Is tomorrow too soon for you?"

"The sooner the better. I want this concern to start making money so that I can get my plane back up here. If we can find a crackerjack mechanic, half my worries will be over."

"What about the other half?" she asked.

"I wouldn't want things to get too dull."

"Angie!" A burly male in a leather flight jacket loomed over them, hauling Angela up out of her chair and enveloping her in a bear hug that looked as if it might crush a slighter woman. "Where the hell have you been the last few days? Ever since you told Rosa you liked lasagne, we've been eating it night after night. The least you can do is suffer with us."

"If the worst torment you ever have to endure is Rosa's lasagne then you've got it made," Angela said, her face alight with pleasure. "What kind of trouble have you been getting into, Stan?"

"Not enough, what with you giving me the cold shoulder," he replied, grabbing a chair and dropping down at the table without being asked. "Who's the new pilot?" He was looking Clancy over with an astute, possessive attitude, but Clancy couldn't figure out whether it was simply older-brother protectiveness or something more basic. Sparks seemed torn between the two emotions, as did most of the men present. As far as he could see, he was the only man whose positive reactions to Angela Hogan were direct and unfettered. He either wanted to fight with her or sleep with her. Not hold her hand or protect her from bullies.

"Clancy," Jack said, holding out his hand.

Stan's broad, Slavic face creased in sudden delight, and he pumped Clancy's hand with such enthusiasm he knocked over a couple of empty beer mugs. "You know, I thought you looked familiar. I've always wanted to meet you. I've followed your career as closely as I've followed Lindy's. Whatcha been doing lately? I don't think I've heard."

"I've been down in South America. Mail routes over the Andes, that kind of stuff."

"No more racing?"

"No more racing. I figure if I'm going to crash, it might as well be for something worthwhile. Not breaking a stupid record."

Dead silence at the table. It was considered bad manners to talk about crashing, and Angela's fiancé had died attempting just such a stupid move. "Well," Stan said, clearing his throat, "you're probably right. We've all settled down in the past few years. Got families to raise, that sort of stuff. You married?"

"Nope. It's not my style. Sooner or later the little lady starts crying and begging you not to fly, and then where are you? No one's clipping my wings." He lit another cigarette, deliberately not meeting Angela's eyes. "But I bet you are, Stan. Got pictures?"

It was all the other pilot needed. While Clancy tipped back in his chair and feigned interest, Stan trotted out snapshots of a dark-haired, cheerful looking woman and two round, blond babies. Clancy'd seen too many photos like that. Left among the effects of too many dead pilots.

"So what are you doing here, Clancy?" Stan asked, after the proper attention had been paid to his family.

"Flying," he said briefly.

"I assumed that. I didn't know anyone was hiring...." His eyes skipped over to Angela's composed face. "You don't mean you're working for Angie?"

"Exactly."

"You sure you want to do that? No offense, Angie, but you've got Charlie Olker determined to drive you out of business, and he plays rough. It's not the sort of life for a woman, anyway. You're a great pilot, Angie, but it takes a man to run a business. You should just go back to your air races."

"You should—" She bit off her retort and managed a pleasant, strained smile. "You should wait and see what happens," she amended. "Ten years ago no one would have thought women could fly. We've proven you wrong. In another ten years no one will be surprised at women running businesses, colleges, banks."

Stan laughed. "Always the kidder, Angie. I tell you one thing, with Clancy working for you your business is going to pick up one hundred percent. You might stand a chance against Olker after all."

It wasn't what she wanted to hear, Clancy thought, though she took it gracefully enough. "Even without Clancy I'm going to make it," she said calmly.

"Of course you are," Stan said indulgently. "We're all pulling for you."

The bar lapsed into a sudden hushed silence, and Clancy pulled his attention away from Angela long enough to glance toward the entrance.

The vision that posed in the doorway waited long enough for customers of the place, almost exclusively male, to appreciate her sheer loveliness, and then she advanced into the room, hips swaying just slightly enough to entice, not enough to outrage. And those hips were headed toward their table.

She was quite a looker, Clancy thought distantly. The kind of woman he liked, with smooth blond hair waved close to her head, pale blue eyes, a bright red, hungry-looking mouth. Her eyebrows were plucked thin, painted with a high arch over those slightly protuberant eyes, and he would have taken a bet that those lush curves beneath the exaggerated shoulders were padded.

A bet he would have lost, he thought, as he belatedly realized this was Constance. She was no aristocrat like her sister Angela. Constance knew exactly who she was and what she wanted in life.

She paused at the table, bestowing a gorgeous smile on all of them. "I've come looking for my big sister," she said, her voice light and slightly breathy, sort of Shirley Temple crossed with Jean Harlow. She was looking across the table, directly at Clancy, with a big, innocent smile on her gorgeous face. "I don't know you, do I?" she murmured, dimpling prettily.

"That's Jack Clancy," Angela muttered, clearly bothered by something. "Let's go home, Constance."

Stan was already in the midst of pulling up another chair. "Oh, let her have a drink, Angie. Don't be such an old maid."

Stan wasn't long on brains, Clancy thought lazily. Either to be suckered by a pretty little piece of fluff like Constance or to think of Angela Hogan as anything like an old maid. "She better go home, Stan," Clancy drawled, paying little attention to the luscious blond newcomer. "We've got a long trip tomorrow and she needs her beauty sleep."

"You're going somewhere?" Constance demanded, still eyeing Clancy with a covert interest he recognized and ignored.

"To find a mechanic. We'll be back in a couple of days."

*"We?"* Constance echoed, clearly astonished as she stared at Angela. "You're going off with him?"

"You bet, honey," Clancy drawled. "Don't worry, I'll take good care of your older sister."

Constance shook her blond head, grinning a likeable grin. "She doesn't let anyone take care of her," Constance said. "She likes to be in charge."

"So do I," Clancy responded, leaning back. "I imagine we'll work it out."

"Clancy's right, we'd better get home," Angela said briskly. "See you tomorrow."

"Tomorrow," Clancy agreed, watching them leave. And realizing, for all Constance's curves and sashaying hips accentuated by the clinging pink dress, he found Angela's slim, no-nonsense stride far more arousing. "Sparks," he said, not taking his eyes off the Hogan sisters. "See if Tony has a bottle of Johnny Walker. I think it's going to be a long night."

Sparks followed his gaze, his own expression both troubled and mournful. "You're right," he said with a sigh. "Endless."

# Chapter Four

Angela was out of the house the next morning by the time Constance even began to stir, her overnight bag stashed in the back of the Packard. The train didn't leave till late that afternoon—she had every intention of getting a full day's worth of work done before they left.

That is, until Charlie Olker walked into her office, as big as brass and twice as hard, and heaved his impressive bulk into her protesting chair.

"Do come in," she said affably, leaning back. "Don't stand on ceremony."

"I thought it was time we laid our cards on the table," Charlie said. "Enough of this pussyfooting around."

"All right. Lay your cards on the table," Angela suggested.

Charlie Olker was an unprepossessing figure of a man. He was big, and what had been muscles in his youth had now spread to sloppy fat and a beer belly. He'd had either the good fortune or the sheer stupidity to have shot down several German planes during the Great War, and the subsequent medals and notoriety had sealed his profession as a War Hero for the rest of his days. He'd started an air-freight business a few weeks after Frank Hogan had died, jumping in while Angela was too distracted by grief and rage to pull her father's struggling business together.

It had been an uphill battle since then, with Charlie's dirty tricks tripping her up when she least expected it. As far as she knew, he hadn't been in an airplane since he'd been smart enough to hire a crew of down-on-their-luck veterans, but he still dressed like one, complete with leather flight jacket, white silk scarf draped casually beneath his double chin, baggy khaki pants drooping low beneath his impressive stomach and dragging behind his heels. He was smoking a cigar, a big, cheap, smelly one, and Angela reached for her Luckies in self-defense.

"I heard you fired Martin and Bellamy."

"I did," she said, blowing a thin stream of smoke in the direction of his piggy little eyes.

"Bellamy's a good pilot. Likes the sauce too much, of course, but then, what real man doesn't? You can't be too picky when it comes to hiring people, Angela. Just a word of friendly advice."

"Then I'm sure you'll have plenty of room to take Bellamy back into your organization."

Charlie batted his colorless eyelashes. "He never worked for me," he said innocently.

Angela's own smile was sour. "Well, he can now. Martin, too."

"That's another thing. You shouldn't ought to go firing people like that. It gives people a bad impression. If you have a little trouble with your employees, you just need to sort 'em out. That's why women can't run businesses. They can't take someone out behind the woodshed and give 'em a tarring."

"And you could?" The thought of Charlie trying to pound some sense into Robert Bellamy was momentarily amusing, and she smiled.

Charlie, of course, misread her smile. "Well, it's probably too late. I don't think you could get them back if you want to. Though maybe if I put in a good word for you, they might be willing to consider it.''

"No, thank you. I don't want them back." She set her cigarette down in the bright pink ashtray and met Charlie's gaze. "Is this laying your cards on the table, Charlie? Why did you come to see me?"

"I hear you hired Jack Clancy."

"Aha," she said. "That's what I figured was bugging you. How'd you hear?"

"There's not much that goes on around here that I don't know about," he said. His cigar had gone out, but even the dead stogie still smelled foul. "Let me be straight with you, sister. It's a losing battle. No woman can compete with a man and ever expect to win. It goes against the laws of nature. This is a man's world, and the sooner you accept it, the happier you'll be."

"Gee, Charlie," Angela said. "It's really swell of you to be so concerned about my future happiness. I didn't know you cared."

He missed her sarcasm completely. "Listen, Angie, you can't go up against a man and expect to remain a woman. And letting yourself get involved with a playboy like Clancy! Your father, God rest his soul, would be whirling in his grave if he heard about it. Take some advice from an old friend. Sell me the pitiful remains of your business and get on with your life."

"Stuff it, Charlie." She stubbed out her cigarette. "And get off my property."

Charlie's moon face creased in anger, and his small dark eyes were bright with malice. "You think you got something with Clancy? Let me tell you, honey, he's been through more women than you could even imagine, and he's left every one of them. He'll leave you, too, just use you up and dump you, and then this place won't be worth spit. I'll just come in and mop up the mess, and you'll have nothing, do you hear me, absolutely nothing!'' His voice had risen shrilly.

"Why, Charlie,'' Clancy's voice broke through Olker's rage. "Long time no see.'' He was lounging in the doorway, an inimical expression on his face. "You busy warning Angel about me?''

For a moment an expression of sheer dread passed over Charlie's face. The effect was oddly comical, particularly since the room was still thick with tension. Angela heard herself giggle.

"Clancy.'' Charlie cleared his throat noisily. "I heard you were in town.''

"So I gather.'' Clancy straightened up and moved into the room with a sort of sinuous menace that left Angela momentarily stunned. "Next time you try to bully Miss Hogan, I'm going to take it personally. She's just doing her job, trying to run a business, and she doesn't need you butting in with threats and warnings and helpful hints. She's got enough going on without you interfering. Get it?''

"Look, Clancy, Angela and I are old friends, and it's none of your damned business—''

"It became my business when you started taking my name in vain, Charlie.'' Clancy's voice was a smooth, silken threat. He turned to Angela. "You want this guy here?''

"No.''

Clancy smiled. "Get out, Charlie. And don't come back without a written invitation.''

"You'll be sorry, Angela,'' Charlie said, heaving his impressive bulk out of the chair and heading for the door, carefully skirting Clancy as one might skirt a wild animal. "Don't say I didn't warn you. He's no good for you. Listen to an old friend....''

Sparks had appeared in the doorway, a very large, very nasty-looking wrench in one oil-grimed hand. "You need someone to show you the door, Charlie?'' he questioned affably.

Charlie turned and ran as fast as his bulk let him. Clancy dropped into the vacated chair, sniffing the air. ''He always did like those cheap cigars.''

''I didn't know you knew Charlie Olker,'' Angela said carefully.

''You stay in the business long enough, you eventually meet everyone. Are you going to ask me whether I'm on his payroll?'' Clancy's voice was almost casual, but Angela wasn't fooled. If she came out with the wrong answer, he'd get up and walk out and she wouldn't see him again.

She didn't want that. She told herself she needed a pilot, she told herself that he knew where the mechanic was and she didn't. And she knew well enough that those were only side issues. She wasn't ready for him to disappear.

That was as far as she allowed her thought processes to go. ''I'm not going to ask you that,'' she said.

''Why not?'' He pushed it. ''You don't strike me as the kind of girl who trusts people, and you sure as hell don't strike me as someone who trusts me.''

''You're right. I just don't have much choice right now. I need you too much to worry about whether you're selling me out.'' The moment the words were out, she wished she could have called them back. In all her twenty-seven years she'd tried very hard not to need anyone, and certainly not to tell them when she did. She'd just placed a very useful bit of ammunition in Clancy's hands, and she could have kicked herself.

Clancy, however, looked bored with her hard-won confession, as if it were nothing more than he expected. ''Glad you realize it, Red,'' he drawled. ''And let me give you a word of warning about Charlie. He's probably just been annoying you, getting in your way, because he doesn't consider you a real threat. If and when you do become one, he's going to get very nasty, indeed. Watch your back. Or I'll watch it for you.''

"Do you intend to be around that long?'' she asked, curiosity and dismay swamping her at that thought.

"Let's just say that if I'm not, either you've given up or Olker has lost.''

"You'll stay around that long?''

"I've always had a soft spot for an underdog. Besides, this place suits me, Tony's suits me, the job suits me. As long as you aren't too big a pain in the tail, and providing we can find a decent mechanic, I'm willing to sign on for the duration.''

"The duration of what?''

"You really like things written in blood, don't you, Red? The duration of your little war with Charlie Olker. I'm an old hand at trench warfare. Though I tell you, his cigars smell too much like mustard gas for my state of mind.''

She looked at him for a moment, rapidly recalculating his age. She would have thought he'd been too young to have fought in the war to end all wars, but clearly she was wrong. Maybe that accounted for the bleak expression in the back of his dark eyes when he thought no one was looking, an expression she'd seen on too many pilots who'd seen action over Germany.

"I'd appreciate your help,'' she said gravely.

He grinned. "No, you wouldn't. You're too proud to appreciate anyone's help. But you'll accept it because you're too smart to turn it down, even if it chokes you. Don't worry about it, Red. Think of it as castor oil. Nasty when it goes down, but ultimately good for you.''

Sparks shifted in the doorway. "Are you two still going to Albany?''

"I'm going,'' Angela said. "I don't suppose you were able to get any of my poor broken birds in decent enough shape to fly?''

"Just the Percival, and we need that if we're going to complete our contract with Hudson Brothers."

"We're going to complete our contract," she said. "There's nothing Charlie Olker would like better than to get that away from us." She glanced at Clancy. "Are you still planning to come with me?"

"You aren't going to be able to find him without me," Clancy replied, still slouched in the chair.

"Well, then, let's go. You're going to have to step on it if you want to have time to change before we make the train."

"I don't." He glanced down at his leather jacket, baggy khakis and rough cotton shirt. "You think I'm going to wear a suit and tie to go rummaging through a shanty town? Sorry, Angel. For one thing, I don't own a suit. For another, even if I did, I would have thrown it out years ago. Ties make me feel like I'm being strangled." He let his gaze run over her, lingering a little too long. "And if I were you, I'd change out of that little frock you're wearing. Silk stockings and high heels aren't made for wading through trash."

"I'll wear what I'm wearing," she snapped, knowing he was right. He had an irritating habit of being right far too often.

"So will I."

Stalemate. "We'd better get a move on, then. I've got reserved seats, but it doesn't hurt to be too careful."

Clancy rose, stretching lazily. "That's the difference between you and me. I'm always just careful enough."

"That's arguable."

"We have a long ride to Albany. We can fight all the way."

"Terrific," Angela said. She had the gloomy conviction they were going to do exactly that.

CLANCY SETTLED INTO his window seat, a stack of magazines in his lap, a half dozen truly estimable Cuban cigars inside his flight jacket. Angela was sitting across from him, slender ankles crossed demurely enough, her hands holding the latest issue of *Colliers*. He'd spied on her choice of reading material, noting with approval that she'd bought the latest edition of *Aviator* and *Air Travel* along with her ladies' magazine. He'd chosen *Black Book Detective Magazine*, complete with a lurid cover of a buxom blonde being menaced by an Oriental villain, and topped it off with the latest editions of *Thrilling Western Stories* and *Secret Agent Detective Mysteries*. It was with a fair amount of relief that he noticed the aristocratic Miss Hogan had purchased a copy of *Western Love Stories* and the issue of *Sky Devils* he'd hesitated over. In his fondness for yellow journalism, he avoided things like *Sky Fighters Magazine* and the like. Most of the writers knew nothing about planes, and the inaccuracies drove him crazy. The writers probably didn't know a thing about the West or secret agents, either, but at least he was equally ignorant and he could read with a fair amount of pleasure.

He glanced over at Angela, who was holding her copy of *Western Love Stories* flat against her slender thighs in the vain hope that he wouldn't notice what she was reading. Were the women who wrote about true love on the range equally ignorant as the men who wrote about flyers? He couldn't imagine there was much of reality to the books—it was probably the chaste relationships that existed in a Fred Astaire movie, where he never even kissed the girl. It must come as a rude shock to the gentle women readers when they're confronted with a real man.

Of course Angela had been engaged. Hal Ramsey had been an okay guy—she had better taste than Clancy would have given her credit for. So she couldn't be as naive as all that. Her long fingers were clenched tightly around the magazine as the train started forward with an uncustomary lurch. Most young women would be thrilled and excited to be traveling on the famous *Twentieth Century Limited*, even if it was only between Chicago and Albany, New York. Clearly Angela was not so thrilled.

"You don't like trains?" He broke the silence, reaching for his cigarettes and holding the pack toward her.

She shook her head, closing her magazine and gripping it tightly. "I don't mind them."

"Of course you don't. That's why you're sitting there with your knees clamped together, your hands gripping that magazine as if it were a lifeline, your face pale and your lips trembling. Don't fight it, Red. None of us likes to be ferried around by someone else. We like to drive it, fly it, ourselves."

For a moment her tension relaxed. "You feel the same way?" she asked, allowing her vulnerability through, and for one crazy moment he wanted to move across, sit beside her and pull her into his arms. He didn't move.

"Always. Pilots are an egocentric bunch. We want everything our way."

"No, I don't—"

"Oh, yes, you do," he corrected lazily, sliding back in the seat. "And it's driving you crazy that I realized you were scared. Look at it this way, Red. At least we can't fall out of the sky."

"No, but we could smash into another train."

"We're in the middle of the train. We'd probably get a few bumps and bruises."

"What if we went off a bridge? Over a cliff, into the ocean?"

"I don't know that we're going by any cliffs or the ocean, Red. If we go over one, I promise to hold your hand."

She snapped the magazine upright, too irritated to remember she didn't want him to see her reading material. The

cover showed a Gary Cooperish man with his arms clasped
tight around a ginghamed blonde, probably the same one
menaced by the yellow peril in his *Black Book Detective
Magazine*. "No, thanks," she said coolly.

"Tell me something, Angel," he said, his voice low and
caressing. "Does Red Rider kiss as well as Hal Ramsey
did?"

Bright red flooded her pale face as she slammed her
magazine back down. "You're despicable."

"And you're real cute when you're mad. Why don't you
lend me your *Sky Devils* while you read about hearts in the
West? If you're real nice I'll let you see my *Secret Agent
Detective Mysteries*."

"Why don't you—"

"Tickets, please." It was lucky for her the conductor interrupted her tirade or the entire car would have gotten an
earful. Clancy lounged back, watching as she handed in the
tickets, well aware of the curious glances from beneath the
conductor's billed hat. Clearly he wasn't used to masterful
women. Neither, for that matter, was Clancy. "The dining
car's to the front, the club car's ahead of that," the conductor said, his voice disapproving. "The porter will be by
to make up your berths at nine. Have a good trip, Mr. and
Mrs. Hogan."

Before she could protest, Clancy moved to sit beside her,
putting his hand on her knee. She jumped like a startled
rabbit. "We will. Won't we, honey?"

And Angela, smiling sweetly, covered his hand with hers
and dug her short, sharp nails into his skin. "We certainly
will, darling," she cooed, and the conductor, having missed
her action, smiled on them benignly.

## Chapter Five

She'd made some mistakes in her life, Angela decided later, but this one had to rank among the very finest of stupid moves. Why hadn't she realized that being cooped up on a train, even one as streamlined and modern as the *Twentieth Century*, would be enough to set her nerves on the screaming edge? Add to that the impossibly disturbing presence of Jack Clancy, sitting across from her as they sped toward the northeast, seemingly oblivious to her very presence, while she couldn't even concentrate enough to read a paragraph without glancing up at him, and it all added up to a raw state of nerves.

Dinner was the worst. He'd sat across from her in the dining car, eating a huge, almost raw slab of steak, while she picked at the chicken breast with no enthusiasm. She hadn't really expected him to be adept at dinner conversation. What she hadn't counted on was his ogling the other women in the car. He seemed to do it every time he realized she was looking, and if she had a more devious, paranoid turn of mind, she would have thought he was doing it just for her reaction.

Of course he had no reason to, she chided herself, poking at the strawberry shortcake she'd been fool enough to order. Why should he care whether his blatant flirtations bothered her? He'd be smarter to worry about whether he was going to end up with a bloody nose when someone's escort took exception.

"Are you going to eat that strawberry shortcake or just mangle it?" Clancy asked, lighting a cigarette.

She glared at him. "Would you mind not smoking? I'm still eating."

"No, you aren't. You're just sitting there stabbing that poor dessert. I don't know why you ordered it—you didn't touch the rest of your dinner."

"I didn't realize you noticed." He grinned and she glanced down at her strawberry shortcake with a wistful expression. She would have given anything to shove it in his handsome face, but her Grandmother Maynard's upbringing was too strong.

"What's that dangerous look in your eye, Red?" Clancy asked.

"Do you remember the scene in *Public Enemy*?" she asked gently.

"When Jimmy Cagney shoved the grapefruit in Mae Marsh's face? Don't even consider it. That's the problem with seeing too many movies, Red. They give you bad ideas."

"Oh, I don't know if it's that bad an idea."

"Trust me. It is. There's no reason for you to be sore. I'm entirely capable of keeping my eyes on every single pretty woman in the car," he said. "You included."

She didn't know quite how to respond to that one. For a compliment it was a fairly oblique one, and she didn't want to be in a position to accept compliments from Clancy. She preferred the enmity.

Dropping her fork, she pushed back from the table. "I'm going to bed."

He raised an eyebrow. "It's only nine o'clock."

"It's an hour later on the East Coast. Besides, the more time I spend asleep on this trip, the better. I haven't been sleeping well recently." She rose, not the least surprised when Clancy remained sprawled lazily in the chair.

"Why not?"

"There are a dozen reasons, Mr. Clancy, none of which I'm about to share with you," she said. "Good night."

"Sweet dreams, Angel. I'll try not to wake you when I climb on top of you."

It took all her self-control to turn and walk away, knowing he was watching her. She wanted to tug at her skirt, make sure her stocking seams were straight, smooth her hair. Resolute, she kept her back straight, walking out of the dining car like a debutante.

The berths were already made up in the sleeping car. It took her a moment to find hers, and for the first she allowed herself to react to Clancy's deliberately taunting statement. She was almost tempted to take the upper berth herself, if it weren't for the fact that there were no windows up there. She was feeling claustrophobic enough on this train that was probably driven by some incompetent. She at least wanted to be able to see out a window as she crashed to her death.

The washroom was empty that early in the evening. She washed quickly, tying back her hair, deciding to change into her nightclothes once she crawled into her berth. Most people changed in the washroom, having no qualms about traversing the corridors in bathrobe and slippers, but Angela had no desire to run into Clancy in dishabille. She could just imagine those dark, disturbing eyes lingering over her body, suggestive without his having to say a word.

Of course, he'd already said any number of suggestive words to her, she thought, diving into her berth and pulling the green serge curtains around her. She still wasn't quite sure whether he meant them or not. Probably not. She knew full well she wasn't the sort to arouse overtly lustful feelings in men, and thankfully she hadn't been bothered by too many of her own. If she had, she wouldn't have kept putting Hal off when he'd made a few suggestions about increasing the intimacy in their engagement.

Most, if not all, of her friends were men, and she preferred to keep it that way. Nothing would make her happier than to end the barbed enmity between her and Clancy, letting things settle down to a comfortable working relationship. She'd done it with most of the other men she'd worked with. Why did she keep thinking it was a losing battle when it came to Jack Clancy?

It was tricky enough to undo those tiny buttons when you were pretzeled up in a lower bunk, she thought, staring out at the darkening countryside as the train sped east. Shimmying out of a girdle was also an experience, not to mention climbing into the enveloping nightgown she'd deemed modest enough for a brief fling at communal living. Indeed, there was more material in the nightgown than there was in the Vionnet day dress. So why did she feel so exposed?

Lack of underwear, of heavy cotton bra and girdle, neither of which she actually needed, was part of it. And the knowledge that Jack Clancy would be sleeping above her was the other part. She slid beneath the sheets, pulling them up around her, and reached for her magazine. She'd barely read a sentence before she closed it again. She couldn't read about Red Rider's thrilling kisses without thinking of Clancy's barbed comment. About Clancy's mouth.

She threw the magazine toward the foot of the berth, wincing as the next person down cursed her. Turning off the small wall light, she snuggled down in the bed, her arms wrapped tightly around her. She was never going to sleep, she told herself. She was going to lie there and worry about Constance; she was going to worry about the doubtless inexperienced engineer who was going to plunge them all to their death the moment they came to a wide enough river;

she was going to worry about Charlie Olker and the fact that he seemed to be winning the battle they'd somehow become engaged in. And she was going to worry about Clancy. She wasn't quite sure why, but she knew without a doubt that she would, and those worries would keep her wide awake until dawn....

She didn't know what time she woke up. It was too dark to see her watch and she didn't want to risk turning on her light. Clancy had finally come to bed, disdaining the short ladder the porter usually provided and landing up there with a decided thump that had woken Angela from the sound sleep she was certain she never would have enjoyed. She lay there, hoping to recapture it, but the creaks, the thumps from overhead couldn't be ignored.

She didn't know how long she lay awake. The time passed as endlessly as the landscape outside, the throbbing of the train beneath her no longer soothing but maddening.

One thing was certain—she wasn't falling back to sleep on her own accord. The bar car usually remained open all night long for fellow insomniacs or sailors on leave or the like. Her only recourse was to pull on her clothes and go find herself a couple of very strong whiskeys. Then she might be able to recover at least part of her night's sleep.

Grabbing her clothes, she slid from the berth onto the floor, secure in the knowledge that she wouldn't be running into anyone in the middle of the night. She stood up, reaching for her bathrobe in the darkened, swaying car, when the curtains directly in front of her face opened and Clancy stuck his head out.

"Where do you think you're going?" he whispered.

"To the bar car. I can't sleep."

"The hell you are. This isn't Tony's Bar and Grille, Angel. Ladies don't go to bar cars alone, particularly not at three o'clock in the morning. You're not one of the boys on this train, and I'm not getting up and coming with you to protect you."

"Nobody asked you to," she shot back in an angry whisper. A sleepy voice two berths down ordered her to shut up.

"Listen, Red, you need a drink, I've got a flask. Dump your things and come on up."

"I will not."

"Suit yourself. I've got crackers and cheese up here, and you didn't eat any dinner."

Angela didn't move for a moment. She was absolutely starving and hadn't realized it until he said something. "You are the devil incarnate," she told him.

"I do my best. Come on, Red. Your virtue's safe with me." Before she realized what he was doing, he reached down, caught her arm and yanked her up onto the upper berth, her body sprawled across his, her legs thrashing out in the corridor.

She gave up the fight, more because she was afraid of rousing the other passengers and the porter than because she actually thought this was a good idea. Pulling her feet in after her, she scuttled across him, ending in the corner at his feet as the serge curtains closed back around them, plunging them into inky darkness.

"Mind if I turn on the light?" he inquired politely, turning it on before she could reply. He pulled himself up in the bed, but his long legs were almost touching her, and there was no way she could make herself any smaller. "That your idea of slinky nightwear? I would have thought you'd be wearing silk pajamas at the very least."

"I would have thought you'd be wearing pajamas at the very least," she shot back without thinking, and then blushed. She hadn't blushed in years and she could only hope the dimness of the yellow light couldn't penetrate into the far corners of the upper berth.

"I don't believe in 'em," he said, sitting up, the covers dropping to his waist as he handed her a silver flask.

"Apparently not." It was all she could do to tear her eyes away from his chest, from the unexpected silver cross that hung around his neck, and it took all her concentration to focus on the flask. "You don't believe in undershirts, either?"

"I figured if Clark Gable could get away without one, then so could I." In the shadowy darkness his eyes were hooded, a faint smile played around his mouth, as if he knew just how disturbing she found him.

He had hair on his chest. The few men she'd seen shirtless, most of them in the movies, were all hairless. Even Clark Gable, when he'd shed his shirt in *It Happened One Night* and plunged undershirt manufacturers into a depression of their own, had been surprisingly smooth skinned. Most men still wore shirts over their bathing suits when they swam in Lake Michigan, and she'd had no brothers, no uncles and not much of a father to see shirtless. She couldn't keep from stealing fascinated gazes as she tipped back the flask and took a generous gulp.

"Easy with that, Angel," he chided. "I don't know if you're used to stuff that strong."

"I can drink you under the table," she scoffed. He didn't have too much hair, she decided, taking another gulp and leaning back against the wall of the berth. She wouldn't have liked it on his shoulders or his back. Not that she could see his back, she realized. He was leaning against the opposite wall, but from what she could see of him, she imagined that the hair wasn't too much. Just a wedge of dark curls across the center of his chest, then arrowing down in a thin line and disappearing beneath the white sheet. She jerked her eyes upward quickly, but not before he'd caught her watching.

"Taking inventory?" he inquired casually.

She'd already had too much to drink on an empty stomach. She took another swallow, then managed a brave smile. "I'm not used to seeing men with hair on their chests," she said blithely.

"Then I don't imagine you're used to seeing men without shirts on. Most men have hair on their chest."

"Do they?" she questioned ingenuously, leaning forward. The tie to her hair had been lost sometime during her few hours of sleep and her hair fell forward over her face, obscuring her vision for a moment. She pushed it out of her way with slightly tipsy impatience. "How far does it go?" She wasn't so drunk that she didn't realize the outrageousness of such a question the moment it was out of her mouth, and she slapped a hand over her lips in comic dismay.

"All the way." He flipped the sheets away, and Angela let out a muffled shriek. Someone in the car shouted, "Shaddup, lady."

At least Clancy was wearing something, albeit only baggy linen boxer shorts that reached halfway down to his knees. He had very nice legs, she thought for a moment, until she realized he was reaching for the row of buttons on the shorts, waiting for her reaction.

"Cut it out," she whispered fiercely.

He flung the covers back over him, shrugging. "You asked. I guess you'll have to take my word for it."

"I will," she said hastily. "Why do you wear a cross? You don't strike me as the religious sort."

"I'm not."

"Then why...?"

"Superstition, Angel. Most pilots have their own. This is my lucky piece. I never fly without it, I never go anywhere without it."

"Where'd it come from?" She leaned forward to touch it, then belatedly realized she'd be touching him, too. She snatched her hand back. "It looks very old."

"A remnant of my Catholic boyhood."

"You want to tell me about it?"

"Not particularly. But you're dying to know, aren't you?" He slid down in the bed so that his leg was almost touching hers. "I was a foundling. I grew up in an orphanage, then moved up to a home for wayward boys. I was heading toward reform school when Father Robbins beat some sense into me. And showed me airplanes. After that the army and the war finished the job."

"Do you ever see him?"

"Father Robbins? He died years ago, just before the war. That's where the cross came from. I couldn't swallow his religion, but he was the closest thing to family I ever had. Am I breaking your heart, Angel? Ready to comfort me?"

"Go to hell." She took another gulp from the flask. "What is this stuff? I've had bootleg liquor but this tastes far better. Where'd you get it?"

"That's not bootleg, Angel. That's one hundred and fifty proof rum, direct from the Caribbean. If you were standing you'd be flat on your tail right now."

She giggled. "Isn't that a contradiction?"

"I didn't know you could giggle."

"I didn't know I could, either." She shoved her hair out of her face, ignoring the fact that Clancy looked different in the shadowy recesses of the upper berth. More dangerous somehow, with the overnight growth of beard darkening his face. She leaned forward across the bunk and placed a long finger on his cleft chin. "How do you shave in there?"

"Red, you're sloshed."

"Too much rum on an empty stomach," she said with a sigh. "Where are those crackers you promised me?"

"Come and get them."

She didn't even hesitate, crawling up the bed and plopping down beside him as he handed her a wax-paper twist of crackers. She leaned back, her head whirling slightly. She started nibbling, eyeing him covertly. "I should have known you'd be the type to eat crackers in bed," she said.

"Isn't it a lucky thing you don't usually sleep with me?" he replied, taking the flask out of her unresisting hand and taking a generous pull himself.

"Very lucky," she said. "Am I sleeping with you tonight?"

"I think you'd better. If you tried to crawl out of this bunk you'd fall flat on your keister."

"You could always be a gentleman and climb down yourself."

"I thought we'd already established that I'm not a gentleman." He took the crackers away from her. "Get under the covers. We have four more hours before we reach Albany."

She complied without thinking, sliding down beside him. He smelled of tobacco and rum and warm skin, and she was just thinking what a nice combination that was when he reached over her and turned off the light, plunging them back into darkness.

"This berth is awfully small," she said in a tiny voice.

"That's because you're trying to put three feet between us. Come here, Red. I promised I wouldn't make love to you, and I won't. But I'll be damned if I'm going to sleep with my tail hanging out in the aisle."

She didn't move, so without ceremony he pulled her against him. It was a shock that almost sobered her for a minute. His long, bare legs were entwined with hers. His hips were against her stomach, his strong, muscled arms around her, and his chest was against her face.

She reached out to push him away, and then stopped, as her hand came in contact with warm, hard skin and hair. The hair on his chest was crinkly but softer than she would have expected, and for a moment she let her fingers drift through it, exploring.

His hand shot out and caught her wrist. "Don't," he said in a rough voice.

"Don't what?"

"Push me. Or I may not keep my promise."

"Yes, sir," she said meekly.

"One more thing before you sink into a drunken stupor...."

She didn't bother to deny it. She was too comfortable to argue against what she suspected was the truth. "What is it?"

"Just this." He put his hand under her chin, pulled her face up to his and put his mouth on hers.

She lifted her face willingly enough, expecting a sweet salutation on her lips before she fell asleep. She was unprepared for the hot, seeking dampness of his mouth on hers, for the pressure that was far removed from Hal's gentle salutes.

Clancy pulled away, a few inches, and she could feel his breath on her face, warm and frustrated. "Open your mouth, Red," he whispered.

"Why?"

"Just do it." He set his mouth back on hers, his hands reaching up and holding her head in place, and this kiss was even more startling. His mouth was open against her, moving against her, and his tongue touched her lips, her teeth, then swept into her mouth with sudden force. She struggled for a moment, startled, but his hands held her still beneath him as he kissed her, lengthily, thoroughly, with his lips, his tongue, his hands, his body.

When he finally pulled away, her hands dropped limply to her side. She was hot and trembly all over, and deep inside her, in the pit of her stomach and lower, was a burning that had nothing to do with temperature and everything to do with the man beside her. She was feeling just drunk enough and aroused enough to want to reach out and touch him, to taste his mouth again, when his distinctive drawl interrupted her.

"God, Red, didn't you ever make out in the back seat of a jalopy? You don't know diddly-squat about kissing."

She jerked away, enraged, wanting to scramble out of the upper berth, but her legs were trapped beneath the cover. "Let me out of here!" she demanded in a fierce whisper.

It took him no effort at all to get her flat on her back, her hands held by her head, as he loomed over her. "Don't get sore, Angel," he whispered. "I'm going to enjoy teaching you." And he kissed her again, a slow, leisurely kiss that drained her anger, drained her embarrassment, leaving her nothing but a soft, melting mass of emotions.

She wanted more, she wanted so much more. Her body ached; she told herself she wasn't sure for what, but deep down she knew. She wanted Clancy as she'd never wanted anyone in her life, including Hal Ramsey.

Clancy had released her wrist and his deft fingers were already on the third button of her high-necked nightgown when she reached out to stop him.

He pulled his mouth away, but even in the darkness she could see the glitter in his eyes, hear the slow, heavy pounding of his heart, feel the strained exhalation of breath against her face as he struggled to control himself.

"Clancy, you promised," she said desperately, knowing that if it were up to her, she couldn't stop him.

For a moment he didn't move. "We've established that I'm no gentleman. Who says I keep my promises?" he replied, but she could tell by the torment in his voice that he would.

She reached up and touched his cheek, the rough texture of unshaven skin curiously arousing. She wished she dared ask him for more of that rum, but she knew that instead of assuring her a quick night's sleep, it would seal her fate for certain.

"I do," she said. "I trust you."

"You don't trust any man."

"I trust you," she said again, meaning it.

"Angel, you really know how to get a man where he lives," he said wearily, flopping over onto his back. "It's going to be a long four hours."

She leaned over him, suddenly anxious. "Do you want me to go back . . . ?"

"I want you to come here." He hauled her across him, pushing her head down against his shoulder with just a touch of unnecessary force. "Go to sleep, damn it."

For a moment she didn't know what to do with her hand. The other one was tucked up underneath her, but she wasn't quite sure what was safe to touch.

Clancy solved the problem for her. His big hand wrapped around her narrow one, holding it against his chest. And before Angela could think of one more complication, she fell asleep.

## Chapter Six

Angela's first feeling was panic when she was suddenly, instantly awake. She felt as if she were suffocating, trapped in a dark cave, alone, with noise all around.

She almost tumbled out into the crowded corridor before she was able to take her bearings. She was alone in Clancy's claustrophobic upper berth, and obviously everybody else in this car was already up and about and talking in the most piercing tones.

Angela fumbled for the light, switched it on and groaned. She had the most colossal, super-duper queen of hangovers. Demon rum, they called it, and now she knew why. For a moment she pulled the pillow back over her head and let the shards of pain slice through her skull. The nausea came next, and Angela held herself very still. She certainly wasn't going to toss her cookies in Jack Clancy's bed, and there was no way she was going to manage to thread her way through the cheerful throngs who seemed more than ready to face the day.

Gradually the nausea receded. Gradually the headache diminished to manageable proportions so that she could move without moaning. And then realization sunk in. She'd actually been fool enough to crawl up into bed with a skirt-chaser like Jack Clancy, gotten soused and practically passed out in his arms. It was sheer luck she'd escaped with nothing more than a fairly overwhelming kiss.

Slowly she raised her head, shoving the pillow to one side. Luck, or the fact that Clancy didn't find her the slightest bit attractive. Well, perhaps the slightest bit. He had kissed her, after all. Several times. With more devastating expertise than any of the other men who'd kissed her had ever shown.

Of course, Clancy probably had more practice. And it could very likely have simply been force of habit that made him kiss her. And what the hell was she doing, lying in bed worrying about whether Jack Clancy found her attractive? That kind of hooey had absolutely no importance in her immediate or long-term scheme of things.

She had no intention of ringing for a porter to bring the ladder. Peering out into the corridor, she discovered it was relatively uninhabited. With an agility that her poor, pounding brain paid for, she swung over the edge and dove into the bunk below, disappearing before anyone had a chance to notice.

Pulling up her shade, she discovered it was just past dawn on a surly day in early May. She had no idea when they were due to arrive in Albany, but chances were she didn't have a whole lot of time. By the time she'd managed to scramble into her clothes and stumble out into the swaying corridor, her need for the ladies' lounge was becoming an emergency. She made it just in time, ridding herself of Clancy's rum and crackers with expediency.

By the time she'd brushed her teeth, washed her face and run a comb through her shoulder-length page boy, she felt almost like a new woman. She'd forgotten to wind her watch the night before, and the Patek Philippe watch her grandmother had given her had stopped sometime around three in the morning. Just around the time she'd crawled into bed with Clancy.

The porter in the corridor gave her the time, informed her they were half an hour out of Albany, that the dining car was open for breakfast and that he hadn't seen Clancy. The thought of putting food on her ravaged stomach was almost enough to send Angela back to the ladies' lounge, but she gritted her teeth and moved on ahead through the swaying railroad cars in search of her erstwhile companion.

She found him on the railing beyond the bar car, smoking a cigar with one of the Pullman porters, engaged in lazy conversation.

Angela barreled onto the platform, stopping short in surprise. Never in her life had she seen a black man and a white man sharing a morning smoke and a casual conversation. The sight was so extraordinary that for a moment she was lost for words.

"Hi, Red," Clancy said, blowing smoke away from her. "I was going to come and make like Prince Charming if you hadn't appeared. This is Langston."

"Ma'am," Langston said, back suddenly straight and expression uneasy as he tossed his cigar out into the countryside. "I'd best be going. You take care, Clancy, you hear?"

"I hear," Clancy said, reaching out his hand. Langston hesitated for a moment, then shook it. "You, too, pal."

With a subservient nodding of his head toward Angela, Langston disappeared into the train, leaving the two of them alone. For a moment Angela almost followed, then she straightened her back, determined to bluff it out.

"Take that look off your face, Red," Clancy drawled.

"What look?"

"That 'what are you doing talking to a colored man' expression. Langston and I go way back."

"Do you?"

"Why, sure, honey. He used to work for my pappy, down at de ole plantation. Why he'd—"

"Cut it out, Clancy. Don't put words in my mouth or thoughts in my brain that aren't there. I don't give a damn who you talk to."

"As a matter of fact, you ought to give a damn. You ought to thank your lucky stars that Langston happened to be on this train. Otherwise we would have spent a lot of time looking for Will Parsons."

"Your friend knows where he is?"

"Sure. They've got a lot in common. Both of them love airplanes."

Angela stared back toward the car where Langston had disappeared. "That wasn't Langston Howard?"

"First man of his race to hold a pilot's licence. Exactly. We worked together down in Peru in '34. He was fool enough to come back, knowing he wouldn't be able to fly."

"Why?"

"Why'd he come back? Family. He had a wife and two kids, and the money he was sending wasn't enough. I guess he missed them too much. Marriage is a sucker's game, Angel. Once you get caught, you get grounded for good, one way or the other." He took another puff of his cigar and blew the smoke skyward.

"You're probably right," she said. "You don't see me getting married, do you? Hard as it is to believe, I've had offers."

"I know. I'm sorry about Ramsey. He was an okay guy."

"You knew Hal?" Somehow the idea of that was unsettling.

"In this business everybody knows everybody sooner or later. Unless they die first." He stared down at his cigar in meditative silence for a moment. "I'd offer you one of these, but I gave Langston my last."

"I can do without cigars, thank you," she said. "And I didn't mean why did Langston come back. I mean why isn't he able to fly?"

Clancy stared at her with undisguised disgust for a moment, then sent the cigar hurtling out into the early-morning air. "You're pretty damned naive, aren't you? That's the problem with women pilots. You're all spoiled little rich girls with nothing better to do than play with airplanes. You probably haven't ever talked with someone of another race unless it was to give them orders. No one will hire a black pilot, Red, even if he's one of the best around."

"Don't be ridiculous," she shot back, stung both by the truth of his accusation and the unfairness of it. "I'd hire anyone who's as good as Langston is supposed to be."

"Then you'd be a fool. You have trouble enough getting contracts being a woman, not to mention Olker putting a spoke in your wheels every chance he gets. How many people are going to use you if they know you've hired a colored man to fly their precious cargo? Not many. And even if you offered Langston a job, he'd turn it down. He's learned his lesson. He's damned tired of being a pioneer and getting the stuffing kicked out of him. All he cares about nowadays is taking care of his family and bringing in a decent wage. Too many people are out of a job. If he took work with you, we'd all be out of a job."

"It's not fair!"

"Honey," Clancy said wearily, "whoever said life was fair? Come down out of the clouds. Life is mean and dirty down here in the trenches. If you haven't found that out yet then you're about to."

"I've found it out." Her voice was flat, unemotional, but Clancy's hard expression softened for a moment.

"Yeah, that's right. There's Ramsey and there's your father. I never met him, but I heard he was all right. I guess you've been through your share in the last few years."

She straightened up, glaring at him. Pity was one thing she wasn't about to take from him. "You said Langston knows where this mechanic is?"

"Back to business, is that it? The colored section of Albany isn't very far from the shanty town. Convenient that way. He ran into Parsons a few days ago and they got to talking. If he's still around, it shouldn't take long to find him."

"Why wouldn't he be around?"

"People don't stay put when they're out of work. Why do you think shanty towns crop up around the railroad lines? He's been riding the rails. There's no guarantee that he hasn't decided to strike out for something better."

"You mean we made this trip for nothing?"

"I don't mean anything. I'm just warning you. You go through life expecting everything to go your way and you're going to get kicked in the teeth." He pushed away from the railing.

"And if you go through life expecting the worst then there's no reason even to try," she shot back.

His dark eyes raked her face for a moment. "Then I guess we're at a stalemate. You dream too much, I dream too little. Or maybe my dreams are just a little more practical. A Pan American Clipper crossed the Pacific last week. The first commercial aircraft to do so. That's where the future is, Red. Not hotheaded barnstormers breaking speed records and endurance records for the hell of it."

"Are you talking about me?" Her voice was frosty.

"No, Red. I'm talking about me." He moved past her, but the space on the tiny platform was too small to avoid touching her. She had the sense that if he could have, he would have, but she was damned if she was going to squeeze herself into a corner just to avoid him.

"Where are you going?"

"We're coming into Albany. I'm getting our bags."

"I thought you weren't a gentleman," she said, thanking heaven she'd thought to repack before coming in search of her traveling companion.

"I have my moments. Meet you on the platform." He disappeared into the darkened bar car with such speed that Angela might almost have thought he was trying to get away from her. Impossible, she told herself. He didn't care enough about her one way or another to want to run away. With a tiny mental shrug, she followed him, her high heels just slightly wobbly in the swaying car.

CLANCY WANTED TO GET as far away as fast as he could. The steady thrum of the train beneath his feet and the innocent, seductive sway of her slender body as she maintained her balance were driving him absolutely insane.

He'd had one holy hell of a night. He thought he'd gotten over his love of risk, his daring of fate. Why he'd hauled Miss High-and-Mighty Hogan up into his berth in the middle of the night couldn't be anything but sheer cussedness. Why he'd kissed her was even more unfathomable. Except for the fact that he'd wanted to kiss her ever since he'd seen her, glowering at him in that makeshift office inside the hangar.

How many times did he have to remind himself that she wasn't his type? He liked blond, busty babes with bright red bee-stung lips, china-blue eyes and enough intellect to wipe their nose and not much more. At least, that was what he liked in bed.

Women like Angela Hogan were better as friends, and surprisingly enough, he'd had a number of women friends over the years. Fliers, all of them, and he'd viewed them with the same lack of lust that he viewed Sparks. So why couldn't Angela join that select band of sexless women? Why did he want to...?

With a muffled curse he grabbed the two flight bags from their berths as the train began slowing its headlong pace. The less he thought about Angela Hogan, the better. He needed to concentrate on finding a decent mechanic, one who understood Wasp engines and Percivals as well as Avians and Lockheed Vegas. Not to mention his own precious Fokker. He needed to remember that planes, that flying, came first, way above anything else. Certainly far beyond anything as paltry as his overactive glands.

He did his own double take when he stepped out on the platform as the train pulled in to Albany. Angela was carrying on a friendly, low-voiced conversation with Langston, and for once his old friend had dropped his defenses. She had gumption, Clancy had to grant her that. And persistence and her own kind of charm to be able to get through Langston's determined pride. She hadn't bothered to bestow any of that charm on Clancy, which was a damned good thing. She was a potent enough package wrapped in hostility.

Langston flashed Clancy a rueful grin, shutting up as other passengers crowded onto the tiny platform, and for once Angela had the sense to follow his lead. Even in the free-thinking north, people might not like to see a white woman and black man having a casual conversation, and she knew that as well as Langston. And knew he'd be the one to suffer for it.

Clancy jumped down first after Langston lowered the steps, moving out of the way as his old friend helped the passengers down. Clancy had no intention of offering Angela a hand—she'd probably slap it away. He watched with surprise as she accepted Langston's assistance onto the high box on the station platform, and she pressed something in his hand, something he took with a bob of his head and the deftness of a magician.

Clancy didn't say anything until they were halfway down the almost-empty platform. Angela was managing to keep up, despite her shorter legs and ridiculous high-heeled shoes, and it wasn't until they were at the end that he turned and glared at her.

"Don't tell me you were fool enough to tip him?" he demanded, whirling around with sudden ferocity.

She stood her ground, not even flinching. "With a wife and family, doesn't he need the money?"

He cursed then. "I thought you were smarter than that, Red. How much did you give him?"

She just looked at him, her eyes calm and clear, saying nothing, and then it sank in.

"You didn't give him any money," he said.

"Of course I didn't. I figured he needed his self-respect more than he needed a handout. I gave him a card with my name and address and phone number on it. In case he wants to find work flying again."

"He won't."

"Maybe. But at least he's got a choice."

"He has no choice at all," Clancy said bitterly. "Don't you realize that you're just dangling a carrot in front of his nose, one that's forever out of reach? That's not being kind, Red. That's being damned cruel."

"If you spend your life knuckling under to bigots then you might as well give up trying," she said fiercely. "But then, we've already covered that ground, haven't we? I dream too much, you dream too little."

There was nothing he could say. He stood, fuming, exasperated, knowing he was right and yet wishing he weren't. "We're wasting time," he said finally. "We've got less than a day to find your mechanic before the *Twentieth Century* comes back through. Let's get moving."

"How are we going to get to the shanty town? I didn't see any taxis."

"We don't need a taxi, Red. Look over there." He pointed to the left, to a vast, sprawling mass of tents, shacks, lean-tos and the like, the smoke from hundreds of campfires swirling lazily into the early-morning air. "People without a home stay as close to the tracks as the railroad bulls will let them. You never know when you'll need a quick getaway."

She looked up at him with sudden curiosity. "Have you spent time in one of these places?"

"Honey, that's none of your damned business." He took a step away from her, away from the teasing scent of her perfume. He wasn't used to women who wore perfume, not such a subtle, tantalizing fragrance. They either used something musky and overpowering or nothing at all. Angela Hogan was a confusing mix of femininity and pilot, and he began to think that Hal Ramsey had been a lucky man, even if he'd gone west before his time.

As they came to the edge of the hobo encampment, the smells rose in the air as well as the smoke. Beans and coffee, woodsmoke and poverty, unwashed bodies and pride and despair filling the air like a thick cloud. There were fewer families, thank God. Fewer people all together. Back in 1932, when the Depression had been at its worst, this Hooverville would have been twice the size. If prosperity hadn't been just around the corner when F.D.R. and his alphabet soup took office, at least things had improved for a number of people.

Fewer able-bodied men, too, though work was still scarce. Clancy strode at an easy pace through the encampment, always aware of Angela trotting along at his heels. He didn't spare her a glance, but if anyone had touched her, even looked at her in a way he didn't like, he would have known it and been on the man instantly. He'd lived on the edge long enough to know how to trust his instincts.

She slipped and he caught her instantly. A light drizzle had begun to fall and her usually smooth hair had begun to curl in the humidity. Her shoes were a wreck, with twigs and garbage clinging to them, and her stockings were splattered with mud. Her dress was shrivelling in the dampness, and he looked into her face, expecting a tirade.

"How do you know we're going in the right direction?" she asked calmly enough, instead of the tantrum he'd been fearing.

"Langston said he was over in the west corner last he heard. If he's still here, we'll find him." A thin, ragged woman was moving past, her cotton housedress soaked with the rain, her hair straggling down around her scrawny neck. Clancy reached out and caught her arm, and she stared at him out of vacant, hopeless eyes. "We're looking for a man named Will Parsons," Clancy said. "Have you seen him?"

The woman pulled away, shaking her head. "People don't use their last names around here." And she started to move away.

"Wait," Angela said, moving after her. The woman stopped, watching numbly as Angela spoke to her in low, hurried tones. A moment later what almost passed for a smile crossed the woman's face, and then she was gone.

"I suppose you gave her money," Clancy said with a sigh as Angela rejoined him. "You know how stupid that is, in a place like this? There are people here who'd kill their own mother for two bits. You start flashing money around and we may not make it out of here...."

"These aren't criminals, Clancy. They're just people who've run out of luck."

"What do you think makes some people criminals, Red? No luck, no job, no hope. You can't afford scruples and honesty when you can't feed your kids. You're just lucky it started raining. If you looked like Miss Society from Chicago instead of a half-drowned kitten, she wouldn't have given you the time of day."

"Maybe. Women tend to help each other, despite their backgrounds."

He shook his head. "You'll never learn, will you? I suppose she told you where to find Parsons. And I suppose you believed her?"

"You're not having much luck so far, Clancy. Let's try it my way."

Now it was his turn to follow her through the muddy paths of the makeshift city. The rain was coming down more heavily now, forcing the weary inhabitants back inside their rude dwellings, but Angela scarcely seemed to notice it. Her hair hung in wet rats tails over her padded shoulders, her feet slipped in the mud and the dress clung to her subtle curves with a stubborn tenacity. Clancy tried to concentrate on that, on the way the lavender material wrapped itself around Angela's hips, instead of the way the rain was sliding down inside his collar. It would be a damned lucky thing if neither of them got pneumonia.

She came to an abrupt stop by a rough lean-to. The fire in front of it was sizzling and hissing in the rain, not quite out, and the battered coffeepot balanced on top of it was putting forth wonderful smells. There was no sign of humanity anywhere around the shack, and Clancy was just about to open his mouth and tell her just how wrongheaded she was when he noticed the photo of the airplane just inside the open doorway. Clancy's experienced eyes recognized a Lockheed Vega, practically identical to the one Angela flew. The picture looked as if it had been ripped from a magazine, and he took a step closer to see whether it was Amelia Earhart's famous Lockheed or one of its humbler cousins, when a man's gruff voice stopped him cold.

"Who the hell are you?" the man demanded in a rough, scratchy voice. "And what do you think you're doing, poking around my digs?"

## Chapter Seven

Angela stood there, rain plastering her hair against her skull, and surveyed the man she'd traveled so far to find. What she could see was scarcely reassuring. He was of average height, dressed in old, patched clothes, a wide-brimmed hat keeping the rain off his face. That face was obscured by a huge, bristling, gray beard and thick, bottle-lensed glasses, and she thought she could see the red tracery of scarring across his nose and cheekbones. She was overcome with the strangest sense of emotion, of déjà vu, of deep, inexplicable sadness that vanished as quickly as it came.

"Are you Will Parsons?" Clancy asked, standing his ground.

"What if I am? Who wants to know?" The old man barely glanced in Angela's direction, stomping past her into the makeshift lean-to, and ripped a picture of an airplane off the wall, tossing it into the hissing, spitting fire.

"My name's Clancy. We've come a long ways to see you, Mr. Parsons."

"You didn't fly in this weather?"

"What makes you think I know how to fly?" Clancy countered smoothly.

"Stands to reason." Parsons hunkered down by the fire, pouring himself a cup of coffee into a battered tin mug. "You wouldn't be coming to see me for any other reason.

You must be looking for a mechanic. And I'm guessing you're Jack Clancy."

"You're guessing right. And no, we didn't fly. We took the *Twentieth Century*. Not because of the weather. Because we need a mechanic. Our planes are grounded. Got any more of that coffee?"

"Plenty of coffee. Only one other mug." He glanced over at Angela and his expression was no more than faintly interested. "Your wife mind sharing?"

"I'm not his wife," Angela said sharply. "And I'd share a mug with Adolf Hitler."

"Hey, Red, I'm not quite that bad," Clancy drawled, sounding surprisingly at ease as he took the second cup from Parsons gloved hand. "Why'd you throw that picture into the fire?"

"What picture?" Parsons said, staring at Clancy, staring into his oily black coffee, staring everywhere but at Angela.

"The one of the Lockheed Vega."

Parsons shrugged. "What can I say? I like Amelia Earhart."

"That wasn't AE's plane. Hers is painted bright red to help people find her if she's in trouble."

Parsons scratched his head in an elaborate show of surprise. "Gee, you can't trust anybody nowadays. And I thought for sure that was Amelia Earhart."

"If you like lady fliers, I've got one here you can do a favor for."

The old man glanced over at Angela then, and she thought she could feel animosity behind those thick lenses. She was almost ready to tell Clancy to forget it, that she didn't want any favors from such a nasty old man, when she noticed had badly his hands were shaking.

"I don't like lady fliers," Parsons said in his raspy, ruined voice. "They should be married and having babies. You have any babies, lady?"

"I'm not married." She was tired of this pussyfooting, tired of standing in the rain with mud oozing through the open toes of her ridiculous high heels, the shoes she was too damned stubborn to admit she should have left behind. "My name's Angela Hogan, Mr. Parsons. I own a small air transport firm just outside of Chicago. I've got a Percival, a Lockheed Vega and an Avian, and Clancy's got a Fokker coming up from South America before long. We need a mechanic, a good one."

"I'm not a good mechanic, Miss Hogan. I'm the best there is."

"Then you're what we need."

"Sorry, not interested."

She opened her mouth to protest, but Clancy forestalled her, handing her the half-empty mug of coffee. "Why not? Angela can pay you what you're worth."

"John D. Rockefeller himself couldn't pay me what I'm worth," Parsons said. "Can't you find any mechanics in Chicago? There must be a dozen of them swarming around. If they've already got a job, steal 'em away."

"Angela has a little problem."

"Who says I care?" Parsons shot back.

"A man named Charlie Olker is determined to put her out of business. He's scared all the mechanics away, hired them away, fixed it so that all she can get by with is rum-soaked old has-beens."

Parsons set his cup down in the mud, and there was no ignoring the trembling in his hands. "So you thought you'd see if you could find a rum-soaked has-been named Parsons instead of hiring a local one?"

Clancy glanced at his hands, and there was sympathy in his dark eyes. "Rough night?"

"I'll be okay in a few hours. Just as soon as I find the hair of the dog. You don't happen to have a little nip on you?"

"No," Clancy lied.

"Do you drink all the time?" Angela asked.

"What the hell does it matter to you, lady? I'm not working for you."

"It means I can be relieved instead of disappointed," she snapped, taking a sip of the awful coffee, letting its warmth sink into her chilled body.

"Shut up, Angel," Clancy said. "Why won't you work for us, Parsons?"

"I'm sick of airplanes."

"I beg your pardon?"

"You heard me. I'm sick of the damned things. I need more challenge in my life. I've decided airships are the wave of the future."

Clancy stared at him in disbelief. "You're kidding me! After all the disasters involved with dirigibles, do you think people still want to travel in them?"

"Nobody's done 'em right. The durn government spent millions on two big, showy pieces and what happens? They go down, taking over a hundred lives between 'em. Same thing's happened all over the world. England, France and Italy have all backed out after a little bad luck. The thing is, there's still incredible potential and I think I can lick their problem. I've had a thought or two that might just turn the tide."

"But no one's building airships anymore," Angela pointed out.

Parsons shook his head and the rain that had collected on the wide flat brim sprayed around him. "Only Germany's sticking with the thing, and I intend to be in on it. The *Hindenburg*'s proven everybody wrong—they've already made two trans-Atlantic crossings with as smooth and safe a flight as anyone could hope for, and they've just started on the third. When it docks in New Jersey in a few days, I intend to be there, to offer my services. Eckener himself is rumored to be aboard. I know if I can just talk to him, I can give him a few pointers on how to solve the airships' vulnerability to lightning and storms."

"You'd move to Germany? You'd work for Hitler's crew, when you know all the trouble they've been causing?"

"Hitler doesn't want war any more than we do," Parsons said flatly, his opaque glasses fixed unnervingly on Angela's face. "He just wants to scare everybody into leaving Germany alone. And part of his plan is to spend a fortune on defense, including airships. He'll never use them."

"What if he does. Won't you feel like a murderer?"

"Miss Hogan, I worked at the Lockheed factory in Burbank, building bombers for this country and half the countries in the world. If the Great War wasn't really the war to end all wars, then I'll already have done my part to add to the death toll."

"But . . ."

"And Hitler's not our enemy, at least not yet. If that happens to change, then I'll hightail it out of Germany. In the meantime, if this country's too shortsighted not to keep working on airships, I have no choice but to turn to the one country with the vision to do so." He squatted back down and poured himself another cup of coffee, ignoring them.

Angela watched him for a moment, the trembling hands, the obscured face. "You didn't answer my question," she said quietly.

He glanced up at her again, his face inscrutable through the heavy glasses and beard. "No, I don't drink all the time. I'm just like anyone else—I have a bad night now and then. God knows there's not much else for comfort in my life."

"I still don't understand why you're here. If you're the best mechanic in the world, why aren't you working?"

"Get her out of here, Clancy," Parsons snapped in his harsh voice. "You can fill her in on the rumors during your trip back to Evanston."

Something wasn't right, but Angela couldn't quite figure out what it was. "How'd you know we came from Evanston?"

"It stands to reason. Most of the small airfields around Chicago are in Evanston. I know the business, Miss Hogan. I just chose to leave it. Now would you leave an old man in peace?"

Angela opened her mouth to speak, but Clancy once again forestalled her. "Any chance you'll change your mind?"

Parsons glanced up at him. "I've been kicking around this mean old world long enough to know that you never say never. I'm heading down to New Jersey in a couple of days. The *Hindenburg*'s due to dock at Lakehurst on Tuesday and I want to be there to watch it land. If by any chance Eckener doesn't want me, maybe I'll give you a ring. Then again, maybe I won't."

"I guess we'll have to settle for that." Clancy held out his hand and after a long moment, Parsons took it.

"I'd like to say I appreciate your coming all this way," he said in his raspy voice.

"But you don't," Angela piped up, moving her frozen mud-encrusted feet with some difficulty. "You wish we'd left you the hell alone."

The rusty sound Parsons made could have almost passed for a laugh. "You got it, girly. Have a nice trip back."

"Let us know if you change your mind," Clancy said, taking Angela's damp arm in his. She was too cold and miserable to object, slogging through the mud feeling like a foot soldier from Parsons's Great War. They were about to turn a corner, disappear from sight in the great rabbit warren of shacks and tents, when something made her stop.

She turned, expecting to see Parsons's fire deserted. He was still standing there, watching them, his face almost completely obscured by his hat brim. But she somehow got the impression of longing, of an aching need that couldn't be filled.

The moment he saw her watching him, he disappeared, diving into his shanty without a backward glance. And Angela wondered whether she'd ever see him again.

"What's holding you up?" Clancy tugged at her arm.

She started moving again. "He was lying."

"Yeah? What makes you say that?" Clancy's voice was carefully neutral, but she had the impression he knew far more than he was saying.

"He hasn't given up on airplanes. He wanted to come work for us, I know he did. I could feel it."

"Don't tell me you're some kind of fortune teller, Red! If so, I'm going to find myself a shack and stay right here."

"No, I mean it. Couldn't you feel it, Clancy?"

"I couldn't feel anything but cold rain down my neck and annoyance that we came this far for probably nothing."

"What do you mean, probably?"

"Parsons might still show up. You're right, you know. He hasn't given up on airplanes. He thinks they've given up on him. There's a reason why he's been riding the rails. He's had a rough few years. He was in that fire in the Lockheed factory a few years back. Got badly burned, including his eyes. A bunch of men died, and when Parsons recovered, he just took off. He's worked since, but he's had a run of bad luck. Nothing was ever his fault, but there've been too many crashes, and he's got the reputation of a jinx. I think he needs to start a new life."

"I suppose we don't want a drunkard and a jinx hanging around," she said slowly.

"I don't think he'd drink if he had a job. And I don't believe in jinxes."

"Neither do I."

Clancy stopped, looking down at her with a lopsided grin. "Well, will wonders never cease? We actually agree on something."

"We agree on something else," Angela said wearily. "These clothes were a stupid idea."

"You know, Red, there's hope for you yet. You look like a drowned kitten. Let's go find a nice warm restaurant with a good juke box and soup that comes from a back burner and not a can. We've got a long wait before the *Twentieth Century* comes back through."

And Angela, remembering the upper berth and what had happened in it the night before, was suddenly filled with foreboding. It wouldn't do to get too friendly with Jack Clancy. She already got in enough trouble when they were practically enemies.

"Drowned kitten, eh?" she managed to squeak out.

"Don't worry, kid. I won't tell anyone you ever admitted you were wrong. Now let's get the hell out of this rain." He took her arm again and began hauling her through the muddy paths of the shanty town. And while she knew she should protest, try to manage on her own two muddy feet, it was nice to have something strong to hold on to. For balance, she told herself righteously, clinging tight. Just for a few moments. And then she'd stand on her own again. As always.

THE RESTAURANT ACROSS from the railroad station had terrific coffee, oxtail stew, Vienna Roast with beans and fresh strawberry-rhubarb pie. The jukebox had the latest Benny Goodman, Count Basie and Artie Shaw, the cigarette machine had fresh Luckies, and by the time Angela changed into her jodhpurs and leather jacket in the ladies' room, brushed her sopping hair into a semblance of order and even went so far as to put just a slash of lipstick on her pale mouth, she was feeling much more in charity with the world. She even thought she could face the trip back without any danger of traveling between berths.

That is, if Clancy continued smoking cigarette after cigarette, drinking cup after cup of coffee and staring out the window into the dreary Albany weather. Angela was almost sorry they weren't fighting. At least that would have been more interesting than picking at the crust of her pie and listening to "Harbor Lights" for the seventeenth time.

"Penny for your thoughts," she said finally, desperate. Clancy lifted his head, his dark eyes momentarily abstracted, and then they focused on her.

"You wouldn't want to know," he said, stubbing out his cigarette and reaching for the crumpled pack.

She put her hand over his, stopping him, and immediately regretted her gesture. He had hard hands, strong hands, disturbing hands. She pulled away quickly, reaching for her lukewarm coffee. "Haven't you smoked too many of those things?"

"When did you appoint yourself my mother? They help me think."

"What are you thinking about?" He grinned then, and she flushed, knowing he was deliberately taunting her. "Don't give me that. You weren't thinking of anything pleasant."

"Who says sex is pleasant?" he countered, lighting the cigarette with deliberate defiance.

"I wouldn't know," she said in her frostiest voice, and immediately regretted it. Of all the stupid things to say, to him of all people! She wished she could kick herself under the table.

"Oh, really?" He leaned across the table with that charming smirk that she wanted to slap off his face. "You know, I guessed that might be the case, given your lack of experience in kissing. Sparks said you were engaged to

Ramsey. What'd you do, keep him on a leash? Or did he have some old war wound I never heard about?''

"You're disgusting," she said furiously.

"Yeah?" He blew a smoke ring with a casual expertise Angela would have envied if she weren't so angry. "Well, sister, there's a word for women like you, and it's not a nice one. I won't sully your sweet little virgin ears with it, but I bet you can think of it all by yourself if you put your mind to it. Or I can always enlighten you—"

She did slap him then. The sound was loud in the deserted café, over the muted trumpets of "Harbor Lights." She knocked over her coffee cup when she'd slapped him, and the small amount pooled on the table between them.

"Do that again, Red," he said between his teeth, "and I'll knock you halfway across the room."

She was tempted to do just that, to call his bluff. The problem was, she didn't think he was bluffing. The tired looking waitress wasn't around, but even her presence wouldn't have stopped Clancy if Angela pushed him too far.

She sat back against the banquette, knowing she should apologize, knowing she'd die before she did so. "What are we going to do about a mechanic?" she said instead.

"It's still we, is it? You aren't going to tell me to take my ill-bred presence from your sight?"

"You aren't going to walk out in a huff?" she countered. She could see the mark of her hand on his strong, tanned cheek, and she felt ashamed. And still angry.

"I never back down, Red. Not from a challenge, not from a dame. I told you I'm in it for the duration. We'll find a mechanic. I'll put out the word and see what I can come up with. But I still wouldn't count Parsons out. I have a feeling he's going to show up in Evanston before long."

"What makes you say that? Don't you think the Germans will want him?"

"They'd be fools not to. But I'm willing to bet he won't be on the *Hindenburg* when it flies back to Berlin."

"How much?"

"I beg your pardon?"

"How much are you willing to bet?" she repeated patiently.

Clancy slouched back in his seat, a speculative expression on his face. "So the lady likes to gamble? You could have fooled me. I would have taken you for a girl who doesn't take chances."

"I'm a flier, Clancy. Every time I climb in an airplane I'm taking a gamble. I do what I can to minimize the risk, but it's still a matter of odds."

"That's right, I keep forgetting. You'll have to take me up sometime, Red, so I can check you out. Maybe then I'll be able to keep it straight."

"I thought you didn't like to fly with other people."

"I don't. But if I'm tying up with you for a while, I'd better know what kind of talent I'm getting involved with. If you're just a fancy amateur with heavy hands, then the deal's off. If you're any good at all, then we have a bargain."

"What do you think?"

He glanced at her through half-closed eyes, and the effect was oddly unnerving, deep in the pit of her stomach. When would she learn not to ask leading questions of this disturbing man?

"The truth, Red?" he asked, stubbing out his cigarette.

"Always, Clancy."

He grinned. "Then I hate to admit it, but I expect you're one hell of a pilot. Maybe almost as good as I am. Sparks says you are."

"And you'll take his word for it?"

"He'd be the one to know. But no, I won't. That's why we're going up together as soon as we get the Lockheed in working order. That jake with you?"

"Certainly."

"And then you can check out my talents. See if I'm overrated."

"We're talking about flying skills, I trust?" Her voice was caustic.

Clancy's expression was positively angelic, belied by the glint in his dark, devilish eyes. "What else, Angel? What else?"

SHE WAS A DAMNED DANGEROUS woman, Clancy thought, listening to her rustle around in the berth beneath him as the *Twentieth Century* barreled its way back toward Chicago. And if she did turn out to be a terrific pilot, things were going to get even worse. He liked his women compartmentalized. Pilots were pilots, dames were dames, and the two weren't supposed to cross over. Not that he had anything against women pilots. He just didn't want to be attracted to one as he was attracted to Angela Hogan.

He wasn't going to waste any more time denying his attraction. The fact that she was still a virgin made her even more of a challenge, a challenge he wasn't about to accept. She was the kind to tie a man down, to weep and wail when he had a dangerous flight, to make him settle down and raise a family and get strangled with a mortgage and a dog and a backyard.

He'd figured long ago that that sort of life wasn't for him. And a woman like Angela Hogan wasn't for him. The problem was, she was making him forget that.

He could hear her sliding out of her pants in the narrow bunk, and that finished him. He swung his legs over the side and dropped down on the floor with a thud, almost landing on a bathrobed matron with curlers in her hair. She gave a frightened little shriek and dove into her berth.

"Sorry, toots," he said to her disappearing feet.

Angela stuck her head out of her berth, her long dark hair rumpled from having pulled her nightgown over it. He could see the white lace of its high collar, and he remembered the soft feel of it, the feel of her body beneath it, sleeping in his arms. "Where are you going, Clancy?" she hissed.

"To the bar car. Just for your peace of mind, Red, I'm going to spend the night there. You might have to pour me off the train, but at least your virtue will be safe."

She opened her mouth to object, and then shut it again. A trace of her bright red lipstick lingered, and he wanted to lean over and kiss it off her mouth. "That's probably a wise idea," she said.

"Afraid you can't resist me, Red?" he taunted.

"No, Clancy. I'm afraid you can't resist me." And with an impish grin she disappeared back behind the green serge curtains of her lower berth.

He almost dove in after her. If it weren't for the matron with her curlers peering out at him, he would have done so.

"Go back to bed, toots," he snapped at her, and the woman disappeared promptly. And then he headed off for the bar car, knowing he'd better not hesitate any longer. Angela was right. When you were a pilot you always took risks. But you learned to minimize those risks if at all possible, and spending even another moment near Angela Hogan was a risk not worth taking.

Maybe the bar car had one-hundred-fifty-proof rum. And maybe the night wouldn't be endless. But he wasn't about to count on it. Not for a moment.

# Chapter Eight

Clancy straightened up, running his grease-stained hands down the legs of his coveralls. Sparks was on the other side of the Wasp engine, tinkering with the manifold, and Clancy stepped back, thinking he might step outside for a cigarette, when the sound of the radio penetrated his abstraction.

It was evening, past seven, and they were all working late. Angela usually kept the volume turned up loud enough for them to hear it if they weren't testing an engine. At first he thought she'd turned on a soap opera, *Helen Trent* or something of that ilk, when the voices began to coalesce into something he didn't want to hear. His eyes met Sparks's for a moment, and they stood there, listening.

"I'm going to turn that damned thing off," Sparks said hoarsely, dropping the wrench with a loud clatter on the cement floor.

"I'll do it," Clancy said.

ANGELA SAT FROZEN AT her desk, her fingers gripping a broken pencil as she listened with blind concentration. The newscaster was sobbing in horror and in the background, through the static, she could hear the screams of people in pain, people dying, people plunging to their death from an airship that was disintegrating.

She didn't look up when his shadow darkened her office door. It was early evening on May 6, and she was listening as the *Hindenburg*, the pride of the German airships, crashed and burned. She should have switched the station when they began covering the landing, but curiosity had stayed her hand. She'd been wondering whether Will Parsons was in that crowd of onlookers at the New Jersey hangar, whether he'd get a chance to work on the huge dirigible.

And then, in a matter of moments, triumph had turned to disaster as fire and death rained out of the sky onto the tarmac below. And Angela was too sickened to move, an unwilling prisoner to the radio, as she listened while terrified victims faced her worst nightmare.

Suddenly the sound cut out and Angela looked up at Clancy. He'd switched off the radio. For a moment he kept his back turned, and she could see the tension thrumming through his body. And then he faced her, his expression remote and unreadable. "Tough break," he said. "I wonder whether Parsons was hurt."

It took all her energy to say something and her voice came out hoarse and strained. "Maybe he didn't make it down there."

"He was there, all right. He's the sort of man who does what he says he's going to do. Listen, Red, why don't you go home? This has shaken you up—hell, it would shake anybody up. You should see Sparks. His hands are shaking so hard he can't even light a cigarette."

She didn't say anything for a moment. A small, very tiny part of her wanted to do just that, to get in the old Packard and drive straight home, climb into bed and pull the covers over her head.

But that was only a tiny part, that tiny kernel of fear that lived inside everyone, a part she was used to ignoring. She rose, pushing back from the desk, and was pleased to see that her hands were steady and calm.

"Go on home, Red," he said again. "You're not going to accomplish anything tonight, and I'm willing to bet half our lessons won't show up tomorrow, not if our budding pilots have a radio or a pair of ears. I don't know how this is going to affect business in the long run, but right now things are clear."

"That's good," Angela murmured, moving past him.

He caught her arm and she looked down at his hand clamped across the white linen shirt she usually wore. He'd been tinkering with one of the engines and his long fingers left dark grease marks across her lower arm. "What're you doing?"

"What do you think I'm doing, Clancy? I'm going flying." And she jerked her hand out of his arm and kept going, out into the hangar.

The Lockheed Vega was already out on the tarmac, waiting for tomorrow morning's student pilot, the one who wasn't going to show. She'd checked it over herself, earlier, and Sparks had done the same. Without hesitating she grabbed her leather jacket and flight helmet and headed out, vaulting into the cockpit without looking back. She just got the Wasp engine into a confident purr when the door opened and Clancy heaved himself up beside her. He'd managed to change out of his oil-stained coveralls and grab his own jacket, but he still didn't look any too pleased to be there.

"Don't be a sap, Angel," he said. "You're in no condition to fly."

"Don't condescend to me, Jack Clancy," she said fiercely, gunning the motor and starting down the runway. "I can't think of a better thing to do right now." Her eyes met his for a brief, challenging moment. "Can you?"

She half expected him to come up with an argument. She'd forgotten that one good thing she could say about Jack Clancy was that he was honest. "No," he said. "I can't." And leaning back, he strapped himself in, bracing himself for her takeoff.

She would have thought she'd be nervous, self-conscious, ham-handed with Clancy beside her, watching her every move, judging her. But she wasn't. As the plane gathered speed and hurtled down the short runway, she could feel the old familiar sense of rightness seep into her bones. She was one with her pretty blue bird, getting ready to hurl herself into the twilight sky, and no one else mattered as she felt the familiar rush of excitement shoot through her.

She knew he was watching her out of those hooded eyes. As she brought the plane up, up and then began to level off, she was suddenly aware of him beside her. Her feet on the rudders, her hands on the throttle were suddenly clumsy and she muttered a small, daring curse under her breath.

"Forget about me, Red," Clancy ordered. "You're doing fine."

"Go to hell, Clancy," she snapped. "Of course I'm doing fine. I'm a pilot, damn it, not some wet-behind-the-ears student."

"I know that. You're not bad, either."

"Kind of you to say so. I really appreciate compliments coming from old-timers like you."

"Feeling feisty, are you?"

"I'm feeling angry. Angry at the waste of human lives. Why can't those stupid Nazis realize that occasionally we know what we're doing? We've lost hundreds of people in airship disasters. Anyone with any sense would have given up long ago."

"Haven't you noticed how stubborn governments get? No bureaucrat has ever admitted he was wrong."

She glanced over at him. "You're pretty cynical, aren't you?"

"I've been kicking around this world for thirty-six years. It's enough to make anyone cynical. Look on the bright side, kid. At least you've got yourself a mechanic."

"Why do you say that? Parsons flat-out said he didn't want to work for me. Just because the *Hindenburg* crashed doesn't mean he'll show up here. The damned thing might have even landed on him."

"He'll be here. Call it a hunch. I'd say two days at the outside." He leaned forward. "Aren't you accelerating a little too much?" He frowned at the control panel.

"No," she said, and promptly did a faultlessly executed double loop. The wind was perfect, the day clear and cloudless, and her heart soared with her airplane as it dipped and swirled and spun.

"Okay," Clancy drawled as she leveled off again. "So you can get a job at a carnival. That doesn't mean you're a great pilot."

Try as she might, she couldn't conjure up her usual knot of anger. She was too happy to be out, flying. It had been too long. "Believe it or not, Clancy, I wasn't trying to impress you. Scare you, maybe."

"You can't do that, either. I've flown with too many student pilots to let anything frighten me. Besides, I know when someone's got it."

"Got what?"

"'It.' That special something that separates the flyboys from the real pilots. I don't know where it came from, Red, and you sure as hell don't deserve it, but you've got it."

She glanced over at him, startled. "Why, Clancy, is that a compliment?"

"Nope. Simply a statement of fact. Now why don't you land this baby," he suggested lazily, "so we can get ourselves a drink?"

TONY'S WAS MORE CROWDED than usual that night, and all anyone could talk about was the *Hindenburg*. Someone had recorded the commentator's voice as he described the awful sight, and that recording was played over and over again on Tony's radio, reliving the awful moments.

"Shut that damned thing off, willya?" Sparks shouted drunkenly. Tony was doing a land-office business in boiler-makers that night, and even the usually officious Rosa was turning a blind eye to the heavy drinkers.

"Someone said they were making a record of that newscast," Stan said bleerily. "Put it in all the jukeboxes, in between Benny Goodman and Fats Waller."

"You hear that, Tony?" Clancy called out. "If you put it in this one I'm going to shoot the damned machine."

"Sure thing, Clancy," Tony said in a somber voice. "No Hindenburg on my jukebox, you bet."

"Where's Angela?" Robert Bellamy demanded.

Clancy glared at him. The pilot had come in with Stan and joined them a few minutes ago, and Clancy had let him stay, despite Sparks's obvious animosity. "She went straight home. She was tired."

"Angela doesn't get tired," Sparks said flatly.

"No, I can believe it," said Clancy. "I think maybe she wanted some time alone. Say, Sparks, why didn't you tell me she was such a good pilot?"

"I told you, Clancy," Sparks said bleerily. "You just didn't listen."

"I listened. I guess I had to see it for myself."

"She's swell, isn't she?" Stan said soulfully. "She's got such a light touch on the controls, delicate but sure."

"Yeah," Bellamy said with a grin on his pretty face. "I bet she'd be hell on wheels in bed."

Without hesitation Clancy sent his fist into Bellamy's jaw, sending the handsome man sprawling backward onto the floor, glasses and beer bottles and half-empty plates of spaghetti flying after him.

"Hey, what's going on here?" Tony demanded, emerging from behind the bar. "You trying to break up my place, Clancy?" Rosa was right behind, scolding like an angry Italian magpie.

Sparks had managed to grab his drink before the table went flying and he was still sitting, like a drunken potentate, clutching his glass. "You don't wanna yell at Clancy," he announced with great dignity. "Bellamy made a smutty remark about Angela. Clancy was just defending her honor."

Tony was in the midst of helping the downed pilot to his feet, but instantly his solicitous care disappeared and he hauled the dazed flier up with brute force and carted him to the door. "You learn to treat Miss Angela with respect if you come in my bar," Tony said sternly, dumping Bellamy outside and slamming the door behind him. Tony came back into the room rubbing his hands together briskly. "And now, we have a bottle of our best Chianti for Clancy and drinks all around. And we will drink a toast to Miss Angela."

"God bless her," Rosa said fervently.

Clancy wasn't about to voice the same sentiment. In fact, he felt the opposite. Angela Hogan's presence was a thorn in his side and an ache in his gut, and he wished that right now he weren't so inextricably entwined with her.

In the ensuing fuss no one stopped to notice how absurd it was to think of a womanizer like Clancy defending any woman's honor. And it wasn't until several hours later, when Clancy was lying stretched out on his sagging double bed in the room over the bar, that he thought about what had sent the white-hot bolt of fury spiking through his brain. Not outrage that Bellamy had had impure thoughts about Saint Angela but the knowledge that he'd been thinking the very same thing.

He lit another cigarette, tipped his complimentary bottle of Chianti to his mouth, drained the last drops and then slid down farther on the bed. He'd kicked off his shoes but that was it, too lazy to undress. He liked the wine. He'd learned to drink it in France during the war and he still liked it. This red stuff was rougher than he was used to, but nice, nonetheless.

He'd put off flying with Angela for days, his instincts, his wonderful, infallible instincts, warning him. He knew she'd be good. Despite what he'd said to Sparks, he took his old friend's word in matters like that. He already had a grudging admiration for her. That, mixed with his nagging, inexplicable attraction to her, was making things hard enough. Going up with her might be the final straw.

It had been, all right, but not in the way he'd expected. Sure, she flew like a dream, like a cross between Amelia Earhart and Wiley Post. Stan was right, her touch on the controls was sure and delicate, and Bellamy was right, too. She would be hell on wheels in bed.

She certainly wasn't going there with a two-timing two-bit pilot like Bellamy. She wasn't going there with anyone but him, and not even that, if he could help it. She was trouble, trouble, trouble, and he was looking for peace and quiet.

She probably didn't know what happened to her when she flew. He'd watched her, covertly enough, as she taxied down the runway and lifted off. He'd seen the subtle change in her eyes, the slightly glazed look of pleasure, the speeding up of her pulses, hammering away at her slender white neck, the flush of excitement on her high cheekbones. She might not think she knew what sexual excitement was all about, but she felt it every time she flew, and more strongly than anyone he'd ever seen. By the time they landed it was all he could do not to rip off her leather flight jacket and that prim white shirt beneath, not to...

"Damn it," he said out loud, stubbing out his cigarette. He'd been plagued by erotic thoughts ever since he'd gotten in that airplane with her. He'd never realized what a sexual thing it was to fly with a woman, having her in control as they soared far above the world and everyone in it. He wondered if he could talk her into being on top.

His wry bark of laughter broke the silence of the darkened room that was laden with the ancient aromas of garlic and onions and beer. He wasn't going to talk Miss Angela Hogan into a damned thing, least of all his bed. He was just horny, is all. He needed to find himself a woman, his kind of woman. And then Angela Hogan's long-legged, cool-as-a-cucumber charms would no longer have the ability to move him.

CLANCY WAS WRONG. Will Parsons didn't show up in two days. It was almost a week later when he appeared in Angela's doorway, neatly dressed, full beard trimmed somewhat, battered felt hat in hand. "You still got a job?"

Angela put down the unpaid bills she was fretting over and leaned back in her chair. The radio was tuned to NBC's red network, and someone was playing Bing Crosby singing some song about the beach at Waikiki. She'd almost given up hope of having Parsons show up, and it took all her formidable self-control to keep the relief from showing on her face. Sparks and Clancy were doing an adequate job of maintaining the Avian and the Lockheed, but the Percival was proving beyond their capabilities, and the Percival was Angela's largest plane. She needed it up and running, needed it desperately, and her savior stood in front of her.

"I've still got a job," she said carefully. Savior or not, he might prove more trouble than he was worth. She couldn't rid herself of the notion that there was more to the man than appearances. Couldn't rid herself of the notion that maybe she'd met him before.

"Mind if I take a seat?" He moved to the vacant chair, his left foot dragging slightly, and sank down wearily. "It's been a long trip."

"If you'd wired me I would have sent the money for your train fare."

"If I'd had the money for a telegram, I would have had the money for the train. Besides, I like riding the rails. You meet a better class of people that way."

She stared at him. In the full light of day, without the enveloping fedora covering his grizzled gray hair, he looked even more familiar.

"Do you fly?" she asked abruptly.

"You need two good feet, two good arms and two good eyes to fly, Miss Hogan. I stopped flying years ago. Why?"

"A couple of reasons. I think a good mechanic has to know what a pilot's up against, not just understand engines."

"True enough."

"And I can't get rid of the feeling I've met you before. Maybe at an air race, something like that."

He didn't seem discomfited by the notion. "Could be. I've met a lot of people over the years. You might be one of them."

"That's probably it," she agreed, still not satisfied. "How much do you drink?"

"That's my business."

"If you're working on my engines it's my business, too. I can't have a drunken mechanic responsible for the safety of my pilots and students."

"I've quit drinking."

"Just like that?" she asked cynically.

"Just like that. I figure if I've got a good job and a decent place to live I won't need to drink."

"We haven't decided on that. How much do you want?"

"I want fifty dollars a week. That's what I was getting at Lockheed. However, I know you're not going to be paying me that much. From the looks of things, you aren't over-run with business. Things should pick up a bit once people get over their scare about the *Hindenburg*. And once they hear you've got a decent mechanic. Let's start at twenty-five and see how things work out. Once you get Charlie Olker licked, you should be raking in the money." He glanced around him. "So what's it to be, Miss Hogan? Have I got a job or don't I?" His raw, raspy voice sounded no more than vaguely curious. He'd traveled more than a thousand miles under less-than-ideal conditions, and it didn't seem to make the slightest bit of difference what the outcome was.

"You've got a job," Angela said, wondering whether she was making a huge mistake. "But the first time you show up drunk, you're out of here."

"Fair enough." He glanced out the windows to the hangar beyond. Clancy was climbing down from the recalcitrant Percival, a disgusted expression on his face. "Who else works for you besides Clancy?"

"Another pilot who helps with the maintenance. He'll answer to you, of course. His name is Thomas Crowley, but everyone calls him Sparks."

"What about the office? Does your sister help out here?"

A sudden chill swept over Angela's back. "How did you know I have a sister?"

If he was discomfited by her question, he didn't show it. "I've been in town for a while. It made sense to check you out. Clancy's got a good reputation, at least for work, but you were a question mark."

She didn't believe him. She didn't know what else she could say, though. "If you heard I had a sister, then you should have heard that she works at Woolworths. She doesn't like planes or flying or anything about them. Our father was a pilot, and he died badly."

"Does anyone die well?"

"My fiancé did," she said flatly. "He died trying to make a run, but his altimeter was broken, he flew too high and his wings iced up. You know what happens next."

"He went into a spin. That's tough." His rough voice was filled with sympathy. "What happened to your father?"

"He was a cheat, Mr. Parsons," Angela said coldly, the anger still burning deep inside her. "He was running bootleg liquor and he decided to cheat his employers. His employers countered by blowing him up, along with my stepmother and an innocent bystander. So Constance doesn't care much for pilots. They remind her of the man who was responsible for her mother's death."

"That's pretty harsh."

"Life can be pretty harsh."

"Do tell." He sat forward, and for a moment Angela was ashamed of herself. This was a man who knew even better than she did how tough life could be. If things worked out, they'd both of them be a lot better off.

"Thirty dollars a week to begin with," she said briskly, getting back to business. "We'll raise it to thirty-five when things begin to pick up. We've got to find you a place to live."

"I've taken care of that. There's a boarding house over on Canal Street. The place is clean and decent and I gather the food is good."

"You must have been pretty confident I'd hire you."

"You don't strike me as anybody's fool."

She couldn't help it—her eyes riveted to Clancy's lean body as he crouched over the Percival's landing gear. "I'm not," she said, wishing she believed it.

Parsons's gaze followed hers, and it didn't take a college professor to read her mind. "You're lucky to have Clancy, you know," he said. "He's one of the best."

She looked back at her new employee. "Word has it the same thing could be said about you."

"Then we'll make a hell of a team."

She thought back to Hal Ramsey, decent and good and brave. And dead. And now she had Clancy, brave, certainly, but not very decent or good. She thought of her father, feckless and wild and dead. And now she had Parsons to take care of her airplanes, to keep things going. A man she was going to have to rely on the way she'd never relied on anyone since her father was killed.

It was a frightening thought. But Angela Hogan didn't let things frighten her. "You're right," she said coolly. "We'll make a hell of a team. Come on out and meet Sparks."

# Chapter Nine

She should be feeling more optimistic, Angela chided herself two weeks later. Things were going well, almost dangerously well. The *Hindenburg* disaster hadn't had the effect they'd worried about. While the entire world now seemed convinced that airships were an unqualified failure, it only seemed to reinforce the belief that airplanes were the travel mode of the future. If things could just keep going as well, if there were no major air crashes, then maybe her instruction business would pick up.

The air-freight-transport situation had improved slightly. While Charlie Olker still maintained a stranglehold on the majority of the business outside Chicago, a few brave souls were switching. Word of Clancy's tenure had spread, and with it had come business, just as Clancy said it would. The knowledge that Hogan Air Transport also employed a reclusive, brilliant mechanic also helped matters.

Angela would have liked to have turned down some of the jobs. Particularly ones like Woodward Chemicals. Josiah Woodward had been grudging, insulting and cheap, haggling her down to the lowest possible rate, demanding on guaranteed flights or no payment for any of the previous deliveries and insisting that only Clancy or Sparks pilot his precious cargo. Women might conceivably have their place in an office, though he had his doubts. They certainly had no place in an airplane, particularly one carrying his chemicals.

She'd wanted to throw him out of her office. But she couldn't afford to. The total tab for eight flights from Evanston to Detroit would be enough to cover all the outstanding bills and even put something aside for her Newfoundland-to-Havana run. She couldn't let pride get in her way.

Sparks had made two of the runs, Clancy three. Each time they took off, she held her breath, crossed her fingers and prayed. Woodward Chemicals didn't go in for anything innocuous. Her planes were delivering cylinders of highly toxic gas, one she couldn't even name. She only knew that in an accident, even a rough, forced landing, they would be deadly.

Not that Woodward could be talked into coughing up money for hazard pay. She expected that was why he'd shown up at her place—Olker had demanded too much money for the dangerous duty. And if she had held out for it, he would have simply gone back to Olker and paid the extra to a man.

Leaning forward, she ran a weary hand along the back of her neck. The last delivery was this afternoon, and they could count on a hefty sum from skinflint Woodward. And maybe, if her flight was successful, she could tell people like Woodward to go take a flying leap.

"The Percival's all set." Parsons's rough voice distracted her. She looked up, squinting in the shadowy afternoon light. It seemed strangely dark for the middle of the afternoon on a day in May, a fact she hadn't noticed.

"Thanks," she said. "How's the Lockheed doing?"

"I replaced the fuel line. You ought to think about trying out some of the new deicing systems. They're expensive, they're experimental, but they're better than nothing."

"You're probably right," she said wearily. "Money's so tight right now. Maybe if we can just get a little ahead. Chances are we won't need it until fall, not if we fly low enough. If things go the way I hope they will..." She let it trail off.

Parsons walked into the office, shut the door behind him and sat down in the chair opposite her. "You want to tell me about it?"

She stared at him blankly. "Tell you about what?"

"What you're planning. I know pilots too well. You've got something in the works, some flight, and you haven't wanted to tell your pilots. That's jake with me, but you'd damned well better confide in your mechanic."

Angela hesitated. She had a superstitious fear of talking about the flight. Hal had talked to everyone, for months and months, about every little detail, and it had all ended in disaster over the cold Atlantic. She had the crazy notion that if she just made her plans in secret, kept them to herself, then her chances of success were increased tenfold.

But Parsons was absolutely right. It was one thing not to broadcast your plans to the world, it was another to keep them secret from the one person a pilot needed most. She didn't even bother to ask Parsons whether he could keep a secret. In the two weeks he'd been in town, he'd kept a very low profile, keeping his distance from Tony's Bar and Grille, even keeping his distance from Sparks and Clancy. But he was an absolutely inspired mechanic, seeming to know by instinct or crystal ball what was wrong with an engine, what was about to go wrong with an engine, what was hopelessly outdated in an engine. She couldn't ask for a better confederate.

"I'm going to fly from Newfoundland to Havana, Cuba. I'm planning to do it in two hops, and I'm going to beat the current record by a wide margin. It's stood for more than five years—planes are faster nowadays, and I'm a hell of a pilot.''

"You want to complete the run Ramsey was attempting when he got killed?'' Parsons said shrewdly. "Is that a wise idea? You don't want to get too emotional about your flights. Why don't you pick something different, like Chicago to Denver? I could get your Lockheed hotted up—''

"I'm doing Hal's flight,'' she said flatly, not even questioning how Parsons knew about her fiancé's death. He seemed to know just about everything worth knowing. "Are you going to help me or are you going to come up with unwanted suggestions?''

He sat there looking at her through his thick lenses. "I'm going to help you,'' he said finally.

"Aren't you going to ask me why I haven't told the others?''

"It's none of my business.''

"Aren't you going to ask me why I'm doing it?''

"I know why you're doing it,'' he said in his raspy voice. "I was a flier once myself. I still think you should talk to Clancy about it.''

"He's the last person I'd discuss it with,'' she snapped. "When do you think I should do it?''

"Depends on the plane and weather. Since I can't do anything about the latter, I'll keep going on the plane. You're going to have to figure out how you're going to explain what I'm working on. Clancy's no fool, Miss Hogan, and neither is Sparks. If they don't figure something's going on, then they're not the men I think they are.''

"I know that. I just want to keep them in the dark as long as possible. Sparks will fuss over me like a mother hen.''

"I can't see Clancy doing that.''

"No,'' she said. "Clancy will try to stop me.'' She shook her head. "That's a silly thing to say, isn't it? He understands flying, and he certainly doesn't have any special feeling for me. He's been hanging around with a blond waitress from Tony's. But I can't get rid of the feeling that he'll try to throw a monkey wrench into my plans if he can.''

''You think he's that petty?''

''No. I can't explain it. I have hunches, instincts, Will. Don't you know what I mean? A feeling I get when there's no logical reason for it.''

''I know what you mean.'' Parsons's rough voice softened for a minute. ''Listen to those voices, Angela. They can tell you a lot.''

''People would probably think I'm crazy,'' she said with a nervous laugh.

''Let them. Those little voices have saved my life more than once. Saved yours, too, when it's come to problems with your airplanes. I'll help you, Miss Hogan. I'll get your plane in tiptop condition to fly from Newfoundland to Havana, at speeds which'll darn well frighten the birds. The rest is up to you.''

''The rest I can handle,'' she said confidently. ''If I can just come up with the money.''

The door to her office slammed open and Sparks stormed in, his hair standing up in tufts, his heavy eyebrows creased in a worried line. ''Angie, I think you better come out here and talk to Clancy. He thinks he's taking those chemicals to Detroit.''

''Of course he's taking those chemicals to Detroit. Will says the plane's all set, and you're scheduled for a lesson this afternoon. What's the problem?''

''The problem is the damned weather!'' Sparks practically shouted. ''Have you looked outside in the last half hour?''

''I don't have a window in my office, Sparks,'' she said mildly enough, rising from the desk. ''What's up? A little rain?''

"A GD hurricane! He can't go up in this stuff, I don't care how good he is." Sparks was following behind Angela at a fast trot. "No contract is worth dying for, Angie, you know that. Tell him he can't do it."

Sparks hadn't exaggerated. By the time she reached the huge sliding doors of the hangar, she could feel the wind whipping through the metal building. They'd already pushed the Percival out onto the tarmac, and the quiet thrum of the engines was almost inaudible through the galelike winds.

The sky was black overhead, a roiling mass of inky clouds. Clancy was nowhere in sight, and for a moment Angela wondered whether he'd had second thoughts.

A moment later he appeared, wrapped in leather flight gear, a tightly folded parachute swinging nonchalantly from his arm. "Hi, Red. Come to see me off?"

"See what I mean?" Sparks shouted over the churning winds. "You can't do it, Clancy."

"Shut up, Sparks," Angela said. She stepped up to Clancy, the wind whipping her hair into her face. "The weather looks pretty bad, Clancy."

"It is. Unfortunately it's not going to get any better, not for a couple of days. Might as well go now before all hell breaks loose."

Angela glanced up at the sky. "I think it already has."

"Hell, no," Clancy said with an easy laugh. "They're talking about hailstones the size of golf balls. Now that should be exciting."

"Don't go."

"Don't be ridiculous. That shipment of chemicals has to go out today, and I know it as well as you do. Old Woodward isn't going to pay the freight if it doesn't, and we've put too much work into it to just kiss that money goodbye. I need my share to pay the shipping costs for my plane. I'm not going to roll over and play dead."

"How did you know that?"

"I listen at keyholes. Out of the way, kid. I've got a flight to make." His dark eyes were alight with excitement, the kind of excitement she knew too well, had felt herself.

"I'm forbidding you to go," she said. "It's too dangerous."

"It's up to me whether I want to risk my life or not. Hell, you should know that every time we go up it's a risk. Besides, I've got my lucky cross with me. Can't crash with a lucky piece on you."

"It has to be a reasonable risk. And it's up to me whether you risk my airplane or not. I'm telling you you can't do it. We'll just have to accept the loss of Woodward's money. There are other jobs around."

"Not if you get the reputation for folding under adverse conditions. On the other hand, if people know they can count on you no matter what the conditions, you'll start pulling in a lot more business." The wind was taking his voice and hurling it away from them, and his dark hair was rough and tumbled in the stormy air.

"No, Clancy." Her voice was flat, firm. "And that's final. Sparks, go and turn the engine off and help Clancy get the plane back in the hangar. I'll call Mr. Woodward and tell him what's happened. Maybe he'll be reasonable."

"And maybe hell will freeze over. All right, Red. This is your show," Clancy said with an easy smile. "Come on, Sparks. Let's get this baby back under cover."

She should have known. Deep inside, she did know. She'd turned away, heading back for her office and the telephone, when over the rush of wind she heard the unmistakable sound of an engine revving. By the time she raced back to the open doorway, Clancy was already taxiing down the runway.

Sparks was sitting up by the time she reached him, rubbing his jaw and cursing a blue streak. "That was a sucker punch, Clancy," he shouted at the airplane as it lifted up into the dark, dangerous sky. "I'll get you for that."

"I hope you do," Angela said numbly. "I hope you get the chance."

Sparks hauled himself to his feet. "Hey, Angie, don't worry about him. Clancy could fly anything in any kind of weather. He's a fool to go out in stuff like this, but I'm not really worried about him. He'll make the drop safely enough. I'm going to get on the radio and give him holy hell."

"Give him holy hell for me, too," she said weakly. "And tell him to stay put once he gets to Detroit. No one's going out on this end until the weather clears."

"I'll tell him, Angie."

The radio was set up in a corner of the hanger, close enough to hang the antenna out a window. Sparks hunkered down, glued to the radio, while the sky darkened further, and fat, angry raindrops hurled themselves downward.

Angela could hear Clancy's jaunty voice as she headed back for her office. "Tell Red she can tear a strip off me when I get back. Things aren't too bad yet, but I think I'm going to take her up a bit and see if I can get above the storm."

"I hope to hell he knows what he's doing," Angela muttered under her breath.

Sparks looked over his shoulder. "He knows. The wings aren't going to ice up in May."

"Not unless he goes too high. You know as well as I do wings can ice up on the hottest day in August if you go high enough." Her voice was cold and unemotional. It had been a hot day in August when Hal Ramsey had gone down.

"He's not going to join the circus. He's just going to have a hell of a ride, and I hope it scares the socks off him," Sparks said angrily. He turned back to the radio set. "You hear that, Clancy? I hope this takes ten years off your life!"

"Won't happen, Sparks." Clancy's voice came back through the static, and Angela thought she could hear a strange rattling noise. "I thrive on danger. This'll only make me feel ten years younger."

"Not after I get through with you," Sparks grumbled.

"What's that noise, Sparks?" Angela demanded with sudden urgency. "Is it the engine? That rattling noise...?"

Clancy was talking again. "Gotta concentrate on my flying, boys and girls. This idle chitchat has been swell but I gotta go. I'll check in in about half an hour." And the radio went dead.

"Damn him!" Angela fumed. "That noise, Sparks..."

"It wasn't my engine," Will said, coming up behind her. "It was hail."

"Oh, God," she moaned.

"Now, Angie, a little hail isn't going to stop a man like Clancy," Sparks said, his blue eyes dark with worry.

"It didn't sound like a little hail."

"Maybe he'll climb above it."

"And his wings'll get iced up."

"Maybe it'll clear once he's a little farther away."

"Maybe he'll die," Angela said.

"Maybe he will," Sparks said. "There's nothing we can do about it from down here, now is there?"

For a moment a cold wash of fear swept over her and she could feel her body tremble. And then she snapped out of it, straightening her back, stiffening her resolve. "Not a damned thing," she agreed. "I'm going back to work. Call me if you hear anything."

"You bet."

It was a two-hour flight to Detroit in the best of conditions. What with hail, rotten visibility and having to fly high, Clancy probably wouldn't make it in less than three. If he was lucky.

She was counting on that luck. Or at least his own belief in it, which was half the battle. She was also counting on his ability. She hadn't been up with him yet—something had kept her from checking out his fabled skills firsthand. But if anyone could make it through the storms crackling overhead, Clancy could. She just wasn't certain anybody could.

She finally gave up trying to work as the hours passed. Her office darkened, but she didn't turn on the light. Instead she sat there, her booted feet up on the desk, and smoked cigarette after cigarette until her throat was harsh and dry. If she'd thought there was a chance that Clancy had left his flask behind, she would have helped herself to some of his powerhouse rum.

But Clancy was a man to ignore regulations, and this time she couldn't blame him. If she were flying into what he was flying into, she would have taken a flask along with her, too.

The hangar was still and silent. She'd long ago turned off the radio, and as seven o'clock came and went she even ignored the siren call of *Amos and Andy*. Nothing would be able to distract her, not until she knew that Clancy had landed safely. Or crashed.

But the radio in the front room was as silent as the cathedral-style in her office. If Clancy was still aloft, he wasn't talking.

After three and a half hours, she couldn't stand it any more. She headed out to the front, running her cold damp hands along her trousers, to the two men sitting crouched by the silent radio.

"His radio's out," Sparks said, his usually cheery voice hopeless.

"I thought so. What do you think happened?"

"The radio was working fine when he left," Will announced without a trace of defensiveness in his voice. "Any number of things could have happened. He could have been hit by lightning. If he flew too high and everything iced up, the antenna might have snapped. The engine might have overheated . . .''

"He might have crashed," Angela supplied.

"There's that, too," Will agreed calmly. "I think we'll just have to wait and see."

"How long has he been out?" Angela asked.

"Three hours and fourteen minutes," Sparks said. He spoke into the microphone again with the air of a man expecting not much. "Hogan Air Transport calling Clancy, flight 3. Come in, Clancy."

Nothing but static. Sparks had been calling, over and over again, for more than an hour, and his voice was hoarse with strain and despair.

Suddenly a strange voice filtered through the static. "This is Stan Jansen, Transamerica Freight. That you, Sparks?"

"It's me, Stan. We're looking for Clancy. He was headed for Detroit in this mess and we've lost contact."

"I should have known it would be Clancy." Even through the static Angela could hear the resigned admiration in Stan's voice. "I just heard over the radio—he landed in Detroit not five minutes ago. Came down as gentle as a lamb in the midst of a hailstorm. Detroit was teed off."

Angela put a steadying hand on the back of Sparks's chair. "Thank God," she muttered, feeling suddenly dizzy.

In a second Will was settling her gently in his own chair. "You all right, Angela?" he asked, his rough voice solicitous.

By that time Sparks had gotten off the radio. "Geez, Angie, I've never seen you go all pale like that. You doing okay?"

"I'm fine," she said, taking a deep breath, willing the color back into her cheeks. "I just didn't want to lose that airplane."

The two men looked at her in silence for a moment, and she couldn't meet their knowing expressions. Two men, both with failing eyesight, and they could see her far better than she would have wished.

"Sure, Angie. You didn't want to lose the Percival," Sparks agreed. "I'm going to call Detroit. See if we can roust the maniac before he takes off to celebrate."

"Do that. And tell him when he gets back here I'm going to kill him."

"I'll do that." Sparks headed for the office telephone.

"And Sparks," she called after him.

"Yeah, Angie?"

"Tell him thanks."

THE RAIN WAS STILL COMING down at a steady pace, battering against the tin roof of the hangar. Angela was alone in the semidarkness, staring sightlessly at the papers in front of her.

It had taken all her self-control not to grab the phone and start screaming at Clancy when Sparks had finally gotten through. Instead she'd stood in the background, listening as Sparks joked with him, knowing that if she took the phone she'd burst into tears. Instead she walked back out into the hangar, into the shadows where no one could see her and wonder why in the world the indomitable Angela Hogan's eyes were wet with unshed tears.

"He's fine," Sparks announced when he found her staring at the Vega. "He was heading out to a bar with a bunch of the pilots there. They wanted to buy him a drink to celebrate. Apparently that was one hell of a tricky landing."

"I imagine it was." Her voice sounded only slightly strained, and she was hoping Sparks wouldn't notice. "I hope you told him to stay put until the weather improves."

"I did. Jim Manning was there, and he has a sister who's just Clancy's type. Short and blond and plump. I guess he'll keep busy waiting out the storm."

"Swell," Angela said sourly.

There was a moment of silence. "Are you crying, Angie?"

"What the hell would I be crying for?" she replied fiercely. "The plane's okay, isn't it? Clancy's worthless hide is okay, too. Everything's positively copacetic."

"Sure, Angie. I told Clancy you were pretty upset."

"Thanks a lot. I hope you told him it was the plane I was worried about?"

"Sure," Sparks said again. "You coming to Tony's? I find I'm in need of a good stiff drink after all this. I think I even managed to talk Will into joining me."

"You go ahead. I wasn't able to concentrate this afternoon and I'm way behind on the paper work. And I want to call Woodward and tell him his precious cargo is delivered and he owes us a nice fat check." She managed to feel positively cheery at the thought.

"If you're sure."

"I'm sure."

But she wasn't accomplishing anything. She was sitting alone at her desk with not enough light from the goosenecked lamp on top of the steel file cabinets to accomplish anything more than eyestrain. And she was thinking about the damnable thing that had happened to her.

Clancy mattered to her.

It was the last thing she needed, the last thing she wanted. She'd been through enough heartaches, lost enough friends, to know that she never wanted to get involved with a flier again. Particularly not a womanizing, cynical barnstormer like Clancy. Somehow, when she least expected it, he'd begun to worm his way into her thoughts, into her heart, and she didn't dare let that happen. She had to force him out, ruthlessly, turn all her concentration on the flight she was planning to make. Sooner or later Clancy was going to end up dead in the twisted remains of whatever plane he was flying. She didn't want to be the one to mourn him.

But for right now, for a few hours, she was going to sit alone in her deserted hangar and do just that. Mourn Clancy, mourn something she wasn't going to allow herself to feel. And then she was going to head over to the liquor store, go home and get gloriously, stinking drunk. And by tomorrow she'd be hung over and back to normal.

When she first heard the sound she couldn't believe it. Over the steady beat of the rain came the faint whisper of an engine. An engine she knew far too well. She'd flown the Percival enough times to be able to pick out its engine with unerring accuracy. And it was the Percival flying overhead in pea-soup fog, planning to land.

## Chapter Ten

Angela slipped once, racing to the radio set in the front of the hangar, skinning her knees through her trousers. "Hogan Air Transport calling Clancy, flight 3. Come in." Nothing but static while the unmistakable sound of the Percival droned overhead.

Throwing down the microphone, she ran over and flipped on what meager runway lights she could afford. Hogan Transport wasn't really equipped for night flying, but she'd been putting lights in whenever she had cash to spare. Clancy hadn't tried landing there at night, but he knew the runway as well as anyone by this time, and besides, there was his incredible luck, the luck that served as his copilot time and time again.

Back to the radio, for one last futile try. And then, to her relief and exasperation, Clancy's voice came through, filtered by static, calm and seemingly amused. "Anyone down there? Must be, since I see what passes for landing lights. I'm coming in. Tell Red she can bawl me out in person."

"Clancy, there's no ceiling. It's fog all the way down," she said desperately.

"Anyone there? Or don't you want to use the radio? Maybe you're all out on the tarmac waiting to see me crash. I'm coming in now. Let's see how I do with Blind-man's Bluff."

"Clancy, don't . . ." But it was obvious he couldn't hear. The radio in the Percival could only send, not receive.

She ran back to the huge, sliding metal doors, pulling them open and letting the rain and fog roll into the hangar. And she waited, listening, knowing exactly what the plane was doing without having to see it, knowing the sounds of the engine too well.

"Be careful," she muttered under her breath. "You're coming in too fast, Clancy, pull up. Pull up, damn you. That's it. Try it again. You've flown this enough times that you can do it blind. Try again, and this time come in a little lower. That's it, Clancy. Steady now."

She could hear the rattle of static from the radio behind her, and then Clancy's voice, loud and clear. "Coming in now. If I land this crate safely I'm going to want a stiff drink, Sparks. And a welcome-home kiss from Red."

"I'll cut your throat," Angela snarled to herself, peering through the fog in a vain effort to make out the lights of the Percival. "Don't crash, Clancy," she whispered. "For God's sake, don't die."

And then there he was, dropping down out of the fog with all the grace and precision of a dancer. The wheels bounced slightly, then settled down as the plane taxied to a stop.

Within seconds she was racing after him, oblivious to the soaking rain, the heavy fog, oblivious to rational thought. He was just jumping out the side door when she reached him, and she flung herself at him, shrieking with rage, pounding at him with her fists.

"Damn you, damn you, damn you," she cried, beating on his leather flight jacket, her tears mixing with the rain pouring down from the sky.

He didn't hesitate. He hauled her into his arms, turned her and pressed her against the cold wet metal of the plane, and set his mouth on hers, kissing her with a hungry desperation that matched hers.

Her mind wasn't working. His big, warm body was shielding her from the rain, his arms on either side of her imprisoning her against the plane as his mouth did things she'd never even imagined. His tongue thrust deep into her mouth, demanding a response, and she shivered, twining her arms around his neck and kissing him back. A moment later he'd reached over and yanked the door of the plane open again, and she felt herself lifted up and tossed inside, out of the rain. And then he'd followed her in, pushing her down on the floor and covering her.

His hands held her head still as he kissed her again, his mouth tracing erotic patterns on her face, her eyelids, her cheeks, her lips. He moved his hand down, between their bodies, and captured her breast, his long fingers sending a shiver of reaction through her. She heard the rip of her buttons, but she was too caught up in the sensations his mouth, his hands were coaxing, no, forcing from her. It was dark, velvet dark in the hold of the plane and he was big and strong and demanding, blocking out what light there was as he kissed her again. For the moment she was content to let her mind float, to simply let her body react to the force and passion in his. For a moment she told herself, why not? It was dark and still in the plane, no one would see, no one would know. He wasn't going to stop unless she made a big fuss. It wouldn't be her fault. Why didn't she just give in to the frightening, overwhelming feelings sweeping over her body?

She could feel the unmistakable hardness between his legs pressing against her. And the hardness of his hands against her breast, the hardness of his mouth on hers. And suddenly she was frightened. Frightened by the darkness, by the desire, both his and hers. She began to struggle against him, but he seemed to pay no attention to her futile battings, merely capturing both of her slender wrists in one hand and holding her still while he continued to kiss her and his other hand reached the waistband of her slacks and began to yank at the buttons.

She whimpered then, a tiny sound of fear, and he froze. She could feel the tension rocketing through him, the tightness in his muscles.

And then he lifted his head, staring down at her in the murky light, and she knew the dangerous moment had passed. He'd regained control, and she told herself it was relief flooding her, not regret. "Those aren't tears, are they, Red?"

It took her a moment to find her voice. "Damn you," she said.

"You've already said that. Several times, in fact. How about trying something else? Like welcome home? Of course, you've already given me quite a welcome. Maybe we're better off not talking at all." And he kissed her again, a brief, thorough, teasing kiss, as if he knew she was about to shove him off her.

Which is what she did, scuttling back against the side of the cargo area, out of reach of his hands and unsettling mouth. Out of reach of that frightening passion that flared so brightly between them. "What the hell do you mean, flying back in this weather?" she demanded, her voice only slightly shaky.

"Sparks said you were missing me. I figured I'd better come back and face the music."

"You could have been killed! It was too dangerous."

"Hell, I'm a dangerous kind of guy."

"Not with my airplanes, you're not!" she snapped.

His eyes narrowed. "Are you going to try to convince me it's the airplane you're so worked up about? It won't wash, Red. I know you too well. Besides, my Fokker is on its way from South America, and it's a helluva lot better plane than this tub."

"This tub just got you through some of the worst flying conditions we've had around here!" she shot back, stung.

"It was my skill, not your plane, that got us through. Will had better look at the radio first thing in the morning. Not to mention the rudders—they felt sluggish."

"Don't tell me what to do!"

For a moment they sat across from each other on the floor of the cargo hold, glaring at each other. She could smell the gasoline, the cool damp rain, the leather of his flying clothes. She was trying hard to hold on to her anger for fear that if she stopped being so angry she'd be back in his arms, and that was far too dangerous a place to be.

And then Clancy laughed. "Listen, Red, we don't need to sit here and argue. I promise, I'll be a good boy from now on. No flying into hailstorms, as long as you don't agree to any contracts that hinge on deliveries no matter what the conditions. You shouldn't need to, after this. Word gets around. You can deliver when you have to, and do it safely."

"What do you mean, I can?" she countered. "You can."

He shrugged. "Lady, I work for you. You've already got a decent reputation. With luck and a few more jobs, you should be sitting pretty. In the meantime, why don't I change out of this flight suit and we'll go to Tony's and see whether he's got any champagne? I deserve it after a night like this."

"I can't drink champagne."

"Why not?"

"I'm allergic to it," she said stiffly. "But I'll go to Tony's with you."

"You didn't happen to call that old skinflint Woodward, did you?"

She grinned. "The moment we heard from you. I don't think he was pleased to get my call. He probably took one look at the weather and figured he was going to get the other five deliveries free."

"Did he arrange for future shipments?"

She shook her head. "Nope."

"Why not?"

"I told him we weren't interested. I don't want my pilots endangering their lives for someone like him."

"Am I your pilot, Angel?" he asked softly.

This was getting dangerous again. "One of the best," she said briskly, moving toward the door.

He didn't move. "I have to tell you something. I didn't endanger my life for Woodward."

Her eyes met his in the murky light of the quiet plane. "Then why did you?"

He paused, long enough for her heart to slow, waiting for the answer. "Because I like a challenge, toots," he said with a wry grin.

She ignored the irrational disappointment that flooded her. "Why didn't you stay in Detroit? Sparks said Jim Manning had you all fixed up with his sister."

"I find I'm losing my taste for dumb blondes," he said, putting a long finger under her chin and tipping her face up to his. "I like redheads who don't have any red in their hair." And he dropped a light kiss on her lips before leaping back out into the rain.

By the time she followed him back into the hangar, he'd changed out of his leather flight suit. A cigarette was dangling from his lips, and he was humming under his breath. "You look like a drowned kitten again, Angel," he said. "Maybe I'm a bad influence on you."

She pushed her wet hair back. "Maybe you are. Have fun at Tony's."

"You aren't coming?"

"I've had a tiring day," she said wryly, brushing a hand over her lips. Her mouth felt hot, sore, and then she realized what had caused it.

Clancy was watching her, watching her mouth with an unnerving intensity. And then he shrugged. "Suit yourself." A moment later he was gone, without a backward glance.

She moved slowly, flicking off the bright landing lights, turning off the staticky radio, locking the big sliding doors and the small side door. The Packard didn't like the dampness, and for a moment she was afraid it wouldn't start. But it did, and a few minutes later she was driving slowly home through the fog-shrouded streets of Evanston. Thinking about Clancy.

HE GOT DRUNK, ALL RIGHT, Clancy thought hours later as he stripped off his clothes and sat down heavily on his bed. But not drunk enough to forget about Angela Hogan's mouth. The feel of her breasts through that wet, clinging shirt, the tears in her eyes that were for him and not her stupid airplane.

And he didn't get drunk enough to take Rosa's waitress up on her very obvious offer. He only got drunk enough to brood about the kind of trouble he was in, falling for the wrong kind of dame.

He shouldn't have let her go in that safe, warm cocoon of an airplane. He could have held her still, kissed her back into submission, into enthusiastic participation. She was strung so tight with nerves and emotion that a devious man could have done anything he wanted with her. And he prided himself on being a devious man.

But he also prided himself on being a man who understood risks. He'd taken enough of them that day, that night. Making love to Angela Hogan could have been far more dangerous than simply flying blind in a hailstorm. If things had gone wrong in the air, if his wings had iced up, all he would have done was crash.

If he got involved with Angela, ended up being her lover, he might never escape. Or if he did, he'd feel guilty for the rest of his life.

Angela wasn't made for lovers. She was made for a husband, for kids, for a house in the country with a picket fence and a mortgage. She might be a hell of a flier, but she was also a woman. And try as she might to squash them down, she still had the emotions, the needs of a woman, and those needs were at complete odds with his.

He was going to have to stop kissing her, even though her mouth was the sweetest thing he'd ever tasted. He was going to have to stop watching her when she wasn't looking, stripping off her clothes with his dirty mind and taking her in his arms. He was going to have to be a good boy for once in his life, when he'd spent almost his entire thirty-six years being as bad as he could possibly be.

Because she was no good for him and he was no good for her. He needed to remember that. And hope that she'd have the good sense to remind him, if it seemed like he was forgetting. Because otherwise they'd have a disaster on their hands and everyone would lose.

SHE COULDN'T STOP THINKING about him. During the long drive home through the fog and rain, all Angela could think about was the rough demand of his mouth on hers. The seductive feel of his tongue. His hand on her breast. No man had ever touched her breast before. She had no idea it would be quite so arousing, almost painfully so.

She couldn't stop thinking about the feel of him, hard against her. She shivered, telling herself she should be outraged, disgusted, even horrified. Instead she kept reliving it, the pressure, the pure demand vibrating through his body. A demand she was too cowardly to answer, much as she wanted to.

She glanced down at her shirt beneath her open raincoat. She had no idea where the buttons were, but it was loose enough that she was able to pull it around her, covering the plain white cotton bra. The thickness of the bra should have blunted some of her reaction to his hand on her breast. How would it have felt on her bare flesh?

The car skidded on the wet pavement and it took her a second to regain control as she turned the corner onto Carroll Street. It was a lucky thing few people were out driving in this weather. It would have looked pretty strange for her to end up in an accident with her shirt torn halfway off.

The lights were on in the bungalow, and Angela didn't know whether to be sad or sorry. She wasn't sure if she was in the mood for a tête-à-tête with Constance. For a while she just wanted to climb into bed and think about what happened, what almost happened tonight.

Constance was stretched out on the battered living room couch, her hair in pin curls, her face creamed of all its usual makeup, her fingernails and toenails glistening with a fresh coat of Max Factor's Vermilion. She was dressed in a faded old chenille bathrobe and reading Angela's copy of *Colliers*, and as usual she looked absolutely beautiful.

"What's an opiate?" she inquired when Angela shut the door behind her, keeping her raincoat held tight around her.

"A drug. Something to knock you senseless. Why?" She edged into the room, wondering whether she could sneak into the bedroom without Constance realizing her state of dishabille.

"I'm reading an article about movies. There was a new Norma Shearer movie down at the Odeum and you know she makes me want to smack her. So I thought I'd catch up with my reading, and this person said that movies are the opiate of the masses. What's that mean?"

"It's paraphrasing Karl Marx."

"The red?" Constance sat up, evincing more interest. Communism was taking the country by storm, much to the chagrin of the New Dealers, and Constance was just as enchanted.

"Uh-huh," Angela said. "He once said that religion was the opiate of the masses. In other words, that common people use church and God to make them forget their troubles. And it's been said that movies do the same thing."

"I guess that makes me a hophead," Constance said with a lazy giggle. "Give me a movie over church any day."

"I'm sure Father Flanagan will love to hear you say that. By the way, he mentioned you haven't been to confession in awhile."

Constance gave her enchanting, elfin grin. "Sweet sister, I have nothing to confess."

"A likely story," Angela said wryly.

"Nothing that would interest Father Flanagan, at any rate. At least you're going to be able to come up with something a little more lively than bad-mouthing F.D.R."

"I like F.D.R.," Angela protested. "What do you mean, something more interesting?"

"Like, where did you get those whisker burns all over your face?" Constance inquired impishly. "Like, why are all the buttons torn off your blouse, and how did you get a lovebite on the side of your neck?"

To her horror Angela realized she'd let her raincoat flap open. She quickly yanked it back around her, and it took all her willpower not to reach up and touch her abraded cheeks. No wonder she felt flushed.

"Your lips are swollen, too," Constance announced critically. "Whoever it was certainly was a demanding sort. Who was it, anyway? Not Sparks—he's too shy. I bet it was Stan."

"Sparks is a friend," Angela shot back. "And Stan is married."

# NO RISK, NO OBLIGATION TO BUY...NOW OR EVER!

# GUARANTEED

## PLAY "ROLL A DOUBLE" AND GET AS MANY AS SIX GIFTS!

# HERE'S HOW TO PLAY:

1. Peel off label from front cover.Place it in space provided at right.With a coin, carefully scratch off the silver dice.This makes you eligible to receive one or more free books, and possibly other gifts, depending on what is revealed beneath the scratch-off area.

2. You'll receive brand-new Harlequin American Romance® novels.When you return this card, we'll rush you the books and gifts you qualify for ABSOLUTELY FREE!

3. Then, if we don't hear from you, every month we'll send you 4 additional novels to read and enjoy.  You can return them and owe nothing, but if you decide to keep them, you'll pay only $2.74* per book - a savings of 21¢ each off the cover price.And, there's no extra charge for postage and handling!

4. When you subscribe to the Harlequin Reader Service®, you'll also get our newsletter, as well as additional free gifts from time to time.

5. You must be completely satisfied.You may cancel at any time simply by sending us a note or a shipping statement marked "cancel" or by returning any shipment to us at our expense.

*You'll love your elegant 20K gold electroplated chain! The necklace is finely crafted with 160 double-soldered links, and is electroplate finished in genuine 20K gold. And it's yours FREE as an added thanks for giving our Reader Service a try!*

# "ROLL A DOUBLE!"

PLACE LABEL HERE

SCRATCH HERE

**?**

**SEE CLAIM CHART BELOW**

154 CIH NBBT
(U-H-AR-10/90)

**YES!** I have placed my label from the front cover into the space provided above and scratched off the silver dice. Please rush me the free book(s) and gift(s) that I am entitled to. I understand that I am under no obligation to purchase any books, as explained on the opposite page.

NAME

ADDRESS _____ APT.

CITY _____ STATE _____ ZIP CODE

## CLAIM CHART

| | |
|---|---|
| 🎲 🎲 | **4 FREE BOOKS PLUS FREE 20k ELECTROPLATED GOLD CHAIN PLUS MYSTERY BONUS GIFT** |
| 🎲 🎲 | **3 FREE BOOKS PLUS BONUS GIFT** |
| 🎲 🎲 | **2 FREE BOOKS** |

CLAIM NO. 37-829

All orders subject to approval.    Offer limited to one per household and not valid to current American Romance subscribers.
©1990 Harlequin Enterprises Limited.    PRINTED IN U.S.A.

**DETACH AND MAIL CARD TODAY!**

## HARLEQUIN "NO RISK" GUARANTEE

- You're not required to buy a single book - ever!
- You must be completely satisfied or you may cancel at any time simply by sending us a note or a shipping statement marked "cancel" or by returning any shipment to us at our cost. Either way, you will receive no more books; you'll have no further obligation.
- The free book(s) and gift(s) you claimed on this "Roll A Double" offer remain yours to keep no matter what you decide.

If offer card is missing, please write to: Harlequin Reader Service®, P.O. Box 1867, Buffalo, N.Y. 14269-1867

Constance shrugged. "I've lived around pilots all my life, Angie. You only showed up when you were eighteen. I never developed much of a belief in pilots respecting their marriage vows. I know who it was, though. Clancy."

"I can't stand Jack Clancy!" Angela said hotly.

"Of course you can't. That's why you kissed him so hard you've got bee-stung lips. Take it from me, it's the ones you can't stand that you fall the hardest for."

"And how would you know, baby sister?"

Constance grinned. "I go to a lot of movies. All Barbara Stanwyck has to do is glare at a man and you know they'll fall in love. Happens every time."

"Not this time."

"Are you going to tell me it wasn't Clancy you kissed?"

"Maybe it was Will Parsons," Angela suggested with just a touch of desperation.

An odd expression crossed Constance's face. "I don't think so."

"Why not? You only met him once, that day last week. Maybe beneath all that hair and glasses he'd be an attractive man."

Constance hesitated. "I imagine he was, when he was young. Right now he's old enough to be your father."

"And yours," Angela said.

"And mine. He's probably older than Frank would have been," Constance said cheerfully, directing her attention to her toenails and proceeding to apply a second coat.

As usual a certain tension filled the room at the mention of Frank Hogan's name. For some reason the two of them had never been able to discuss the death of their mutual parent. Angela wasn't sure if it was a reluctance on her part, or Constance's, or both. All she knew was that after such a harrowing afternoon and evening, she wasn't about to push it.

"I don't like that shade of red," Angela said, changing the subject. "It looks like you dipped your fingers in blood."

"Toes, too," Constance said, admiring her feet. "Though why anyone would want to dip their toes in blood is beyond me. Was it Clancy?"

Angela gave up prevaricating. "Yes, damn it."

Constance's smile was smug. "And was he as good as they say he is?"

"He only kissed me, Constance."

She raised a plucked, pencilled eyebrow. "Some kiss. Then why's your shirt undone?"

There was nothing Angela could say to that, other than "I'm going to bed."

Constance picked up her magazine again. "Go ahead. I have to wait till my nails dry. Besides, there's another good article this month. 'How to Make a Man Your Love Slave.'"

"I don't want a love slave, thank you very much." Angela dumped her rain coat on the hook and headed into the bedroom.

"Not even Clancy?" Constance's voice trailed after her.

"Especially not Clancy," Angela said firmly, looking down at her torn blouse. Crossing the cluttered room, she peered into the mirror above Constance's cheap deal dresser. The glass was wavery, desilvering, and the light was dim in the room. The woman who stared back at her was a wonder.

Her hair was tousled around her face, curly with the dampness, curly from Clancy's fingers lacing through it. Her lips were swollen, her eyes faintly glazed. The mark on her neck was plain as day, and the torn blouse left nothing to the imagination. She looked at the blouse, at her breast through the plain white bra. And with a little shiver she turned away, willing herself to forget.

And knowing, beyond a shadow of a doubt, that the memory, the feel **of** those moments on the floor of her plane were going to be burned into her brain, into her body, until the day she died.

## Chapter Eleven

"So when are you going to fly around the world?" Clancy's voice was lazy, no more than idly curious, but Angela felt her temper rise to the bait, as it always did when Clancy was fishing for a reaction.

She turned away from the engine of the Lockheed, leaving Will alone as he fidgeted with the manifold. "What are you talking about, Clancy?" she demanded wearily. It had been two weeks since Clancy's dangerous flight through the fog and hail, two weeks since those moments on the floor of the Percival. Moments she'd been determined to forget, moments she told herself she had forgotten, until Clancy looked at her with those devilish dark eyes.

He hadn't touched her since. Hadn't said a word about it, only let his glance linger on the love bite on the side of her neck, then slide away as a faint smile curved his mouth. She'd wanted to hit him then, but she'd managed her usual frosty demeanor. And not once since that moment had she had a chance to tell him what she thought of him.

"I'm talking about Amelia Earhart. Haven't you been listening to the radio, Red? She took off this morning for her 'round-the-world flight."

Angela felt a sudden sinking, part envy, part premonition. "She's trying it again? I would have thought she'd give it up after crashing the first time."

"Did you?"

Angela shook her head. "I suppose not. I don't know her that well, but I know she's not the sort to let a minor inconvenience like smashing up her plane stop her when she's set on something."

"AE doesn't let anything stop her when she gets the bit between her teeth," Clancy said mildly. "Rather like another lady flier I know."

It took Angela a moment to realize he meant her. "Clancy, I've done absolutely nothing but push papers around a desk for the last six months and more. Any resemblance between AE and me stops with both of us being members of the 99 Club and owning a Lockheed Vega."

"Not every woman pilot gets invited to join the 99 Club," Clancy observed.

"Don't patronize me, Clancy! I don't need it. I'm very happy AE has gone ahead with her proposed flight, and I wish her the very best of luck."

"I'm sure you do. Apart from the fact that you wish like hell it were you in that plane instead of AE."

"I couldn't care less," she said frostily. "My record-setting days are over. It's time to get down to business."

"Sure, Red," Clancy said. "Sure."

She waited until he wandered away, back over to Sparks and well out of earshot, before she joined Will as he tinkered with the plane. "How soon will she be ready?" she asked.

"Clancy got to you?" Will questioned, not raising his head.

"No, Clancy didn't get to me," she snapped. "I'm immune to him. But Amelia Earhart's flight affects me. I want to finish my run well before she lands back in the U.S. Her flight's supposed to take just over a month. I want to be ready to go in two weeks."

This time Will did raise his head from the engine, and his thick glasses were speckled with grease. "Why?" he asked mildly enough.

"During the next month the world is going to be so wrapped up in Amelia Earhart and her 'round-the-world flight that my tiny little hop from Newfoundland to Havana will seem like nothing."

"I don't get it. Don't you want the publicity? Shouldn't you wait till she gets back, some of the furor dies down, and then reap some of the benefits?"

Angela shook her head. "I'm not doing it for publicity, Will. I'm doing it... I can't explain. But it's for myself, not for the papers and newsreels. It's just something I have to do before I hang it up all together. And I'd just as soon do it as quietly as possible."

Will glanced at the engine, then back at Angela's determined face. "Two days."

For a moment she thought she hadn't heard right. "What?"

"I said two days. The Wasp engine's in good shape, she just needs a little fine-tuning. I'll have her ready by Wednesday. That soon enough for you?"

"Soon enough," Angela said faintly. "Now all I have to do is come up with the money."

"What about flight plans? Fueling stops, maps, all that stuff."

Angela grinned. "You sound like a father sending his daughter out on a date with a boy from the other side of the tracks. I've got all Hal's stuff."

Will was looking strange, pale beneath the grimy glasses and the beard. "Ramsey crashed."

Angela's smile vanished. "That doesn't mean he didn't know what he was doing. He just flew too high and couldn't get out of a spin. I'm making damned sure I keep low enough to avoid icing. I'll only have to stop once for fuel, and I've already talked to the Teterboro Airport in New Jersey. As long as I can come up with the dough, things should be hunky-dory."

"Hunky-dory," Will echoed faintly. "Where's the money coming from?"

Angela looked at him, startled. "I don't know if that's any of your business, Will."

"No, I suppose it isn't," he grumbled, shuffling back to the engine. "I'll do my part, you do yours."

"Count on it," Angela said, wiping her grease-stained hands on her coveralls. "And I'm about to take care of my part."

She closed the door to her office before she sank down in her spring back chair. She'd been putting off calling Cousin Clement, strangely loath to tap into her final source of money, but she no longer had time for second thoughts. Picking up the phone, she waited for the operator to come on the line.

"Lenox three-two-six-six-four," she said, reaching for her cigarettes. "Hello, Clement."

THEIR DAYS HAD FALLEN into an easy rhythm, Clancy thought later, nursing a beer at a back table at Tony's. Too easy. He wasn't a man who liked structure in his life; he wasn't a man who planned ahead. Somehow he seemed to have fallen into it this time around, and it was too damned seductive. Almost as seductive as Angela Hogan.

What he should have done, he thought, was make his move on her. He knew enough about women, about their skittishness and sideways glances, to know when one wasn't immune to him. Angela Hogan was as aware of him as he was of her, and it wouldn't take much more than a concerted effort to get her where he wanted her to be. Upstairs, in his rooms over the bar. Upstairs, in the sagging double bed that was too big for one person.

But something had stopped him from making that move, and he couldn't quite figure out what. Maybe it was the fact that Sparks was so obviously, painfully in love with her and she didn't realize it. Not that Clancy's holding back did Sparks any good. Angela Hogan wasn't the woman for Sparks, but he wasn't ready to realize it.

It wasn't a latent attack of scruples, either, or respect for her innocence. Any woman that pretty who'd lasted until her late twenties was wasting both herself and the best years of her life. She needed to be taught a thing or two about that elegant, slender body of hers, and Clancy was the man to teach her.

It wasn't that he wanted someone else. He'd tried to drum up some interest in Mama Rosa's blond waitress, Betsey, she with the spectacular headlights and the brain like a soap dish. But he'd grown bored long before things had had a chance to heat up. And Angela's little sister, she of the similar endowments and the sweet nature that Clancy didn't believe for one moment. She might have been enough of a distraction, combining Jean Harlow and Angela, but for some reason he'd kept his distance. He didn't trust her, and deep inside he knew that nothing would hurt Angela more than if he messed with her saintly baby sister. And he didn't want to hurt Angela.

Maybe that was his reason for keeping his distance. But he doubted it. He'd never put anybody's well-being ahead of his own animal needs, and he wasn't about to start. No, he'd kept away from Angela Hogan for one very clear and present reason. She was trouble. He'd just about attacked her on the floor of the Percival, and it had been years since he'd lost control like that. Sure, the flight had got him hopped up, and then she'd come running at him like a hot, sweet, avenging angel. It was no wonder he'd grabbed her, no wonder he'd kissed her. No wonder he'd shoved her in out of the rain and started to strip away her wet clothes.

The wonder had been his own reaction. The control he'd come so close to losing wasn't just physical, it was mental, emotional, for want of a better word. He didn't think he had emotions, but something was certainly eating him up inside and he didn't think it had much to do with his intellect. He wanted Angela Hogan so badly he could barely think straight. And for that very reason he intended to keep leaving her strictly alone.

"What are you doing, crying in your beer?" Sparks demanded, straddling the chair opposite Clancy.

"Hardly," Clancy said. "I was thinking about Angela."

"Some woman," Sparks said with a heartfelt sigh.

"Some woman," Clancy echoed dryly. "What's she up to, Sparks? I see her huddled with Will all the time, staring into that Wasp engine as if it holds the secrets of the universe. And I know she's got something planned. Something she's not talking about."

"Beats me. You're right, she's got something up her sleeve, but I don't know what it is. I guess she has to confide in Will, seeing as he's her mechanic. But she sure isn't planning to let us in on her little secret." He downed his beer and signaled for another.

"I hope she has enough sense not to do anything dangerous," Clancy grumbled.

"Are you nuts? How long have you been around fliers, Clancy? How long have you been one yourself? Long enough to know that, of course, she's going to do something dangerous. She's going to weigh her options, make an educated guess and do it. And no one's going to stop her."

"Maybe she needs to be stopped."

"I doubt it. Angela's not crazy, you know. She's all too aware of her responsibility to the business, to Constance, to us."

"She has no responsibility to me," Clancy snapped. "I'm just working for her while my plane gets back into action. She doesn't owe me anything."

"All right, so she doesn't owe you anything. What goes on in Angela's mind is anybody's guess. Constance is old enough and smart enough to take care of herself, and yet Angela still feels she has to act like a mother hen. Duty dies hard in people like Angie." Sparks glanced over at the door. Constance had come in, accompanied by three young pilots vying for her attention, and she was laughing and flirting with them just to the point of outrageousness.

Clancy followed his gaze, his expression sour. He didn't know why he didn't trust Angela's sister, but he'd learned long ago to listen to his instincts. His instincts told him that beneath that demure dress and shy smile lurked a very determined young lady. One who wouldn't hesitate stepping on anyone, her doting older sister included, to get what she wanted.

"Sweet kid," Sparks said with approval.

"Yeah," Clancy muttered.

By that time Constance had seen the two of them in their little corner and, with a graceful smile, she left her three escorts and threaded her way through the crowds to their table. Sparks jumped up, almost knocking over his beer in his haste. Clancy stayed where he was, lounging in his seat.

"Mind if I join you?" she asked with that breathy smile of a voice.

"We'd be honored, wouldn't we, Jack?" Sparks said, pulling out a chair.

"Honored." He tipped his chair forward then. "What can we get you to drink, Miss Hogan?"

"Please, call me Constance," she said sweetly. "And I'll just have a Shirley Temple."

"Come on, honey, you're old enough to drink," Sparks protested in a gruff, father-bear manner that made Clancy want to puke.

"Well, maybe just one little one," Constance said.

Apparently this was an old act, because the waitress showed up with a whiskey sour in a matter of moments. "What's up, honey?" Sparks asked.

"I wanted to talk to you fellows about Angie," Constance said, taking a healthy slug of her drink, then licking her lips with her small pink tongue. Half the men in the room followed the path of that tongue with longing in their eyes. Clancy was bored.

"What about?" Clancy drawled, lighting a cigarette. He didn't bother offering Miss Goody-Two-Shoes one. Even if she was a chain smoker she would have refused, so determined was she to prove what a sweet little darling she was.

"I'm worried about her."

"Where is she tonight?" Sparks asked the question Clancy was longing to. "She left work early and she hasn't been around all evening. She usually stops in, at least for a few minutes, before heading home."

"She went out," Constance said, her high, pretty forehead creased with worry. "I think she went to see her Cousin Clement."

"Anything wrong with that?" Clancy asked.

"No. Except that he's a married man with a great deal of money, and Angela really needs that money if she's going to make her stupid flight."

For a moment Clancy said nothing, eyeing the pretty little beast from behind hooded lids. "Exactly what do you think is going to happen?" he asked finally.

Constance didn't have half of Angela's formidable brain power. She turned eagerly, convinced she had a sucker. "She wore one of the evening dresses I made. Not the Worth one, which is much more her style. She took the Lanvin one, with no back and just about no front to it at all. I'm afraid in her desperation to get that money she might...well, she might..." She allowed words to fail her, dropping her magnificent blue eyes.

"You think she might whore herself to her cousin in order to get enough money to make her flight," Clancy supplied flatly.

"You put it so crudely!" Constance protested.

"I'm a crude kind of guy. Isn't that what you were saying? Isn't it?"

"Don't browbeat her," Sparks protested, his bushy eyebrows drawn together in dismay. He didn't like what his saintly little Constance was saying any more than Clancy did, but he was cursed with divided loyalties. Clancy didn't have any such restraints.

"Isn't it?" he demanded again.

"I suppose it is." Constance said, raising her head to look at him, her eyes swimming with tears. She dabbed at them carefully, not touching her very subtle makeup, and he noticed that she was one of those women who managed to cry well. Her nose didn't run, her eyes didn't get red and puffy. He would have bet a fiver she practiced in front of a mirror.

"I wouldn't worry about it if I were you, Miss Hogan," he said. "Angela isn't about to throw her innocence away for anything as paltry as money."

Sparks and Constance were staring at him in shock. "What makes you think she's still innocent?" Constance demanded abruptly.

Clancy only grinned. "Go back to your boys, Miss Hogan, and don't worry about Angela. She knows how to take care of herself."

The two men sat in relative silence for a while after Constance left them. "You didn't answer her question," Sparks said heavily.

"What question?" Clancy knew full well, but he hoped Sparks would taken the hint and drop it.

"How did you know Angela is still innocent?"

"Isn't it obvious?"

"No," Sparks said stubbornly. "I want an answer, Clancy. If I have to beat it out of you."

Clancy sighed, putting down his drink. "Listen, Sparks, Angela Hogan isn't my type. In case you haven't noticed, I've been keeping a careful distance from her."

"Maybe not distant enough."

"Stop looking for a fight, Sparks. I know enough about women to know who's phoney and who's not. Angela Hogan, for all her tough-guy exterior, is an innocent lamb underneath. As for her sister, she has the soul of a—"

"Watch it, Clancy!"

"What is this? Defend-the-Hogans night? I don't give a damn about Constance, Sparks. Form your own opinion."

"What about Angela?"

"What about her?"

"Do you give a damn about Angela?"

He'd known Sparks for fifteen years, off and on, and in all that time he'd never lied to him. He had a certain code of ethics: you lied to bosses, you lied to superior officers, you lied to policemen and you lied to women. But you never, ever, lied to your buddies.

"Not a spit, Sparks," he said, his eyes wide and honest. "I couldn't care less."

Sparks stared at him for a long moment. "I wish I believed you were telling the truth."

Clancy didn't bother getting mad. "So do I, Sparks," he said obscurely. "So do I."

ANGELA SLID BACK ON THE leather cushions of the Pierce Arrow and giggled. She held on to the half-empty bottle of champagne very carefully, not wanting to spill a single drop.

She didn't know how, and she didn't know why, but stingy Cousin Clement had written her a check without a word of demurral, written it before his battle-ax of a wife, Eleanor, could enter the drawing room and find out what he was doing.

Angela had been dressed to kill for the simple reason that she knew Clement had a weakness for pretty women. It was that weakness that had gotten him involved with Hollywood, a move that had proven very profitable for him. She knew well enough to try to appeal to his baser instincts, safe in the knowledge that their distant blood relationship would keep his animal lust under safe, Catholic control. All during dinner, when Eleanor wasn't looking, he let his dark, pouchy eyes slide down the naked back of the Lanvin evening dress, and it was all Angela could do not to reach for the evening cape she'd brought along with her. She reminded herself that she liked Clement, she really did. And she particularly liked his willingness to fund her next flight.

They'd had champagne to celebrate her upcoming flight, and Eleanor had toasted her, unaware that the money for that flight was coming from her philandering husband. They had champagne to toast Clement's new investment in RKO Studios. They had champagne to toast Eleanor's latest charity drive.

And then Eleanor had sent Angela home in the Pierce Arrow before Clement could offer to drive her himself. The champagne had a dangerous effect on all of them. It made Eleanor more gimlet-eyed and suspicious, with her catty remarks about Angela's sweet little sister. It made Clement forget consanguinity and squeeze Angela a little too enthusiastically as he brushed the chauffeur aside and helped her into the back of the Pierce Arrow himself. And it made Angela giggle most of the way back to Evanston, particularly once she realized that Clement, ever the perfect host, had sent along a chilled bottle of Moet et Chandon to keep her occupied during the long ride.

She surfaced a while later, staring out at the rain-wet streets. She didn't want to go home and go to bed, she wanted to share her good news with someone. She wanted to share this delicious bottle of champagne with someone. She'd left her watch at home and hadn't the faintest idea what time it was. Nonetheless, she leaned forward and gave Eleanor's rigidly proper chauffeur the address to Tony's Bar and Grille. She needed to be with her own kind to celebrate her good news. Not with a stuck-up witch like Eleanor and a lustful stuffed shirt like Clement.

Her legs were only slightly unsteady as she headed up the sidewalk to Tony's. She'd quelled the chauffeur's protests with her iciest glare, then giggled all the way to Tony's door as she heard him drive off. Drunk or sober, she knew how to keep a man in his place, she thought cheerfully, reaching for the doorknob.

It was locked. Leaning against the glass, her eyes focused and belatedly she realized that the bar was almost dark and most certainly silent. It must be much later than she realized. And there she was, alone in the middle of Evanston in the middle of the night, in shoes that weren't working right, and with a bottle of champagne and no one to share it.

She banged on the door, not expecting much of a response. She was just about to sit down on the sidewalk and finish the bottle herself when the door opened, and Clancy stood there in the darkness, staring down at her.

"You better come in," he said after a moment.

And Angela, knowing it had to rank with one of her stupider moves, stepped inside.

## Chapter Twelve

Clancy closed the door behind her, locked it and pulled down the shade. Then he turned, letting his eyes slide down her body, and let out a low whistle. She was dressed to kill, all right. The dress was a midnight blue, studded with beads that caught the light, and the top of the damned thing was just about nonexistent. It was cut low over Angela's small, firm breasts, it was cut to the waist in the back. She was clutching a half-empty bottle of champagne. Her elbow-length white gloves were sagging around her elegant forearms, her hair was loose and wonderful around her face, and her lipstick was unsmudged. Whoever she'd been out to impress, she hadn't kissed him. For some reason Clancy felt some of his frustration fade.

"Angel," he said wryly. "You have had a snootful tonight."

Angela managed a woozy smile as she leaned over to slide off her silver evening sandals, wobbling somewhat as she tried to maintain her balance and not spill the bottle of champagne she clutched in her gloved hand. "It's the champagne," she confided, kicking off the other shoe and wiggling her toes on the bare wood floor that Rosa had just swept.

"I thought you told me you were allergic to champagne."

"I am. Whenever I drink it my brain flies straight out the window."

"You could have fooled me," he muttered under his breath, putting a steadying hand beneath her elbow. "So why drink it?"

"To celebrate." Out of her delectable cleavage she pulled a slip of paper and waved it under his nose. It smelled like her perfume, and he was tempted to warn her that the gesture was tantamount to waving a red flag in front of a bull, but he controlled himself, instead letting his eyes linger over the front of her dress. Why in heaven's name had he ever thought he preferred busty women? Angela was perfect.

"Why don't I find a couple of glasses and I'll celebrate with you?" he suggested affably, moving behind the bar.

She looked doubtful, glancing at her bottle. "I don't have much left."

"What's going on in there?" Tony loomed in the doorway.

"Just me, Tony," Clancy said easily.

"I thought I heard someone at the door."

"You did. It was Angela."

Tony's burly shoulders relaxed. "Oh, Miss Angie. That's okay, then. Can I get you anything?"

"Got another bottle of champagne stashed anywhere? Angela's celebrating."

"Sure thing. I keep it around for special occasions. This a special occasion, Miss Angie?"

"You bet," she said cheerfully, sinking down in a chair, her skirt billowing out around her.

"I'll get the bottle. You'll have to ice it."

"We can wait," Clancy said, his eyes never leaving Angela's face.

A few minutes later a bottle of domestic champagne was chilling in an old mop bucket full of ice and Tony was heading back to the rooms he shared with Rosa, his three young children, his mother-in-law and his uncle. "You'll close up after Miss Angie leaves, won't you, Clancy?"

"You can count on me," Clancy said, forcibly ignoring the brief flash of guilt. He had no intention of closing up after Miss Angie. He was going to continue to ply her with champagne until she could barely walk straight, and when she was ready to fall on her luscious little behind, he was going to make sure she landed in his bed.

He hadn't the slightest qualms about taking advantage of a lady in Angela's condition. It was probably the only way he was going to get her, short of going down on one knee and offering her his heart and hand and dubious income. And that was something he wasn't going to offer anybody.

No, he felt guilty about seducing Tony's beloved saint. He felt guilty about taking what Sparks wanted and couldn't have. He felt bad about betraying his buddies. But he didn't feel bad at all about betraying Angela Hogan.

They had to make do with beer shells. Setting the glasses on the table, he took a chair, deftly turned it and straddled it, watching her out of deliberately enigmatic eyes. "So what are we celebrating, Red?" he asked, tipping the last of the champagne into her glass. "What's the money for?"

"Wouldn't you like to know?" she said archly, draining half her glass with tipsy enthusiasm.

"That's why I'm asking. Who's the check from?"

"My Cousin Clement," she said with a happy sigh. "He's decided to be the soul of generosity. I knew he would. He's investing."

"Investing in Hogan Air Transport?"

"In a manner of speaking. He's underwriting a flight I intend to make."

Clancy felt an unaccustomed edginess pricking at his nerves. "So Amelia Earhart's pushed you into action," he said mildly enough, sipping his own champagne. It was lukewarm, slightly flat, but Angela was drinking it with real enthusiasm.

"You might say so. Now's as good a time as any."

"And what are you planning to do?"

"Uh-uh-uh," she reprimanded him, waggling her gloved finger at him. "It's none of your damned business."

He caught her hand in his. "Watch your mouth, Angela. I don't like women who swear."

"Hell, you probably don't like women who fly, either. Or run their own businesses or wear pants or think they're the equal of men," she said, yanking at her hand. He held it tight. "You probably like women like Betsey. Or Con..." Her voice trailed off.

"No," he said, releasing her hand. "I don't like women like your sister. If I did, I'd have done something about it by now."

"She's probably too sweet and nice for you."

"I wouldn't say that," he drawled. "As for Betsey, I'm surprised you even noticed I was going out with her. It didn't last very long."

"I don't imagine things usually do, with someone like you."

"Hey, Red, I thought we were celebrating, not fighting," he protested, grinning. "Betsey wasn't my type, either."

"Then what is your type?" she demanded. He could tell by the faint flush on her high cheekbones, the faintly belligerent air to her beautiful mouth, that she was spoiling for a fight, saying things she'd certainly thought a lot about but never dared mention when she was sober. The thought of her quietly fuming over him and Betsey was one of the best things he'd heard in months.

"I thought I told you. Long-legged, cold-hearted, acid-tongued fliers."

"Since when?" she demanded, pulling off her gloves and dumping them on the table. "There've been a million rumors about your romantic exploits, and none of them have ever involved a pilot."

"I'm getting better taste in my old age," Clancy said softly.

She looked up then, her eyes meeting and focusing on his for a moment, and something hot, fast and inexplicable shot between them. A moment later she was pushing back from the table. "I should be getting home," she murmured.

"How do you plan on doing that? You're certainly not driving in your condition. For that matter, how'd you get here?"

"Clement's chauffeur dropped me off. My car's back at the house." She gave him a hopeful look. "I don't suppose you . . . ?"

"I don't own a car, Angel. I usually count on Sparks to give me a ride to the hangar." He almost laughed at the look of dismay on her flushed, elegant face. "Don't worry about it. I can always borrow Tony's Hudson. Particularly if it's to ferry his saintly Miss Angie back home."

"I'm not a saint," she muttered.

"What's that?"

"I'm not a saint," she said louder. "I just do the best I can."

"Including taking on all the lost souls in the world."

"What do you mean by that?"

"Sparks, Parsons. Me. A bunch of misfits. Sparks has only a few good flights left in him, and then what? You'll put him to work in the office, won't you, or navigating or something. At the same salary, which I damned well know you can't afford. Same for Parsons. Oh, sure, you needed him. And he's just about the best damned mechanic around. But he's a drunk, even if he's off the bottle right now, and a jinx, and you welcome him with open arms. You would have hired Langston if he'd accepted, a move that would have driven you into bankruptcy faster than anything Charlie Olker can dream up."

"What about you? What makes you a misfit?"

"I'm the worst of all. I don't take orders, I don't listen to warnings, I do things my way and I can't be counted on. Sooner or later, when you least expect it, I'll be off without so much as a fare-thee-well."

"You said you were going to stay until we beat Olker."

"Maybe I lied," he suggested.

She shook her head and the thick chestnut wave tumbled in her face. She brushed it away with an endearing clumsiness, and for a moment Clancy wondered why he was trying to warn her. Why he didn't just pour more champagne down her throat and carry her upstairs?

"I trust you," she said simply.

Clancy swore underneath his breath. "Then you're a fool."

"Maybe. I guess I'll just have to wait until you disillusion me."

"It'll happen sooner or later."

"I imagine so," she agreed. "In the meantime, do you think that other bottle of champagne is chilled?"

*You asked for it, lady,* he thought, not without a trace of grimness. *And you're going to get it.* "It's got to be colder than this stuff. I'll get it."

The beer shell held about three times the amount a flat-bottomed champagne glass would hold. He waited until she drained the first one, then refilled it before heading over to Tony's beloved jukebox. Shoving a nickel in, he pushed C 12.

"You're not playing 'Harbor Lights' are you?" she demanded. "I heard that enough in that little restaurant in Albany. I don't ever want to hear it again."

"Not 'Harbor Lights,'" he said, standing over her as Bunny Berigan's trumpet began the first, perfect notes of "I Can't Get Started." "Dance with me, Red."

"I don't know if I can even stand, much less dance," she said, but he could see the faint tremor of apprehension in the back of her beautiful blue eyes, and he knew it wasn't falling that she was afraid of. It was him catching her.

He took her arm and pulled her slowly to her stockinged feet. "Don't worry, Angel. I'll take care of you." And with infinite care he pulled her into his arms so that her body pressed against his, as Berigan's whiskey-flavored voice started singing.

She stumbled slightly, and he could smell her perfume in the cloud of hair tickling his nose. It was French and expensive and classy and the most erotic thing in the world. He groaned, pulling her closer, feeling her curves mold against him.

"I don't think this is a good idea," she murmured, her face pressed against his shirt.

"Why not?"

"I'm not that squiffed, Clancy. And neither are you." She yawned like a sleepy kitten and snuggled closer in his arms.

"I'm not squiffed at all," he told her. "Try it this way. You'll be able to hang on better." And taking both her arms, he pulled them around his neck so that her body was draped against his. He put his arms around her slender waist, pulling her closer, and shut his eyes for a moment as Berigan began his trumpet solo.

He was being a romantic sap. He shouldn't be romancing Miss Angela Hogan to the strains of "I Can't Get Started." He should be off with his own kind. But she moved so sweetly against him and her head felt just right beneath his chin and his body was strung as tight as a wire. He'd never wanted anyone as much in his life, not even when he was fifteen years old and lost his virginity in the hayloft of a barn in Kansas. Back then he'd thought Elsa Lambert was the hottest thing he'd ever seen, and he'd been in an absolute paroxysm of lust for her.

It was nothing compared to what he was feeling right now. And the damnable thing was that it was more than lust. That was part of it, all right, but mixed in was a grudging respect, an honest liking, a strange, misplaced need to protect. And if his old friend Sparks were to show up at that moment and stop him from what he was planning, Clancy would punch him in the kisser.

She stumbled again, sliding against him, and he wondered if she could feel how hard he was. If she'd even recognize his condition. He couldn't believe Hal Ramsey had been such a sucker to have such a delicious morsel within his reach and never to have plucked it. At least he wasn't troubled with any extraneous sense of honor, Clancy thought.

The record stopped; the room went silent. Clancy stopped dancing, still holding her, and he moved his hand from her waist to her chin, tilting her face up to his. Her expression was solemn, her eyes only slightly dazed. "Are you ready to finish what we started?" he asked softly, giving her one last chance to escape.

The nod of her head was almost imperceptible. But he saw it. Sliding his hand behind her neck, under her hair, he pulled her up to meet his mouth.

Her lips were soft and sweet beneath his. And open. He was so hungry for her he forgot preliminaries, forgot gentle seduction. His mouth ground down on hers, his tongue swept into her mouth, catching hers and demanding a response. He felt a shiver pass through her body, and then she was pressing closer, her fingers digging into his shoulders, her hips pressing up against his.

He moved his head away for a moment, moving his lips back and forth across hers, dampening them. And then he kissed her again, and this time she was ready. He drank in her quiet moan of surrender, and when her tongue reached out and touched his, he almost exploded.

He wanted to haul her up on the wide expanse of polished walnut bar and cover her, take her there and then. His hands were shaking with need and he couldn't get enough of her. "Let's go upstairs." His voice was a ragged breath of sound in her ear.

She looked up at him, her mouth damp and slightly swollen, her eyes confused. "Why?"

He grinned wryly. "I've got a radio up there. We can tune in 'Make Believe Ballroom' and dance."

"'Make Believe Ballroom''s over," she said, scrunching up her delectable face in an effort to concentrate.

"We'll find something else to dance to," he promised, grabbing the bottle of champagne off the table and not bothering with the glasses. He'd have to sneak down after she fell asleep and clean up. Tony would get too suspicious if he left the glasses down here, and he didn't want his landlord to find out he'd deflowered Angela Hogan in the sagging iron bed upstairs. He'd soon find himself out of a billet, and he found Tony's rooms too comfortable to give them up.

Hell, he might be out of a job, he thought belatedly. His plane was arriving by freighter in New York the day after tomorrow—by seducing Angela Hogan he might end up with no place to take it, no mechanic to work on it.

He looked down at Angela, swaying slightly beside him, at the rise and fall of her small breasts beneath the skimpy evening gown. To hell with his plane, he thought absently. Inexperienced, untried and endearingly clumsy, Angela Hogan was going to be worth it.

He put his arm around her and headed her toward the long, narrow flight of stairs that led up to his rooms. She went willingly enough, a faint, otherworldly smile on her face, but the stairs proved to be a little too much for a woman in her condition. Halfway up he hoisted her into his arms, continuing up with barely a pause, kicking open his door and kicking it shut behind him.

"I didn't realize you were so strong," she said as he set her down carefully.

It wasn't a come-on. The silly dame was too damned tight to know what she was saying. She leaned back against the door, a come-hither smile on her wonderful mouth. As he leaned forward to kiss her, she began sinking, still with that smile in place. By the time his mouth would have reached her, she was sitting on the floor, her legs stuck straight out in front of her, that idiotic smile still on her face. Her eyes were closed and she was snoring slightly. Miss Angela Hogan had passed out in the midst of her big seduction.

Clancy leaned his head against the door and cursed. Then he backed away, squatting down beside her and taking one limp hand in his.

He patted it, slapped it. "Wake up, Red. Come to bed."

She responded by slapping at him. "Go 'way," she muttered.

He hauled her up. She was heavier now as deadweight than she was moments before when he'd carried her up his stairs. Of course, he'd had a goal then. Now he had the depressing suspicion that all his evil intentions had gone down the drain.

"Coffee," he muttered under his breath. Maybe he could make some coffee, sober her up long enough to have a little bit of participation. He couldn't actually say he'd never taken advantage of a comatose female, but somehow he couldn't see doing that to Angela. Besides, he didn't just want sex. He wanted her. Body and soul.

That was the kind of thought that scared him. Angela Hogan was coming to affect him more than any female in his long years of existence, and it was time he showed a little sense. It was a lucky thing he didn't believe in anything as ridiculous as falling in love. If he did, he'd be coming too damned close to it. Tonight he'd been given a reprieve from making one of the biggest mistakes of his life. He'd better get out while the getting was good.

He hoisted her up over his shoulder, her luscious little rump beside his face, her arms and legs hanging down limply. "You'll never know how close you came, Angel," he muttered, heading for the outside staircase. If Tony saw Clancy carting a limp Angela from his room, all hell would break loose. He needed to get her home and in bed with the minimum of fuss. And then he was going to take the first train to New York, to his plane, and if he had any sense at all, he'd never seen Angela Hogan again.

There were airplane hangars all over the East Coast, and a man with Clancy's connections and reputation could weasel his way into one. He'd come dangerously close to losing everything tonight. Thank God she'd managed to forestall a disastrous mistake for both of them by passing out. There were no happy endings, no little cottages and white picket fences for a man like him. Besides, he sure the hell couldn't imagine Angela in a frilly apron.

He dumped Angela into the front seat of Tony's Hudson, then moved around to the driver's seat. It started quietly enough and a few moments later he was out on the empty streets of Evanston, heading for Angela's bungalow.

The lights were blazing when he pulled up in front of it, and no sooner had he gotten around to the passenger side when the front door opened and Constance appeared, dressed in a negligee that belonged in some Ginger Rogers movie and not in a working-class neighborhood outside of Chicago. Her fluffy, high-heeled mules tap-tapped on the sidewalk as she rushed to the car, and her voice was high-pitched with irritation.

"What have you done to her?" she demanded. "I was worried sick."

"I didn't do a thing to her," he said irritably. "More's the pity," he added under his breath as he tossed Angela back over his shoulder like a sack of potatoes. "It was her Cousin Clement who got her snockered."

"Clement?" Sweet little Constance's voice got even more shrill. "What was she doing with him?"

"I believe she was conning some money out of him." The house smelled like cheap perfume, not the kind Angela had worn, and coffee. "For some flight of hers. Where's her bedroom?"

Constance gestured to the left. "The only one in the house. Put her down carefully," she said, trailing after them.

Clancy had already dropped Angela down with a touch too much enthusiasm. She was still off in dreamland, that silly smile on her face, and her evening gown had pulled lower, exposing most of one perfect breast.

He was reaching out to touch her when he heard Constance's gasp. She rushed past him, covered her sister with the sheet, then surveyed her critically.

"Who would have believed it of Angela?" she said. "Was she in this condition when you found her?"

"Your cousin's chauffeur dropped her off at Tony's. And yes, she was already pie-eyed."

"I don't mean the drinking. She never could hold her champagne. I mean had she been kissed?"

Clancy leaned over and studied the sleeping woman. Her lipstick was smudged now, her pale cheeks slightly abraded from his own late-evening beard. He just wished the rest of her body was similarly attended to.

"I didn't touch her," he said self-righteously. "It must have been your cousin."

Miss Constance Hogan didn't like that notion in the slightest. "He's Angela's cousin, not mine," she snapped. "I don't believe he'd do it."

Clancy shrugged, wishing Constance would go away so he could pull the sheet down again. Finally he gave up, heading into the living room with only a last, lingering glance. He didn't intend to see Miss Angela Hogan ever again, and he was feeling sentimental.

"Can I get you a cup of coffee?"

He turned, his eyes focusing for the first time on Constance. She'd belted her silky peignoir low over her spectacular figure, and there was no missing her generous endowments or the hint that that peignoir might come off quite easily.

He would have killed for a cup of coffee. "No, thanks. I've got to get going."

"What's your hurry? You aren't afraid of little old me, are you?" She smiled, that cute little-girl expression at odds with her wise eyes.

"Not in the slightest, toots," he said, considering it, just for a moment. After all, he was only human.

"Why don't you sit down and tell me what you find so attractive about my sister? You don't strike me as the type to like forceful women."

"Why don't you tell me what she got that money for?" he countered. "What flight is she planning?"

"You mean she hasn't told you? I guess I got the two of you wrong. I thought there was something between you."

"Not a thing," Clancy said. "What's she planning?"

"To break the record from some place in Canada to Havana. Just like Hal Ramsey tried."

"Hell and damnation," Clancy said bleakly. "I should have guessed."

"Why don't you sit down and I'll tell you all about it?"

His eyes narrowed as he stared down at her sweet little face. "No, thanks," he said. "You might fool your sister and her buddies with that little-girl act, but I've been around. Girls like you are nothing but trouble."

Constance smiled, unmoved. "But trouble can be nothing but fun."

"Sorry. I've got better things to do."

She slammed the door after him, and he half-expected her shrill voice to curse him all the way to the car. Instead the quiet of the early-morning hours settled around him as he started the Hudson, taking off toward Tony's. Things were even worse than he'd thought. He had to get out of here and fast. Before he told Angela Hogan that she was crazy to do what she was planning on doing.

Before he told her that it was his record she was attempting to break.

Before he told her he was falling in love with her.

## Chapter Thirteen

"I'm going to die." Angela heard her own voice echoing from beneath the pillow, and it sounded as if it were coming from beyond the grave. She only wished it were.

"No, you're not." Constance's voice penetrated the thick feather cushion. "You're going to wake up and drink your coffee and face the real world. There are worse tragedies in this life than your hangover."

At the sound of the word *coffee*, Angela surfaced from beneath the pillow, groaning as the midday light speared through her eyes. "Such as?" she demanded, sitting up and holding out her hand for the cup her sister had brought with her.

"Such as the Duke of Windsor marrying that woman," Constance said, fluffing herself down on the bed opposite her sister.

"This is a tragedy?" Angela scalded her tongue on the first sip, but she didn't care.

"It means your sister will never be queen of England."

Angela took a larger sip, burning her entire mouth. "Have I missed something along the way? As far as I remember, King Edward abdicated last December to marry the woman he loved. I don't remember your name being mentioned."

"A girl can dream."

Angela sighed. "Better settle for reality. Why would you want to live in England? I hear it's cold and rainy all the time."

"Maybe I'll have to settle for being a movie star," Constance said in a meditative voice.

Angela laughed, willing to be distracted. "What in heaven's name happened to me last night?"

"Don't you remember?"

"Not much. Clement gave me a check for expenses, we toasted the flight with champagne, Cousin Eleanor was glaring at me—"

"Cousin Eleanor always glares," Constance said cheerfully.

"How would you know that? I didn't think you'd ever met her."

Constance's smile was evasive. "She sounds like someone who glares."

"She is. So how did I get home? Did the chauffeur drop me off?"

"Not exactly."

Angela sat up straighter in the bed. "What do you mean, not exactly?" She looked down at the blue evening dress that was tumbling down to her waist. Somewhere in the mists of her memory she was remembering hands on her, dark hands, strong, arousing hands on her.

"Clancy!" she shrieked, spilling her coffee over the white sheets, over the blue chiffon dress.

"My dress!" Constance gasped, diving for the bed and mopping up the mess.

It took several moments for that overwhelming crisis to be averted, and by the time Angela was standing in the bedroom in her silky underwear, her recalcitrant memory was slowly coming back. "I had Evans take me to the bar," she said. "It was locked and closed, but Clancy was there. Oh, God!"

"So what?" Constance's voice was uncharacteristically brisk as she scrubbed at the coffee stains. "He's scarcely a lust-crazed beast. I'm sure he'd be able to control his evil impulses."

"What would you know about lust-crazed beasts?" Angela questioned darkly. "You've lived a sheltered life. The closest you've come to lust is on the movie screen."

"If you say so," Constance muttered. "Anyway, Clancy drove you home about three o'clock in the morning. You were out like a light. He dropped you on the bed and left."

Angela was prey to conflicting emotions. "I hope you didn't wear that peignoir to the door?"

Constance looked down at the filmy creation. "Are you crazy? I was wearing your chenille bathrobe, with flannel pj's underneath."

Angela wondered for a brief moment why Constance had changed, then dismissed the question as one too many for her poor overworked brain. "I left Clement's before midnight. What was I doing between then and three when Clancy brought me home?"

"You tell me," Constance said, tossing the stained gown over her arm and heading for the kitchen.

Angela looked down at her slender body. The silk stockings were still attached to her garters, the tap pants were in place. Her body looked white, smooth, unblemished, and she knew without a shadow of a doubt that Clancy hadn't had his wicked way with her. He was a man who'd leave a mark, on her flesh, in her mind, in her soul. He already had.

It took hours for coffee, aspirin, a hot bath and clean clothes to turn her into the semblance of a normal person. The Packard was out of gas, but she couldn't bring herself to chastise her sister. Not when she was so busy chastising herself.

It was a cool, rainy day, just the kind of weather to match her mood. She dreaded seeing Clancy again, uncertain how she was going to react. On the one hand, he'd obviously played the gentleman for once in his life, bringing her safely home when she was in no condition to watch out for her own well-being. On the other hand, he'd always insisted he wasn't a gentleman. Was she that unattractive that he wasn't even tempted?

She reached up a tentative hand and brushed her swollen lips. No, he'd been tempted, all right. She couldn't remember clearly, but something told her she'd come awfully close to losing what she'd held on to for far too long. She just wished she knew whether Clancy had desisted out of nobility and a belated caring for her or out of sheer apathy.

She couldn't very well ask him. She'd simply have to pretend nothing had happened and leave it up to him to mention it or not. In the meantime, she had plenty to keep her busy. She had the money, she had the plane, now all she needed was the weather. She squinted skyward into the light drizzle that misted down over her. Maybe things were clearer on the East Coast.

"Where the hell have you been?" Sparks demanded when she walked into the hangar some forty-five minutes after one on June 3. "It's not like you to be late."

Angela smiled tightly. "There were extenuating circumstances. What's the problem?"

"Charlie Olker."

"So what else is new? What's the villainous SOB want now?"

"That villainous SOB has come to give you a friendly piece of advice." Olker loomed out of her office, his impressive bulk rolling with each step, like a sailor on a storm-tossed ship.

"Your friendly advice I can do without. I thought I told you to keep off my property," she snapped, her headache leaping back in full force.

"I don't take warnings from snippy little girls. Especially when my motives are so pure."

"Your motives are as pure as John Dillinger's conscience. Speak your piece and get out."

Olker shook his head sadly. "Such a lack of manners. Your father would be grieved at one of his daughters being so graceless."

"My father's dead," she shot back, enraged. "And I have no intention of discussing him with a reprobate like you."

Olker chuckled deep within his massive bulk. "That's a hell of a way to refer to a war hero, Angie."

"Go away, Charlie," she said wearily, the fight going out of her. "My head hurts too much to deal with you."

He wouldn't drop it, of course. "It's out of respect for the affection I had for your father that I come to you, Angie. I wanted to warn you about one of your employees."

Angela's eyes flew open. What was the old scoundrel up to now? "Which one?"

Olker shook his head. "I'm not going to spell it out for you. A smart cookie like you can figure these things out. I just thought I'd drop you a little hint. One of your employees isn't what he says he is."

"Is anybody?" she countered.

Olker's fat face creased in malice. "I'm talking about running from the law, Angie. I'm talking about you maybe losing your license if the wrong people find out he's working for you. I'm talking about you maybe losing your life if the wrong people find out he's working for you."

Angela's back stiffened in sudden outrage. "I'm not going to listen to your threats, Charlie. There's nothing you'd like better than for me to lose my license, and deep down I don't think you'd give a damn if my life went along with it. So you go and tell anyone you please about the mystery crook who's working for me, and I'll deal with the consequences when they come. Unless you want to be straight with me."

Charlie's little pig eyes were dark with anger in his thick suet-pudding face. "I don't give nothing away," he said, sticking his thick, smelly cigar back in his mouth.

"Just threats and intimidations," Angela said. "Get your nasty cigar and your nasty face out of here, Charlie. Next time you set your fat shadow on my place, I'll be the one to call in the law."

"You'll be sorry, Angie," Charlie said, tossing his cigar away. Tossing it in the direction of an oil spill on the cement floor.

Sparks was ahead of him, stamping it out before disaster exploded in their face. "You heard the lady, Olker. Get out."

"Mighty bold, aren't you? I'm just wondering where her other brave employees are. Afraid to face me." With a chuckle that sounded more like a wheeze, Charlie lumbered out of the building.

Angela didn't move for a moment. "Maybe we should call the fumigators," she said in a meditative tone.

"You were swell, Angie. Simply grand," Sparks said. "Boy, the look on his face when you told him to take his fat shadow out of here was priceless."

"He had a point, though. Where are the others? Clancy and Parsons? I would have thought Clancy would have shown him the door the moment he showed his ugly face around here." She headed toward her office, expecting Sparks to follow.

He stayed put, clearing his throat nervously. "Uh, Parsons was working on the Percival. He said he didn't like arguments and he was going to keep low."

"That's fine." She dismissed him without a second thought. "All right, Sparks, spill it. Where's Clancy?"

"Gone."

For a moment Sparks's words didn't register. "Where?"

"To New York. I think he took the morning train, as near as I can tell."

"That's right, his plane was coming in by freighter some time today." Disappointment warred with relief. "What's the big deal, Sparks? We knew he was going to get it."

"Yeah, but we'd talked about me flying him east to pick it up."

"So he decided to take the train. A man's entitled to change his mind." Something about Sparks's miserable expression penetrated her determined optimism. "What is it, Sparks? What haven't you told me? Did he clean out the safe before he went?"

That stung Sparks into talking. "Of course he didn't. The guy might be a louse, but he's not that big of a louse."

"Okay, Sparks, drop the other shoe," she said with growing impatience tinged with dread.

"He cleared out everything else. His extra clothes, his charts, his tools. Everything's gone. I went by Tony's, to check his rooms, and everything's gone from there, too. He's taken a powder, Angie. He ain't coming back."

Angela took a deep breath, telling herself it didn't matter, telling herself that it was heartburn from her hangover tearing up her insides and nothing else. "All right," she said slowly. "We can deal with that. What flights have we got scheduled?"

"A lot. The work's really picked up since Clancy flew that shipment to Detroit a couple of weeks ago. People learned we can carry through with what we say we'll do."

"And we still will. Bring in the schedule and we'll see what we can do. I'll need to free up a few days as soon as I can, but I guess we can be flexible."

"You planning something, Angie? Clancy said you were, but you never said anything to me. I couldn't believe you'd confide in him and not tell me."

"I'm planning something. And the only person I talked to about it was Parsons. A flier can't keep secrets from her mechanic, can she?"

"A flier shouldn't keep secrets from her best friend, either. It's the Newfoundland-to-Havana run, isn't it?"

"Not hard to guess. I didn't know it was so obvious."

"It wouldn't be to someone who wasn't around when Ramsey bought it. I figured you'd be trying it sooner or later. I just hoped you'd forgotten about it."

"It's not that dangerous a run," Angela protested.

"It's over a hell of a lot of open water." Will Parsons appeared from the darkened hangar. "Why don't you just try for the coast-to-coast record?"

"Flying to break records is always dangerous. Hell, flying is dangerous," Angela said.

"Watch your language, missy," Parsons reproved.

"Stop sounding like a father," Angela shot back, ignoring the old man's sudden wince. "I'll say anything I damned well please. And I'm not changing my mind about this flight. I'm past the point where I want to fly all over the country just to break records. This is just something I have to do, and I don't have to explain it to anyone!"

"Sure, Angie," Sparks said.

But she'd already gone, storming past the two men into her office and slamming the door behind her. The day had gone from bad to worse, but at least one good thing had come from it. Clancy was gone, and she was damned glad of it. Damned glad, she repeated to herself, casting a mutinous glare toward the hangar and Parsons's reproving figure.

She sank down at her desk, leaning back in the oak swivel chair and closing her eyes. A second later she sat forward again, staring at the top of her cluttered desk.

There were her silver evening sandals, her heels encrusted with mud. Beside them lay her gloves and the slightly crumpled check from Cousin Clement.

She hadn't even realized it wasn't still in her possession. She stared at it, horror filling her as she realized how close she came to letting it all slip through her fingers, and all over some man who wasn't worth spit.

There was a note beneath her shoes, brief and to the point. His handwriting was distinctive, thick slashes that reminded her of the way he talked, the way he moved, quick and definite.

Don't make that flight, Red. Breaking records is for suckers.

She crumpled up the note in her hand and tossed it into the wastebasket. "Trusting people like you is for suckers, Clancy," she informed the trash. "You can read about it in the papers." And very carefully she smoothed the wrinkled check, concentrating on it. It took all her indignation to keep from diving into the wastebasket and picking Clancy's note out. He was gone, out of her life for good. The sooner she started appreciating that fact, the better.

CLANCY HAD NEVER BOTHERED to name his plane. He'd been superstitious about it. The twin-engine Fokker was the fourth airplane he'd owned, and he'd named all the others. They'd all crashed with him aboard. Some superstitious part of him told him that as long as he didn't name the Fokker, he'd be safe.

She was in sorry shape, though, one of her wings damaged, her Wasp engines a mess, her Sperry autopilot nonfunctioning and the radio shot. He had her trucked to a tiny airport on Long Island, and while he looked her over, he wondered why he'd bothered to spend the money having her shipped up from South America. It might have made more sense to simply cut his losses and go from there. He'd have no trouble picking up the kind of lucrative work that would enable him to buy a new plane in no time at all.

Instead, he'd gone to work for a penny-ante operation for a fraction of what he could have gotten anywhere else, suckered by a pair of blue eyes and a hard-luck story Angela was too proud to tell him.

It was the same with the Fokker. She was a beautiful lady, down on her luck right now, but he couldn't see putting her out to pasture. She deserved a break just as much as Angela Hogan did.

He just wished he could forget about Angela. He'd put her behind him, along with his quixotic gesture of taking her safely home that last night, but when he least expected it, she'd come back to haunt him.

He couldn't even manage to drum up any interest in the local female talent around Long Island and Manhattan. Some of them looked like Angela, but they didn't talk like her, didn't have her quick intelligence or fierce determination. He gave up trying, gave up doing anything but working on his plane with the local mechanic, a decent enough boy without Parsons's intuitive brilliance.

Clancy left Angela in a hell of a mess, whether she knew it or not. Things were going to come crashing down on that pretty little head of hers, people that she trusted were going to betray her. While she kept planning her fool stunt of a flight, the very people she needed to count on were lying to her.

He wished he could have warned her, but no one likes the bearer of bad news. It would have been a case of shoot the messenger. Besides, Angela was determined to handle things her own way, and the smartest move he ever made was to get away from her and let her do just that. She wouldn't want him interfering in her life, giving her advice. She was probably dancing for joy that he'd taken off.

It took longer than he expected to get the Fokker in decent working shape. Longer, and more money. By the time she was ready to fly again, he was flat broke. He knew what he wanted to do. Now that the Pacific Ocean had been conquered, the fledgling airlines were getting ready to start transatlantic flights. He wanted to be there. He wanted to fly DC 3s, probably the sweetest of the bigger planes; he wanted to conquer the dark, dangerous Atlantic until it was no more important than a puddle. He had the talent and he had the contacts. All he had to do was make the call and the future would be in his hand.

The damnable thing about it was, he wasn't ready. Three times he picked up the phone to call New York. Twice he hung up. The third time he started giving the operator the Chicago exchange before he chickened out. After that he knew.

He wasn't going to start flying the big ones until he took care of unfinished business. Angela Hogan wouldn't go away, even though he'd tried to wipe her out of his brain. The only thing left for him to do was go back, clean up the mess that was about to descend on her chestnut head and say goodbye. Maybe then he could get on with his life.

On Friday morning, June 8, he took off for Chicago with his newly refurbished Fokker purring like a well-fed kitten. And on her fuselage was a name printed in bright red letters. *Angel*.

"WHAT THE HELL DO YOU want?" Angela snarled as Parsons poked his head in the door.

"Watch your language, girly," he said mildly enough. "You've been like a bear with a sore paw the last few days."

"I'm tired," she said, recognizing the defensive note in her voice but unable to do anything about it. "Who wouldn't be with the schedule we've been following? Trust Clancy to leave us in the lurch like that.''

''You miss him, don't you?''

She stubbed out her cigarette. ''I miss having another pilot around that I can trust. Period.''

''If you say so. I can find you another one.''

She stared at him, trying to pierce through the thick glasses to read his expression. ''You can?''

''I have contacts. People who aren't afraid of the likes of Charlie Olker. Good fliers who're tired of barnstorming and would appreciate a decent berth. All I have to do is make a few phone calls. That is, if Clancy isn't coming back.''

She refused to allow herself a moment of hope. ''He's not coming back,'' she said flatly.

''Then should I make those phone calls? You're going to need backup if you want to make that flight.''

She knew he was right. Knew she had no reason to procrastinate. ''Tomorrow,'' she said.

She couldn't tell with his full beard, but she thought the old man might be smiling. ''Tomorrow,'' he echoed. ''I'll check with you first.''

God, was she so transparent? It was a waste of energy to keep denying it. ''Check with me tomorrow,'' she agreed with a rueful smile. ''You still haven't told me what you came in here for. Anything up?''

''Your sister's asking for you.''

''Constance? What's she doing here in the middle of the day? She's supposed to be working. Even jobs at Woolworth's are hard to come by nowadays.''

''I don't know. But she's crying her eyes out on Sparks's shoulder right this minute.''

''Oh, God,'' Angela gasped, leaping from her chair.

''Watch your language,'' Parsons muttered as she raced past him out into the hangar.

The sight that met her eyes was momentarily terrifying. Constance was enfolded in Sparks's burly arms, sobbing loudly. Her flower dress was bedecked with a black arm band of mourning, and Sparks's expression was equally grim.

Clancy, Angela thought, her mind immediately jumping to the one person who'd claimed it for the last few days, few weeks. She ran across the cement floor of the hangar, her booted feet ringing loudly, telling herself it couldn't be him, that Constance wouldn't be crying over a man she'd scarcely met.

"What in heaven's name has happened?" she cried breathlessly.

"Oh, Angie!" Constance wailed, releasing Sparks and flinging herself in Angela's arms. "Such a tragedy! Too young to die. Too young!"

Angela put her arms around Constance's hysterical figure, looking to Sparks for guidance. Belatedly she realized it wasn't grief creasing his rough-hewn face, it was discomfort. "What's happened?" Angela asked again, more calmly now. "Who crashed?"

Constance lifted her tear-stained face indignantly. "Is that all you ever think about? Your stupid airplanes? No one crashed."

Relief flooded her. "Then who died?" she asked evenly.

"Jean Harlow!" Constance wailed.

"Jean Harlow?" Angela echoed blankly. "The actress?"

Constance simply cried louder, and it took all of Angela's self-control not to give her weeping little sister a good hard shake. "That's...a real shame," she said instead, forcing herself to sound sympathetic.

"You ever meet this Harlow dame?" Sparks demanded, still confused.

"Of course not!" Constance said damply. "I just worshipped her from afar."

"So did I," Sparks said with the faint trace of a leer.

"Oh, you men!" Constance dismissed him. "I'm so unhappy, Angie. I had to leave work when I heard about it."

Angela cast about in her mind for something soothing to say. "Well, why don't you take the car and go home and have a nice cup of soup and a nap? You'll feel better afterward."

"You're so strong, Angie. So brave."

Angela controlled her irritation. "Look at it this way, Constance. You'll simply have to go to Hollywood and take her place as the blond bombshell."

She expected at least the trace of a laugh from her watery sister. Instead Constance nodded, intent. "You're right, Angela. You always know the right thing to say."

The tight rein Angela was keeping on her recently volatile temper was coming close to snapping when Parsons suddenly appeared from the doorway of the hangar. "I don't suppose any of you noticed, but there's a bright red twin-engine Fokker circling overhead. Looks like he's getting ready to land, but I haven't been able to raise him on the radio."

Angela released her sister abruptly. "Isn't Clancy's plane a...?"

"Yup."

She moved to the door, peering out into the cloudless June sky. It was Clancy, all right, she knew it in her soul, in her blood. No one flew like that, with just that combination of grace and daring. She turned away, afraid the others would notice her reaction. "I'm going back to the office. I've got work to do and I've already wasted enough time. Let me know who it is when they land," she said calmly.

There was no missing Parsons's grin this time. "Sure thing, Angie. Shall we tell Clancy you missed him?"

"I'll cut your heart out," she said calmly, and turned on her heel, ignoring her tearful sister, stomping back toward her office without checking to make sure Clancy landed safely. He didn't dare crash. She'd kill him if he did. She was probably going to kill him anyway, but she wanted him in one piece for the execution.

## Chapter Fourteen

Angela turned up the radio, loud. It was Artie Shaw's orchestra playing "The Man I Love," not the best song to blast through her untidy office, but she didn't have much choice. If she'd turned to another station, like WLS, she could have ended up with another rendition of "Harbor Lights." Or, even worse, Bunny Berigan singing "I Can't Get Started."

She smoked four cigarettes, one after another. She shuffled twelve bills, wrote checks for three of them and then had to tear them up. She listened to the news, including the latest flash about Jean Harlow's death and the Duke of Windsor's honeymoon in Venice with his American bride. She listened to F.D.R.'s latest plan for economic recovery, she listened to the Andrews Sisters singing about Ovaltine. And she waited for Clancy.

She smoked three more cigarettes, until her throat was raw and her eyes stung and smoke hung heavy in the crowded office. She wrote two more checks, ripped them up, tried balancing her checkbook and came out two dollars and fifty-three cents in the red. She tried again and came out with three dollars plus change in the black. She slammed her checkbook shut, changed the station on the radio and listened to "Amy Andrews, Girl Reporter." And she waited for Clancy.

Two hours later Sparks poked his head in the door. "We're heading over to Tony's. Wanna come?"

"Where's Constance?" She didn't look up from the girdle advertisement she was studying. What she meant was, where's Clancy?

But Sparks never was very good at reading her mind. "She went home hours ago to enjoy a period of mourning. She took the car, by the way."

"That's all right, I'll walk home. It's a nice day."

"It's after five, Angie. And the sky's gotten cloudy. Might rain before you get all the way home. If you don't want to come with us to Tony's, why don't you at least let me give you a ride home?"

She could just picture it, crammed into the front seat of Sparks's aging roadster with Clancy. Or worse, stuck in the rumble seat looking at the back of his head. "No thanks, I'd prefer to walk." She shuffled some papers. "I take it Clancy's back?"

"Sure is. His plane's a beauty, too. Wanna see it?"

"Later."

"Want to talk to Clancy?"

"I don't have anything to say to him."

"Okay, boss. I told him he could run those two bankers up to Kenosha for you tomorrow morning. You've been pushing yourself too hard recently. Give yourself a break, kid. You'll live longer."

She stifled her instinctive protest. "Thanks, Sparks. I may just sleep in tomorrow."

"I'll believe it when I see it. 'Night, Angie."

"Good night, Sparks."

She waited again, waited until the cavernous, echoing hangar lapsed into a thick stillness. She finished her pack of Luckies, tossed the crumpled paper into her wastepaper basket and stood up. Tomorrow, or the next day, would be soon enough to face Clancy. She'd been so convinced she'd never see him again, she couldn't quite shift gears.

They'd pulled the Fokker into the hangar, and its bright red sides glistened in the half light. She stopped for a moment, transfixed.

It was absolutely gorgeous. The *Mona Lisa* of airplanes, the Moet champagne of twin engines, the Sistine Chapel of aircraft. She stood utterly still, drinking in its unearthly beauty as a paroxysm of covetousness swept over her. She wanted that plane, as much as she'd ever wanted anything in her life. Or almost as much.

"Pretty, isn't she?" Clancy murmured, materializing from out of the shadows like a ghost.

"*Pretty*'s too nice a word for her," Angela said, too rapt in contemplation to remember she was angry with him. "Gorgeous. Magnificent. Incomparable. Splendid."

"Yes," he said softly. "You are."

Her brain focused sharply. She turned, looked at him in the half light and promptly slapped him across the face.

Without hesitation he slapped her back. "I told you not to do that again, Red," he drawled, looking not the slightest bit regretful. "I don't take kindly to being slugged."

"Neither do I."

"Then maybe you've learned your lesson."

"What are you doing back here?" She was determined not to put a hand to her face. In retrospect she knew he'd pulled his punch. He could have hit her a lot harder. "Sparks was sure you'd left for good."

"I told you I'd stick until Olker was washed up. I'm a man of my word." He bent his head to light a cigarette, the match flaring briefly in the shadowy light.

"Are you? Sparks said you'd taken everything with you. That sounded like a farewell note you left for me."

He grinned then, glancing up at her over the cigarette. "I figured I owed you something after that last night."

"Nothing happened!"

"No? Your memory's that good after you've passed out?"

"Don't try to con me, Clancy. Are you telling me something happened that night?" She kept her face impassive, fighting down the absolute panic that she might have been wrong after all. She knew immediately that it wasn't the loss of her outdated innocence that bothered her. It was the fact that he would have taken advantage of her like that. That he would have cared so little about her that he would have used her the first chance he got.

He leaned back against the bright red side of his plane. "What do you think happened that night, Angel?"

"Don't play games with me, Clancy."

"Games are fun. You're too serious all the time. Come on, take a guess."

"I think I got drunk, passed out and you drove me home."

He nodded, taking a deep drag of his cigarette. "That about covers the basics. You're missing the best parts, though. You haven't mentioned dancing so close you almost crawled inside my skin. You haven't mentioned making out on the dance floor. You haven't mentioned me carrying you up to my room."

"I guess I forgot about that," she said in a rough little voice, knowing her face was as red as a schoolgirl's in belated embarrassment.

He grinned. "I guess you did. However, you also forgot to mention passing out the moment you got there, so that I had no choice but act like a gentleman, something completely out of character for me. You're having a bad influence on me, Angel."

"Is that why you ran away?"

He frowned, staring at his cigarette intently. "I resent that."

"You mean you didn't run away?"

"I mean I resent your knowing that I ran away." He pushed away from the plane, dropping his cigarette on the floor and squashing it beneath his boot. "Want a tour of the *Angel*? She's almost as pretty from the inside."

"The *Angel*," she echoed, horrified. "What made you name her that?"

"Inspiration," he said.

"I wish you'd change it. People might think you named it after me."

"I did." He reached out a gentle hand and touched her face, his fingers rough-textured and unbearably sensitive. She shivered beneath his light touch, wanting to move closer. "I've marked you," he said, his voice husky. "I shouldn't have done that."

She shouldn't do it, she knew she shouldn't, but her brain and her hand didn't seem connected. She reached up and touched him, the imprint of her hand against the faint stubble of new beard. How he could look so attractive and so unkempt at the same time was totally beyond her comprehension. "I shouldn't have hit you first," she said.

He caught her wrist. "Angel . . ."

She yanked her hand away quickly, moving out of reach before her brain could melt completely. "I'll see the inside of the plane tomorrow," she said hastily. "When it's safer."

He didn't try to follow. "What do you think I am, the Big Bad Wolf? You're as safe with me as you want to be."

"That's what I'm afraid of," she muttered. "Good night, Clancy. See you tomorrow." She was half afraid he'd try to stop her, but he didn't move as he watched her walk away without saying a word.

It wasn't until she'd almost reached the door when his voice broke the silence. "Don't make that flight, Red."

There was no mistaking the seriousness in his voice, but she stalled. "What flight?"

"Don't play games. The Newfoundland-to-Havana flight. There's no reason to attempt it. It's over too much water, it's too dangerous. Besides, you don't need to prove anything to anybody."

She didn't bother asking him how he knew. She'd probably blabbed it herself in her drunken state. "Just to myself, Clancy," she said. And she closed the door very quietly behind her.

CONSTANCE HAD WORN BLACK for three days, carried a lacy handkerchief wherever she went and managed to look both suffering and brave when questioned about her bereavement. But then *Snow White and the Seven Dwarfs* opened at the local movie theaters and Constance quickly cheered up, going around the house singing "Whistle While You Work" until Angela was ready to scream. Or hope some other blond actress would die young and give Angela the blessed relief of another period of mourning.

Angela threw herself into her preparations with fierce concentration. For some reason she was convinced that they were all going to try to stop her. Sparks and Clancy, now that they knew what she planned, were both disapproving and admonitory, doing their utmost to talk her out of it given half the chance. Parsons continued in his own taciturn way, seldom volunteering an opinion other than to tell her it was a damn-fool stunt.

She knew it was. Even the insatiable public had lost interest in record-setting flights that had no other purpose than to fly faster than the last human being. Amelia Earhart's current world-wide sojourn was being followed with intense interest, but Angela suspected, and she knew AE did, as well, that this would be the last of the great flights. From now on, people were going to concentrate on the more practical aspects of long-distance flying. Clancy had the right idea about passenger airlines. In the not too distant future, flying across the Atlantic would be a regular occurrence for anyone with the nerve and the passage.

If she had any sense at all she'd forget about her flight. But this time, for once in her life, she wasn't going to show any sense. She had the money, she had the plane, she had the charts and the connections. She was going to follow Hal's route, exactly, and she was going to beat the current record by hours. And then she'd be able to rest.

"She's as ready as she's going to be," Parsons said, pulling his head away from the engine and closing the cover.

Angela looked up from the chart she was studying. She was sitting cross-legged on the cement floor of the hangar on a blisteringly hot day in late-June. Her office was too hot, the smell of spilled gasoline too strong for her to stomach. The Lockheed was over in the far corner of the hangar by a sliding door that let in what little breeze there was on such a sultry day, and the floor was a relatively cool place to work.

She would have preferred to be flying, but Sparks had taken his usual lesson up in the Avian, and Clancy wasn't back from a run to East Lansing in the Percival. She'd cast a brief, longing glance at the Fokker, then righteously put it out of her mind. Clancy would dismember her if she even touched it without his permission.

"What'd you say?" she inquired lazily.

"I say she's ready. The plane's ready, if you insist on making that fool flight. There's no way she's going to be in better shape."

Angela felt the familiar tightening in her stomach, tension and fear and excitement all wrapped up in one large knot. She set the chart down. "All right," she said with deceptive calm. "I'll check the weather."

"You know where you're going in Canada? Where you're going to refuel along the way? Have you considered . . . ?"

"I've considered everything," Angela said, hoping it was true. "If the plane's ready, so am I."

"I sure the hell hope you know what you're doing," Parsons grumbled.

She glanced at him curiously. "What does it matter to you, old man?"

Parsons shrugged. "This is a pretty good berth. I like the Chicago area, and I kind of like your planes. You're not half bad yourself. So I'd just as soon you didn't take a header into the Atlantic Ocean trying to prove something that doesn't need proving."

"You don't know what I'm trying to prove," she said.

"Do you?"

She didn't answer, busying herself scooping up her papers. But several hours later, after she got the unwelcome word that the weather in the northeast was cloudy and rainy, Clancy asked the same question. And with Clancy, she couldn't duck.

"You're going to do it, then," he said, more a statement than a question as he lounged in the doorway of her office.

She looked up, her face composed. "Have you been talking with Parsons?"

He didn't deny it. "He just said he gave you the green light. I want to make sure you know what you're doing."

"I know what I'm doing. Unfortunately the weather isn't sure it's going to cooperate. There's a storm front heading toward the maritime coast of Canada. If it weakens by the time I get there, I should be fine. If not, I'm likely to be stranded for days."

"So you're going to be sensible for once in your life and wait until all danger is passed."

Angela grinned. "I'm always sensible, Clancy. You know that."

The noise he made was something between a harrumph and a snort. "How about joining us for a drink at Tony's?

Will and Sparks and I have every intention of talking you out of this fool idea."

"Will's going? I didn't think he went anywhere but to his room and to the movies."

"Sparks strong-armed him. Hell, you can't blame the man for avoiding Tony's. He's on the wagon, you know."

"I know. Why do you think I haven't been there?"

A light of amusement danced in Clancy's dark eyes. "Don't tell me you're laying off the hooch?"

"Exactly."

"But you're so damned cute when you're tight, Angel. If you keep on the straight and narrow, there's no way I'm going to have my wicked way with you."

She smiled sweetly. "That's right, Clancy. Better set your sights on someone more available."

He shook his head. "No can do, toots. I'm the kind of man who doesn't give up once he decides he wants something."

She felt a queer little tingling in the pit of her stomach. He looked so cheerful, so casual and friendly lounging against her doorjamb, that she couldn't quite believe he meant what he was saying. "And have you decided you want me?" Her voice was deceptively calm.

He straightened upright and for a moment she thought he was going to advance on her. There was a determined gleam in his eyes, one she'd learned to be wary of, and the knot in her stomach tightened and lowered.

And then he laughed, breaking the sudden tension. "You figure it out, Angel. Meet you at the front in ten minutes, okay? You've got the only working car between us."

She let out the breath she hadn't even realized she'd been holding. "Ten minutes," she agreed. And then, as she watched him saunter away, wondered why in heaven's name she'd been fool enough to agree to it.

TONY'S BAR AND GRILLE was already crowded when Clancy pulled up outside, handling Angela's Packard with deft assurance that hadn't kept her from watching him like a hawk. He shouldn't have held out his hand for the keys when the four of them had left the hangar. But then, she shouldn't have given them to him, either. She hadn't wanted to put up an argument in front of Sparks and Will, and she didn't realize till later that her acquiescence was far more remarkable than any resistance she might have shown.

None of them were in particularly festive moods as they threaded their way through the crowded tables. She knew every person there, up to and including Robert Bellamy, who was busy trying to flirt with Betsey as he nursed a dark whiskey and soda. He glanced over at them when they came in together, and his handsome face creased in a sudden, ugly frown. By the time they'd threaded their way through the crowd of friends and acquaintances to find a table in the corner, Bellamy had disappeared, his drink left half empty on the highly polished walnut bar.

"Are you okay?" she heard Clancy ask in a solicitous voice, and she almost answered, assuming his concern was for her. It took her only a moment to realize it was Will who was in trouble. His scarred skin was pale behind the thick glasses, and he was ducking his head, crammed back into the corner of the room as if this was the last place in the world he wanted to be.

"Fine," Will muttered in his scratchy, ruined voice. "I don't like bars much anymore."

"Do you want to leave?" Angela put her hand on his scarred one. "I can drive you home...."

"No!" He cleared his throat. "Please, I don't want to make a scene. I'll be fine."

"What can I get you folks?" Betsey appeared in front of them, Robert Bellamy forgotten as she sashayed her rayon-covered hips at the appreciative Clancy.

"Vanilla Coke for Angela and Will," Clancy said, in his usual high-handed manner. "What're you having, Sparks?"

"Boilermaker," Sparks said cheerfully.

Betsey leaned forward, displaying her spectacular cleavage. "And you'll be having the usual, Jack?" she asked in a breathy voice.

He leered back at her, Angela thought grumpily. "Sure thing, babe. And why don't you make everyone's a double? We've got hard work ahead of us, trying to talk Angela out of making some damned-fool flight."

Betsey glanced over at Angela with friendly curiosity. "No one's ever talked Angie out of anything. Good luck."

With various levels of appreciation, the three men watched Betsey's magnificent hips wiggle to the bar, while Angela controlled her own sour reaction. If only Betsey weren't so darned nice, she'd be able to despise her. As it was, all Angela could do was be jealous.

"Jack?" Angela said, once Betsey had brought their drinks and turned her attention back to Robert Bellamy, who'd reappeared as if by magic. "She calls you Jack?"

"It's my name," he said with a shrug.

"All his women do that," Sparks said cheerfully, ignoring the undercurrent. "I guess he hypnotizes them into thinking that if they call him by his first name, they can somehow hold on to a piece of him. It's as regular as clockwork—he sets his sights on a dame and they start in with 'Jack this' and 'Jack that.' I wish I could figure out something that easy."

Angela's smile felt frozen to her face. "Well, *Clancy*," she said, emphasizing his last name, "what did you boys want to talk to me about?"

Clancy leaned forward, touching her face, a look of devilment in his eyes. "Call me Jack."

She almost slapped him. He must have read her intention for the sudden blackness of his eyes warned her. He would have slugged her back again, and all hell would have broken loose. The bar was full of men who considered Angela their kid sister. Clancy wouldn't have an unbroken bone in his body.

She put her hands on the table, tapping her fingers against the red-and-white checked table cloth. "Clancy," she said again, deliberately. "I don't have all night."

She knew that was the wrong thing to have said the moment it left her mouth, and she was waiting for his next inflammatory statement when Parsons broke in. "Neither do I. Listen, Angie, this flight is just plain stupid. Why do you want to go do such a fool thing for? The flight's been done maybe half a dozen times in the last ten years, and the record's close to unbeatable. Why do you want to go risking your life just to make a new record that'll stand for maybe a year or two, maybe less?"

"That's not why I want to do it," she said in a low voice. "Sparks understands."

Sparks lowered his bushy eyebrows and stared at his beer. "No, I don't, Angie," he muttered.

She should never have come, she knew that now, but she'd gone too far to back down. Besides, it was time Clancy heard the truth. "It's for Hal," she said finally. "I can't stand the thought that he lost. That he let that last flight beat him. For his sake I want to finish it. To end it in triumph, not in failure." She paused, her voice harsh, as the familiar tears burned the back of her eyes.

If she expected Clancy to be touched, even deeply moved, she'd picked the wrong man. "I don't think that's it, Red," he drawled, toying with his glass of rum. "I think you feel guilty that you didn't really love him and you're trying to prove to everyone that you did."

He caught her hand before it connected with his face, his fingers bruising on her narrow wrist. "Haven't you learned your lesson yet?" he said, leaning closer across the table, oblivious to the two men watching. "I hit back."

"Let go of me, you—you womanizer!" she ground out.

He did, leaning back and laughing. "Surely you can do better than that?"

"Listen, we're not getting anywhere," Sparks said in a troubled voice. "Angie, would you at least consider waiting...?"

His voice trailed off, drowned by the commotion at the front door. "That's all I needed," Angela muttered, draining her vanilla Coke as she watched Charlie Olker's huge form enter the bar. "I'm leaving."

This time it was Will's hand that grabbed hers, forestalling her hasty exit. "Wait," he said, his voice low and oddly anxious. "Don't get his attention."

She didn't even bother thinking about how peculiar that was, too busy noticing Clancy's sudden frown as he glanced over at Will. "I don't think it'll do any good," he said in his low, amused voice. "Charlie didn't come for any social reasons. He came for Angela."

Indeed, as he waded through the greetings of the other pilots and mechanics, it was clear that Olker was making a beeline for their table. For a moment she considered crawling under it, then gave up the notion, straightening her shoulders and meeting his oily gaze as he lumbered up to them.

"Such a happy group," he said, his half-smoked cigar clamped between yellow teeth. "Things must be going pretty well at Hogan Air Transport if you can afford to socialize like this."

"Things are going very well," Angela said evenly. "What do you want, Charlie?"

"Nothing at all, Angela. I'm here on purely social reasons. How are you, Sparks? How's the eyesight?"

Sparks growled at him in sullen response.

Charlie turned to Clancy. "And you, Clancy? How's the famous flyboy? No jealous husbands running you out of town yet? You must have tamed down a bit in your old age."

"I'm just a pussycat, Olker," Clancy said, and if Olker heard the thin thread of menace beneath Clancy's voice, he chose to ignore it.

Olker turned his attention to Will. "And you must be the new mechanic I've heard so much about. What was the name again?"

"Parsons," Will said in a harsh, defiant voice. "Will Parsons."

"That's it. Funny, but it seems as if I've met you before," Charlie mused. "There's something awfully familiar about you."

His words startled Angela momentarily out of her rage. She'd felt the same thing, and if anyone but her worst enemy had said that, she would have said something. As it was, she ignored her sudden shock of recognition.

"What is it you want, Olker?" she broke in. "You don't have a social bone in your body. Who are you out to get this time?"

"You wound me, Angela," he protested. "I just heard you were planning a little flight and I wanted to wish you luck. Buy you a bottle of champagne as a good-luck present."

"No champagne," she said in a strangled gasp, then managed a tight smile. "Maybe after I complete the flight, Charlie."

"Which you will, of course," he said smoothly, an evil smile in his piggy eyes. "How could you fail, with Clancy's assistance?"

"Clancy isn't assisting me, Olker," she snapped, enraged. "I'm doing it on my own."

"Of course you are," he said soothingly. "And why should he help you?" He leaned across the table, pushing his fleshy face close to hers. "After all, it's his record you're trying to break."

## Chapter Fifteen

She left them stranded at Tony's. For one moment everything had seemed to stop, the noise, the sound, everything, as she took in Clancy's guilty expression, Olker's triumph, Sparks's worry. Sparks knew. Parsons knew. Everyone knew but Angela.

No one tried to stop her as she pushed away from the table and stumbled for the exit. It was probably only her imagination that made her think everyone was watching, laughing at her. Or even worse, pitying her for being such a gullible fool.

"Damn, damn, damn," she said out loud, pounding the steering wheel as she drove through the twilight. "Damn them all!"

She hated being lied to. She hated things being covered up, she hated the thought of them all knowing and not saying a word as she planned her stupid little jaunt. It reminded her of Frank, her father, flying whiskey in for the mob, all the while pretending he was making all that money from flight lessons. It was Frank's duplicity that had cost him his life, cost old Mrs. McCarthy and Goldie their lives, too. She hated it, hated him, hated everyone.

She didn't want to go home. For all she knew, Constance knew it was Clancy's record she'd been so sure she'd break. No, that was impossible. The only thing Constance found more boring than politics was flying. If she'd known, she wouldn't have paid any attention. Besides, Constance had never kept a secret in her entire life.

The night was clear and warm, and Angela's rage filled her with such adrenaline that she knew she would never sleep. Without thinking she turned the Packard toward the hangar, the place she always went for comfort, for safety when the world was falling apart. Hugging an airplane was a damned poor substitute for a human being, but right now there was no human being she felt like hugging.

She flicked on all the lights as she moved through the hangar. Her bright blue Lockheed was sitting by the side doors, pretty and perky and ready to go. And so was she, damn it.

The telephone call to the weather services gave her a faint green light. And that was all she needed to hear. She rolled the plane out onto the tarmac herself, grunting and sweating but not unused to the manual labor. She had muscles in her long arms that didn't belong in Schiaparelli evening dresses, and she was proud of them. They served her in good stead that warm June night.

This time she left her flask behind, settling for what was on hand in the tiny kitchenette of the hangar. A can of tomato juice, a box of Ritz crackers, and a jar of Ovaltine. She didn't need food—when she went on a flight like this she seldom ate a thing, but she had enough sense to provide for all contingencies. Even Amelia Earhart sucked on tomato juice while she flew. She probably had to carry a case of it as she traveled through darkest Africa.

Angela wondered where AE was. Almost finished with her 'round-the-world trek, circling the globe at its widest point, with only someone else's husband for company. She'd left her own bullying spouse behind, and Angela wondered again why AE had ever married him. Why someone as independent and fiercely proud as AE allowed herself to be tied to some damned man.

Angela wasn't going to make a similar mistake. She almost had with Hal. Clancy was right, curse his black Irish soul. Guilt had a great deal to do with her need to complete Hal's flight. She hadn't loved him enough to go to bed with him, hadn't loved him enough to marry him. All she'd done was delay and delay, and Hal had died. For some stupid reason she thought completing his flight would make it up to him.

But now she had another, excellent reason. She was going to grind Clancy's record into the dust, and then she was deliberately going to seek out any records he still held and smash them, too. She was going to strip him of every honor until he was nothing but the washed-up pilot she knew him to be.

The Lockheed was gassed up, tuned up sweet and sassy and ready to go. The engine started with a quiet purr, the propellers spun smoothly, and Angela didn't even bother to go back and turn off the lights or relock the hangar. If someone wanted to come in and wreak havoc, they could be her guest. With any luck they'd destroy Clancy's precious Fokker.

She took off into the night with a soaring leap at the sky, and within moments the familiar, queer sort of peace and excitement all rolled into one settled around her. She loved night flying, with the sky purply blue around her, the lights far below, the rich velvet comfort of it all. She loved flying in the day, with the limitless blue sky, the bright glare of the sun, the sheer joy of being alive. Damn, she just loved flying, so much that for the first few hours heading northeast, she could forget how much she hated Jack Clancy.

She was somewhere over the province of Quebec when she started thinking about him again. For an hour or so she planned her revenge, imagining each flight she remem-

bered hearing of him make, fantasizing about smashing
each of those aging records. That image soon palled and the
Sperry autopilot was doing a splendid job, so Angela
scrunched down in her seat and thought about the next
forty-eight hours. She had more than enough gas to make
it to the small landing field west of St. John's. She'd arranged for the tanks of gas to be delivered more than six
months ago, certain that sooner or later she'd be making the
flight. It was money she couldn't afford to shell out at that
time, but she'd done it as a gesture of good faith to herself.
She could only hope that someone hadn't happened upon
her fuel tanks in the forsaken Canadian wilderness and
pumped them dry.

She'd cross that bridge when she came to it. She had every
expectation that things would go as she planned. She'd arrive late morning, catch a few hours sleep in the tiny hut and
then take off. Presuming the weather held. Presuming the
airdrome was in good condition. Presuming a lot of things.

She switched on the radio, flying low enough to pick up
a Canadian station. Fats Waller was singing about
"Honeysuckle Rose," something that wasn't heard too
often on WLS. Radio stations in the U.S. of A. tended to
keep their music tightly segregated, even if the genteel North
didn't go in for the hideous lynchings that had been plagu-
ing the South for the last few years. For a moment Angela
remembered Langston Howard and she muttered a small
curse under her breath for the waste, the criminal waste, of
talent and brains. And then she remembered Langston's
friend Clancy and she got mad all over again.

The sun was rising over the Atlantic, sending pale lavender streams of color soaring across the sky. If her compass
and maps were right, she should be heading up across New
Brunswick now, and Newfoundland wasn't too far beyond. She'd been there before, during the transatlantic hops
she'd flown herself and ridden as copilot for Hal. But this

was the first time she'd been alone, without friends, without a mechanic, without any support at all.

Newfoundland sure was inconveniently located for such a crucial spot on the map, she thought, taking the Lockheed off autopilot and banking into the gentle breeze, heading north. It was the closest point to Europe, sticking out into the middle of the icy cold Atlantic. It should have been an aviation center to rival Chicago, but transatlantic crossings were still too rare to merit even something as fancy as an airport. And she was deliberately avoiding the more populous areas, such as they were. She'd heard too many horror stories about weary pilots crashing into houses and wiping out bystanders to want to risk such a catastrophe. She had no qualms at all about risking her own life. But nobody else's.

It was late morning when she finally sighted the wide stretch of tundra that served as a makeshift landing field. The tiny hut was there; the tanks of fuel were stacked beside it. She could only hope they were still full or she was going to be seeing far more of this still half-frozen wasteland than she ever wanted.

In the end she fouled up. She was more tired than she'd realized and still wound up by hurt and anger and fierce determination. She came in too fast, the turf was wet with recent heavy rains, frozen beneath, and the Lockheed kissed the ground, settled and then began to slide.

She felt the plane go out of control with a curious calm. After all, she was on land. How much damage could she do?

The plane kept going, even with the engine turned off to prevent a deadly oil spill and fire, and Angela gripped the steering wheel, her feet pumping ineffectually on the rudders. And then the plane went down, nose first, into a bog, flinging Angela against the windshield, smashing her forehead and the glass. Her last thought before she lost consciousness was sheer astonishment that such a thing could happen on land. The warm, sticky blood began to pour down her face, and then everything went black.

CLANCY HAD HAD LONG NIGHTS in his life. He'd had miserable flights, flying into ice storms with pellets coating the windshield so that he couldn't see, fog so thick he couldn't even trust his own ears. He'd flown with empty gas tanks, birds smashing the windshield, winds tossing him up and down, engines on fire, wings broken, oil spewing over the propellers, every kind of aviation disaster you could think of. But never, never had he been in such a tight, furious panic as when he followed Angela Hogan on her crazy flight to Newfoundland.

He didn't even stop to consider that she might have simply gone for a ride to calm herself or flown to someplace sensible like New York to get away from her anger. When he finally managed to get to the airport in Tony's borrowed Hudson and found the hangar doors open, the lights blazing and the Lockheed gone, he'd known what had happened. And he'd almost broken his fist pounding with impotent fury on the side of his Fokker.

Parsons was with him, his thick glasses and heavy beard hiding whatever dismay he was feeling. It had taken one threat and a matter of moments before Parsons came up with copies of Angela's flight plan, including damnably vague directions for getting to her proposed jumping off place.

Clancy's only chance of stopping her was there. Even on a bad night he could fly faster and better than anyone on this earth, including Miss High-and-Mighty Hogan, and his twin-engine Fokker had the puny little Lockheed beat all to pieces. He was going to catch up with her in Newfoundland and stop her from making this crazy flight, stop her from killing herself if he had to wring her pretty little neck to do it.

He cursed her halfway across Canada. He cursed himself the rest of the way. If only he'd shown the sense that had first made him run. He should have stayed in New York, stayed as far away from her as he possibly could. She had the ability to get under his skin like no other woman he'd ever known and he should be smart enough to keep away from a dame like that. But he hadn't been showing much brains lately, so why break a losing streak? When he caught up with her, he was going to paddle her until she couldn't sit down for a week. And then he was doing to... Hell, he didn't know what he was going to do. He'd make it up as he went along.

He missed the tiny landing field twice, and the fuel in the Fokker was running low. He'd been in too much of a hurry to tank up completely before taking off after her, and he was paying the price for it now. Hell, it sure would be ironic if he fell into the ocean, out of gas, while he was trying to impress Angela with the foolishness of stunt flying.

The third time he flew over the field it was getting on into afternoon, and even the longest days of the year were shorter that far north. The sinking sun glinted off something down in a ravine, something bright blue, and he realized with sudden horror that that was Angela's plane. Stuck nose down in a bog.

His landing on the spongy ground was more along the lines of a controlled crash. He was out of the plane and racing along the muddy ground before the propellers stopped spinning, and under his breath he kept up a steady litany of curses and prayers, terrified of finding Angela's mangled, lifeless body still strapped in the cockpit of her plane.

He'd seen too many pilots die, men and women alike. He didn't know if he could stand to face another death. And not Angela's—please God, not his feisty Angel.

At least the plane hadn't burned. He yanked open the door, holding his breath, then releasing it with a gust of relief. She wasn't there. She'd managed to get out under her own steam—she couldn't be hurt that bad.

And then he saw the blood. It was everywhere, dried to a rusty brown, covering the leather seat, the instrument panel, the unopened can of tomato juice. He pulled his hand away from the door and realized it was covered with the same stuff, and the knot of fear tightened in his gut.

She wasn't lying in a sodden heap between the plane and the cabin. He forced himself to move with agonizing slowness, searching through the gathering gloom in case she'd somehow gotten disoriented and headed in the wrong direction. If she'd gone farther into the scrubby woods instead of toward the cabin, he'd have a hell of a time finding her. It was cold in the maritime provinces, even in June. And if she was still alive, frostbite wasn't going to help the situation.

He saw the blood on the door of the hut with mingled relief and panic. There was no sound inside, and it took him a moment to steel himself to open the door.

It was dark inside, lit only by the quickly fading daylight. She was lying on a narrow, sagging cot, a green army blanket wrapped around her. He could see her hair matted with dark blood; he could see the deathly pale of her face. He glanced around the room. There was a pot-bellied stove kicking out a feeble amount of heat and a clothesline strung across the tiny room with her clothes hanging from it. Slamming the door behind him, he stepped into the hut, walked directly into the fragile rope and pulled it down.

She sat up instantly, the green blanket clutched in front of her, her face blank and panicked. And then her eyes focused on him and she made a sound that was somewhere between a squeak and a snarl. "What the hell are you doing here?"

She'd cut her forehead, but somehow she'd managed to clean it up. Head bumps always bled like crazy, but her angry eyes looked clear and steady, her color was slightly pale but all right, and the hands clutching that stupid blanket in front of her looked strong and steady.

"I would have thought I'd at least be greeted with a little relief, not to mention gratitude," he drawled, stripping off his leather flight jacket and dumping it on the only other piece of furniture the hut offered, a tiny straight-backed chair that wouldn't hold his big frame for more than a minute. "You sure as hell made a mess of your landing, Red. How'd you think you were going to get out of here?"

"My radio still works. I was going to call for help. From anyone but you," she said.

"Why?"

That stopped her cold. "Because," she said finally.

"Because," he echoed. "Not good enough, Red. Did you think to bring any water? You haven't done the world's greatest job cleaning that cut on your head."

"I didn't have a mirror," she said frostily. "And there's plenty of water around. I took a damned bath in it when I fell out of the plane. Go get some of that if my face offends you."

"You fell out of the plane...."

"When I was trying to climb out," she explained with limited patience. "Why do you suppose I was trying to dry out my clothes?"

The significance of the clothes line began to register. He looked at her with renewed interest, realizing that she was naked, or damned close to it, underneath that scratchy wool blanket. "I'll get some water," he said, not bothering with his jacket. He suddenly felt quite warm. "You got any food in your plane besides the tomato juice?"

"I already ate the crackers," she said defiantly.

"Then it's lucky for me I brought some. Stay put."

"Where did you think I'd be going?"

"Watch your smart mouth, Angel," he said mildly, "or I'll take care of it for you." And he headed out into the gathering twilight.

It was going to be a cold night, he thought, humming under his breath. Angela wasn't going to want to share that blanket, and the few puny pieces of wood stacked outside the hut weren't going to go very far. He grabbed his emergency satchel from behind the cockpit, grinning to himself. He'd seen the look in her eyes when he'd mentioned food. Maybe this god-awful twenty-four hours was going to end more pleasantly than he'd ever imagined. But then, he'd been imagining a lot of pleasant things with Angela Hogan ever since he met her. He doubted she'd live up to the fantasies.

But he had every intention of finding out. He'd been a gentleman long enough. Angela Hogan wasn't going to stay alone beneath that blanket for very long. And when he was through with her, maybe then he'd be able to get her out of his system.

He was honest enough with himself to know that that was a feeble excuse. To know whether Angela Hogan was a sexual tigress or a shrinking violet had nothing to do with his ability to get clear of her. He'd never get clear of her, damn it. No matter how far or how fast he ran.

His mood wasn't quite as cheerful as he stepped back inside the cabin, a bucket of icy water in one hand, the satchel in the other. He looked over at Angela and stopped. He should have taken her clothes with him when he went out to the plane. She'd managed to pull on a pair of damp long johns, and she sat there in the bed, shivering, mistakenly thinking she was decently dressed. The damp cloth clung to her skin, outlining her with delicious exactitude, and her nipples were hard against the wet, chilly cloth. He allowed himself a small, satisfied smile before dropping down on the cot beside her, placing the satchel in her lap.

"What's this?" she said, deliberately ignoring the fact that the cot sagged ominously beneath his added weight.

"Emergency rations. Don't you carry something like this with you?" He unfastened it, pulling out chocolate bars, a flask, malted milk tablets and most precious of all, a tin of Nescafé.

Angela couldn't keep her distance any longer. "Coffee," she moaned. "God, Clancy, I could just kiss you."

"Be my guest."

Her wariness immediately returned. "Do you think we dare use the water?"

"I have every intention of risking it. At least I'll die happy. Lie down."

Her magnificent blue eyes took on a cold gleam. "Why?"

"So I can ravish you, of course. There's something about long johns that turns me into a lustful beast," he drawled, his irony disguising the fact that her long johns were having precisely that effect on him. "I have to clean that wound a little better. There's a first-aid kit in that package, too. I don't suppose you carry one of those with you, either."

"Sorry," she muttered, lying down with more obedience than she'd ever shown. "And I do have a first-aid kit. I just wasn't in any shape to look for it. The landing knocked me out for a bit."

"Damn," he muttered, peering into her eyes with clinical detachment. The pupils were even, appropriately dilated against the dimness of the hut. "How long were you out?"

"Not long. I don't think I've got a concussion." She winced as his fingers began to probe her scalp.

"What makes you the expert?"

"I've had concussions before in my life, Clancy. I'm a pilot, remember? I've had worse crashes than this one. If the ground hadn't been quite so slick, I would have been just fine."

"A good pilot takes all the ifs into account. You must have come in too fast."

She couldn't very well deny it. "Get your hands off me, Clancy. I've got a bump on the noggin and a bruised hip, and apart from that I'm just hunky-dory."

"You want to show me your hip?" he said, tipping some of the icy water into a tin cup and dampening a cloth in it.

"Dream on." She let out an anguished shriek as the ice water dripped down the front of her long johns. "Couldn't you have warmed that on the stove?"

"I wanted to make you suffer," he said, his gentle fingers at odds with his bantering tone as he cleaned away the dried blood. "You've got quite a lump there, kid. Bet you have a hell of a headache."

"It's terminal," she agreed, shivering.

"I happen to have salvation in the form of aspirin. You want to risk the water, or would you rather use the contents of my flask?"

She glared up at him. "I'm not touching a drop of hooch, thank you very much. I've sworn off it, anyway, and I'm certainly not going to change my mind when I'm stuck in this hut with you."

"Afraid you won't control your own lustful impulses, Angel?"

Her response was impressive, reminding him that she'd spent most of her adult life around pilots and mechanics, men not known for their euphemisms. "Go away, Clancy," she said, much more mildly. "I can take care of myself."

"So I noticed." He stood up, moving away from her, stretching his cramped body in the tiny confines of the hut. He'd just spent the last fourteen hours in the cockpit of his Fokker, and even that splendid aircraft had space limitations. "I'm going to check out the lay of the land. Are those gas tanks full?"

"They're mine!" she said fiercely.

"Honey, your plane isn't going anywhere for a while. If we're getting out of here, it's going to be in the *Angel*, and she's a little short of fuel."

"I'd rather walk."

He was getting a little tired of this. "I might just be tempted to let you do that. But I'm taking the fuel with me. Why don't you finish cleaning yourself up while I scrounge around? If you stop snapping at me, I might be persuaded to make dinner."

Her face was almost pathetic. "Dinner?" she said. "You mean, apart from the candy bars and the malted milk tablets?"

"I happen to have a can of beef stew with me," he said. "Tucked in the back of the Fokker for emergencies like this one. If you're nice to me, I'll share it with you."

Angela's eyes misted over. "Real food," she breathed. "Take me, I'm yours."

Clancy allowed himself a brief, wry grin. "I intend to." And he stepped back out into the darkening night.

# Chapter Sixteen

By the time Clancy had finished refueling his plane using the tedious hand pump, cleaned himself off in the icy stream and fetched the battered can of beef stew from the plane, he was in less than a charitable mood. When it came right down to it, he didn't really expect to get Angela Hogan out of those scratchy long johns anytime in the near future. It was probably best all around if they spent the night at opposite ends of the tiny hut, keeping their armed truce going. She was already mad enough at him for not volunteering the information about his record-setting Newfoundland-to-Havana run. When she found out what else he hadn't informed her about, she was going to be beyond livid. If she found herself seduced in the bargain, there was no telling to what lengths she might go.

No, he'd be a wiser man to keep his mind above his waist and remind himself what a stuck-up, coldhearted pain in the rear Angela was. Of course, that was a little hard to do when he stepped back into the cabin and found she'd managed to get most of the sticky blood out of her hair and comb it into a damnably seductive cloud around her pale face. She'd put some sticking plaster on her forehead, and it gave her a rakish look. Her lips were pale without her usual lipstick, her eyes dark and questioning, and even though the long underwear had dried in the heat of the wood stove, he could still see, and imagine all too vividly the feel of, her small, perfectly shaped breasts.

She looked at him with a nakedly hungry look on her face, and then he realized she was staring at the can in his hand. He shrugged, dismissing his disappointment. "Dinner for madame," he said with a flourish. "Got anything as useful as a can opener around here?"

"I thought you were Tom Swift, complete with every tool known to man," she countered, her earlier anger fading into light mockery.

He controlled his smutty response. "My trusty pocket knife will take care of it, I imagine." He glanced around the cabin. She'd rehung the clothesline neatly down the middle of the cabin, and on the floor was the blanket, folded neatly, clearly symbolizing his pallet for the night. "What's this?"

"I'll take the cot, you can have the blanket. Unless you'd rather switch?" It took someone who knew her intimately to recognize the anxiety beneath her cool voice. He knew her intimately.

"The blanket's fine," he said. "How come we have the Walls of Jericho? You've seen too many movies, Red. I'm not about to jump you without a direct invitation."

"And I'm sure you have enough sense not to hold your breath waiting for that remote eventuality," she said coolly. "I just thought we both might like a little privacy. I'm not used to sharing a bedroom with someone of the opposite sex."

"I am," Clancy said, deliberately provoking her as he set the opened can of stew on the stove. He reached up and felt the clothes, the gabardine trousers and cotton blouse, the leather flight jacket and long thick socks. With a gentle tug he pulled the clothesline down again, dropping the almost-dry clothes onto the floor. "I don't need privacy, I need something more comfortable than a thin wool blanket to lie on. Since you don't seem disposed to share your cot, I'm going to use your clothes for a mattress. Got any objections?"

She opened her mouth, clearly ready to state a few, then shut it again. "I'll argue with you after dinner," she said, eyeing the can.

"Smart move. It's never wise to bite the hand that feeds you before you've actually eaten."

"I'm a smart cookie," she said, her voice sounding oddly bleak.

They ate their meal companionably enough, considering the tension running through the room. Clancy sat crosslegged on the floor, leaning back against the narrow cot, Angela sat above him, her long legs curled under her, as they shared the can of beef stew, using the pen knife as an eating utensil. She smelled like flowers, he thought absently. How could a woman who'd flown for twelve hours, crash landed her plane, taken a dunking and been covered in blood still smell like flowers?

They split one candy bar, saving the second one for breakfast, and drank the instant coffee with an appreciation seldom felt for something they usually took for granted. Then Clancy lit two cigarettes, passing one to her, and they sat there in an oddly companionable silence, the faintly fragrant smoke swirling upward in a lazy spiral.

"I'm sorry I didn't tell you it was my record you were so intent on breaking," he said finally, the apology sounding harsh and forced even to his own ears. No wonder. He was a man who seldom apologized to anyone for anything. "You didn't happen to confide in me, you know. If you'd asked my opinion, even bothered to talk about it, I would have told you."

"It doesn't matter now," she said, stretching out on her stomach on the concave cot, rather like a sleek cat in baggy underwear. "It's just that I hate being lied to."

"I didn't lie, Red."

"I suppose you didn't. But I hate being spared things. I hate lies of omission, I hate being kept in the dark about things that I'd be much better off knowing and facing. I can't stand being spared things only to have them come up from behind me and knock me down when I least expect it." Her voice was a fierce undertone.

Clancy thought back to the situation, the people he'd left behind at the hangar and knew an uneasy settling in his gut. If she didn't like being kept in the dark about something as innocuous as this, how was she going to respond to what was going on under her nose?

"Okay, so I won't spare you," Clancy said, leaning forward and stubbing out his cigarette against the old iron stove. "Don't make the flight. It's a stupid risk for nothing."

"That's for me to decide, isn't it?" she asked coolly, not moving from her innocently tempting stretch on the cot.

He wanted to jump on her, shake some sense into her, do a lot more things to her. Instead he stood up, fighting his own temptation. "I'm going for a walk," he said, his voice cool and distant.

She glanced up at him. "There's an outhouse behind the shack."

"Did I ever strike you as a man who beat around the bush? If I wanted to use the can I'd say so. I'm going for a walk." Grabbing his leather jacket, he headed for the door.

"You want to leave me another cigarette?" she asked.

"Nope. I'll share my food, my booze and my candy bars with you. But I'm a bit more partial about my cigarettes." And he slammed out of the hut.

He shouldn't have turned so crabby, he told himself as he headed off across the semifrozen tundra. It was guilt, pure and simple, that made him that way. Not that Angela Hogan wasn't an infuriating human being. But she hadn't done anything but slither like Little Eva on that damnably narrow cot and remind him, without realizing it, what a liar he was. It was no wonder he was in a bad mood.

Of course he knew full well what was at the heart of that bad mood, along with guilt. He wasn't going to get Angela Hogan. He wasn't going to be able to unbutton all those tiny buttons and have his wicked way with her. He was going to have the worst night of his life, even worse than the previous night when he'd flown through the darkness, terrified that she'd crashed somewhere along the way. Tonight he'd have to lie on a pile of clothes on a damnably uncomfortable wood floor within inches of her, breathing in her flowery scent, listening to her breathe, the shift and rustle of her clothes as she turned over, the sighs and sleepy murmurings.

And he wasn't going to touch her. Because if he touched her, he'd take her. And if he took her, he wouldn't ever want to let go. If he made love to her, he'd fall in love with her. A simple, never-before equation that he couldn't risk.

He glanced over at the *Angel*, tanked up and ready to go. He could fly away from there, now, head for St. John's or an even bigger city and send someone after her. Hell, he could just keep going, as he should have done the first time he ran away from her.

At the very least he could sleep in his plane. It wouldn't be the first time he'd done so, and on colder nights than the fiftyish air surrounding them. He could do whatever he had to to keep his hands off her.

He lit a cigarette, noticing with absent wonder that his hands were trembling slightly. It wasn't that cold. They were trembling with the effort not to go in there and grab Angela and overcome all her resistance.

An oil lamp was burning through the small, smoked up window, sending a warm glow out into the eternal twilight. It was only a little past eight, but he was worn out. He hadn't slept in thirty-six hours. Maybe if he just sacked out, fate would take care of the problem.

She'd made his bed up carefully, folding her clothes evenly beneath the thin blanket. She was sitting cross-legged on that damnable cot, rubbing her arms against the chill of a room that was too warm and looking up at him out of wary eyes.

"I thought you were going to fly away and leave me here," she said.

"I considered it."

"Should we both fly out? It's not that dark...."

"No, but I'm too damned tired. I spent all last night in an airplane flying after you. And I'm not trusting my plane in anyone's hands, much less someone who's been conked on the noggin. We'll wait till daylight, till after I get some shut-eye."

She nodded. "I appreciate that. It's very kind of you—"

"It's not kind at all. I haven't a kind bone in my body," he snapped, sitting down on the rickety chair and pulling off his boots. "What're you going to use for a cover?"

"The room's warm enough."

"Then why are you rubbing your arms like you're at the North Pole?"

"I have a slight chill," she said defensively. "It'll pass."

He stripped off his jacket and hurled it at her with just a touch more force than necessary. "Take this and stop arguing. I need some sleep." And he dropped down on the makeshift mattress, cursing out his awkward nobility and sense of self-preservation.

The room lapsed into silence. She was still sitting on the cot, his jacket across her lap, not moving. "Do you want me to turn off the lantern?" she asked in a very small voice.

"Do what you please."

"I don't suppose you'd feel like sparing one more cigarette...?"

He sighed, a long-suffering sound. "The pack's in the jacket," he said. "You might as well hand me my flask while you're at it."

She climbed off the cot, stepping over him very carefully as she headed for the oil lamp that stood on the tiny table next to his flask. She blew it out, plunging the room into darkness, and it took a moment for his eyes to adjust. The bright orange flames of the wood stove danced behind the door, the midsummer twilight filtered in the one window with a ghostly charm. And every move she made was torment.

She held the flask out to him and he took it, his hand brushing hers. Her flesh was icy cold in the warm room and he knew a sudden panic. Maybe she was hurt more badly than she'd said. It would be just like her to cover up.

"Why are you so cold?" he demanded angrily, sitting up. "Have you been lying to me about your injuries?"

"I don't lie," she said stiffly, moving past him to stare out the window into the darkness. "I told you, I have a chill."

"Nerves," he said flatly.

"What have I got to be nervous of?" she demanded, not bothering to turn around.

"Not a damned thing," he replied. "Have a swig of the flask. It'll warm you up and put you to sleep in one fell swoop."

"What's in it, a magic potion?"

"Just hundred-and-fifty-proof rum, sister. It works wonders."

"No, thanks," she said distantly. "I've sworn off the stuff. It's too dangerous."

"I thought it was champagne that made your brain melt," he said, tipping the flask back for a long pull.

"No," she said in a voice so quiet he almost couldn't hear it. "It's you."

SHE SHOULDN'T HAVE SAID IT. She knew the moment the words were out of her mouth it was a major mistake, one of the worst in her life of major mistakes. She'd known from the grumpy expression on his handsome face, the stern set of his shoulders, that he was going to let her sleep alone on that cot. He had no intention of seducing her, and that noble resolve was putting him in a towering rage.

Unfortunately she wasn't any fonder of that resolve. She'd resigned herself to being overwhelmed, even overpowered, the future of her outdated innocence no longer in her control. She expected to be swept off her feet, and instead the notorious womanizer had chosen to be saintly.

She focused on the outline of Clancy's plane in the purple twilight. It was a beautiful plane, almost as pretty as her Lockheed. She'd only flown Fokkers a few times and they had handled beautifully. They were the right plane for a man like Clancy, large and powerful and swift, graceful and direct. Maybe he hadn't heard what she'd muttered beneath her breath.

She felt his hands on her shoulders, large, strong hands. "You want to repeat that?" His long fingers were stroking her shoulders, the curve beneath her collarbone, and a tiny shiver swept over her.

"I don't think that would be wise," she forced herself to say. "I'm going to bed." She turned, meaning to move past him to her cot, but he blocked her way.

He was very big in the semidarkness, bigger than she realized. He was no longer touching her, holding her there with the sheer size of him, and she was afraid to push past him, afraid to start it, knowing there'd be no going back once it happened.

And then it was no longer an issue. His dark, dreamy eyes caught hers, a steady promise, and his hand reached out and began to unbutton the tiny buttons that traveled down the front of the baggy long johns. He unbuttoned past her breasts, down to her waist and beyond. And she was shivering, despite the warmth of the room, despite the heat prickling beneath her skin.

He slid his other hand beneath her hair and pulled her face up to his, her mouth to his. It was a very gentle, almost experimental kiss, a tasting, teasing sort of kiss, his lips soft, damp, brushing against hers, nibbling gently. Her hands came up, almost of their own volition, and rested lightly on his shoulders, and she could feel the tension in his muscles, the heat and muscle, bone and sinew; and the reality of him made her shiver.

He kissed her eyelids, he kissed her cheekbones, he kissed her wounded forehead with the softness of a butterfly. He kissed her ears, her chin, her neck, as he pushed the clinging cotton material off her shoulders, down her arms.

"I don't think we should do this," she said in a whisper as he pulled the long johns down to her waist. She reached out and began to unfasten the buttons on his shirt.

"No, we shouldn't," he agreed, sliding the cloth off her hips, down her long legs, so that it pooled around her bare ankles. He put his arms around her waist, pulling her close against him, and dipped his head down to hers. "Want to stop?" he whispered against her lips.

"Yes," she said, and kissed him.

This was no gentle wooing. This wasn't like anything she'd seen in the movies. His mouth was hot, demanding, open against hers, and his tongue was touching hers. And she was kissing him back, no longer shy, no longer uncertain.

He swung her up in his arms, and the world spun crazily for a moment. And then she was on her back on the cot, and he was following her down, covering her with his large, strong body.

A second later the cot collapsed beneath them, tumbling them to the floor amid a welter of ripped canvas and splintered braces. She felt herself begin to shake, and she buried her face against Clancy's shoulder, clinging tightly as she tried to control herself.

"Red, are you all right?" he demanded fiercely, trying to pull away from her tight embrace. "Are you hurt?"

"I'm fine," she managed to choke out.

His eyes narrowed as he peered down at her in the darkness. "Are you laughing?"

"I can't help it," she said, giggling. "This never happens to Joan Crawford."

He supported himself on his elbows, his body still pressed intimately against hers, and his hands brushed the hair out of her face. "How many times do I have to tell you, Angel?" he said softly, "this isn't the movies. There isn't going to be some sweet fade out. You're naked, and I'm about to be. This is real."

She stopped laughing abruptly. "Clancy," she said in a very quiet voice, "don't hurt me."

He frowned. "You're a virgin, Red. The first time always hurts, at least a little."

"I'm not talking about my body, Clancy. I don't care what you do with that. I'm talking about me. Don't hurt me. I don't think I could bear it."

She had no idea what he was thinking. There wasn't really much he could say to her unexpected plea. She should never have asked. The moment she met him she knew he was going to hurt her. He was that kind of man. It was a waste of time to ask.

Then he grinned. "Honey, by the time I'm finished, you're going to care a great deal about what I do with your body. Trust me. Just lie back and I'll take care of everything." And he slid his hands down her body to cup her breasts.

She arched her back in surprised reaction. A moment later his mouth followed his hands, catching her breast and suckling it deep into his mouth. She murmured a strangled cry, half of protest, half of pleasure, and then it was all pleasure. Her hands reached out and cupped his head, holding him against her, as his other hand moved down, past her waist, between her legs with sudden daring.

She squirmed, trying to close her legs against him, but he was having none of it. "Either we're going to do this or we're not," he murmured, lifting his head and watching her out of hooded eyes.

She bit her lip. "Clancy," she said, her voice a helpless confession, "I'm frightened."

She should have hated his grin. Instead she fell in love with it. "Not my fearless Angel," he said, kissing her lips. "Not the woman who's won the Bendix Cup for flying across the country." He kissed her collarbone. "Not the woman who flew that Atlantic in record time." He kissed both breasts. "Not the woman who started her own airline and is holding her own against a creep like Charlie Olker." He kissed her lower belly. "Not the woman who's planning to beat the pants off me by flying from Newfoundland to Havana. That woman isn't afraid of anything or anybody, including something as warm and natural as making love." And he kissed her between the legs.

She shoved him away in shock. "Don't do that," she gasped. "That isn't warm and natural."

"Of course it is. You'll get used to it." But he moved up, his hand stroking down over her hip, moving between her legs again with deft sureness.

This time she didn't protest. She was still so astonished by his intimate kiss that she remained passive as he touched her, stroked her. And then suddenly she wasn't passive. Suddenly she was burning up, clutching at his shoulders as her hips arched off the pallet.

"That's right, Angel," he murmured in her ear. "That's what I want to see." He'd managed to shrug out of his shirt, and in the darkness she heard the rustle of clothing as he kicked out of his pants. She didn't have time to be frightened again. Things were burning out of control, her body was covered with a fine film of sweat and she was no longer content with waiting.

"Clancy," she said, her voice a strangled cry.

He loomed over her in the darkness, between her legs, and he seemed huge, frightening and out of reach, his strong legs between hers, heat and hardness pulsing at the very center of her.

"Just close your eyes and think of flying," Clancy muttered beneath his breath, and he surged forward, into her, his hands catching her legs and pulling them around him.

She shrieked, a small, anguished sound of pain and surprise as she felt his tearing invasion. He held very still against her, his hard chest against her softness, his head cradled against her neck.

She wanted to shove him again. She wanted to scream at him, to hit him, and she reached up her hands to push him.

He caught those hands. "Keep still," he said in a harsh voice.

"I don't like this. Get up, Clancy. Go away."

He laughed, and she could feel his laughter over and inside her body. "Too late now, Red. Calm down, you'll get used to it."

"I don't want to." She could feel the tension vibrating through his body, the body that was capturing her, imprisoning her against the rough wood floor of the hut, the body that was impaling her and owning her. The pain was gone now, but she was too upset to notice.

"Tough." He let out a shaky sigh, lifting his head to look down at her.

"Hurry up and get this over with, Clancy," she said between clenched teeth. "It was a terrible mistake and I just want—" His mouth stopped hers midspate, covering hers, silencing her. She realized vaguely that she was no longer pushing him away. That she was clutching him fiercely. That she was kissing him back with a fiery determination and that the pain and embarrassment were fading into oblivion.

He began to pull away and for a moment she panicked, afraid he really was going to leave her. She clutched at him, but he sank back into her, driving deep. His hands were beneath her hips, pulling her tighter, and she moaned deep in her throat as he did it again, moving away, then sinking back in. That tension was building again, that burning need she couldn't understand, and all she knew was that she wanted more of him, more and more and more. They were both slippery with sweat, she was trembling, he was trembling, and her anger was no longer even a memory as she strove for something she couldn't even understand.

He reached his hand between their bodies and touched her. She clutched him as her body exploded into something beyond her comprehension. She could feel his body as he arched against her, rigid, as lost as she was. Countless moments later he collapsed in her arms, pulling her tightly against him with an instinctive, protective gesture. And she let him, burying her tear-stained face against his chest, wanting to hide from a world that had suddenly gone off kilter.

A little while later he rolled off her, and while she was glad to be able to breath again, she missed the dark possessiveness. He ended up on his own, softer pallet, and for one horrible moment Angela wondered whether he was simply going to go to sleep. She'd heard enough of her friends complain about their husbands, their boyfriends, that she had to be prepared for just such a deflating outcome.

She'd misjudged Clancy. She was just about to curl up in a miserable ball when he grabbed her arm and hauled her over against him. "Come here," he said, tucking her up against him. She could smell the leather from her flight

jacket beneath them, a familiar, comforting smell mixed
with all the strange scents that filled the room. "Those
aren't tears, are they, Red?" he said, touching her face
lightly. "I didn't think you knew how to cry."

"I don't," she said in a wobbly voice, keeping her damp
face against his shoulder.

He sighed, and his hands on her were almost frighten-
ingly gentle. The Clancy she knew wasn't a gentle man.
"Time for the next lesson."

"Next lesson?" she whispered, her body still trembling in
belated reaction.

"Lesson number one was to enjoy it. Still don't care what
I do to your body?"

"Shut up, Clancy."

He laughed. "Lesson number two is you always smoke
after sex." He reached for his pack of cigarettes, shook one
out of the pack and lit it, all without letting go of her. He
took a drag, then set it between her lips.

"What if you make love to someone who doesn't
smoke?" she asked when he'd taken the cigarette back to his
own mouth. She'd never shared a cigarette with someone
before. Somehow it seemed almost more intimate than what
they'd shared with their bodies.

"I pick my women carefully."

"Do you?"

He must have heard the doubt in her voice. He cupped her
head, tilting her face up so that he could look her in the eyes.
She met his gaze unflinchingly, knowing her face was still
streaked with tears, knowing what had just passed between
them was still rocking her world on its foundations.

"Sometimes," he said in a soft voice. "And sometimes I
make a mistake."

She didn't move. "Is that what I am? A mistake?"

He nodded gravely. "A very big one. For a man like me,
you're the worst thing that could happen. I don't like

strings, I don't want to be tied down, I don't want to get married or have children or a cottage in the country. And most of all, I don't want to fall in love with you.''

Each word was a knife in her heart. ''Who's asking you?'' she said, pride keeping her voice steady.

''Red,'' he said, leaning over her and cupping her face in his hand, ''The damnable thing is, I'm afraid it's too late. I already have.'' And he kissed her again before she could say what she wanted to so desperately, before she could say what she knew he didn't want to hear.

Before she could tell him she was in love with him, too.

# Chapter Seventeen

Considering the fact that Clancy woke her up in the middle of the night to make love to her again, this time with a little less delicacy and an even greater degree of pleasure, and considering the fact that they were lying entwined on a welter of clothing with a scratchy wool blanket as their only covering, and considering that she'd never before slept with a man, and certainly not on top of a leather jacket with its zipper digging into her bare back, considering all those things, Angela slept surprisingly well.

When she woke, her cheek was pressed against Clancy's chest, his arm was around her, securing her against him, and her hair spread out around them. And her poor bruised forehead ached like crazy. Along with certain, less public parts of her body.

She stretched, very carefully, not wanting to wake the man sleeping so peacefully beside her, and to her amazement she found she had a lazy grin on her face. Not that it should have amazed her. After the night that had just passed, any woman would be smiling.

What did surprise her was the depth of her own passion. She hadn't thought she'd been missing much, particularly since, though she'd loved Hal Ramsey dearly, she hadn't really been interested in making their relationship more physical. She'd always assumed she'd marry and that sex would be a minor part of that relationship, something men liked to do and something that gave women babies whether they wanted them or not. She hadn't realized quite how powerful an experience it could be. Or how it would tie her even closer to a man who wanted no ties at all.

She sighed, snuggling against him and placed a gentle hand on his chest, on the dark matting of hair that never failed to fascinate her. His body was so different from hers, hard where she was soft, dark where she was pale, hair-covered where she was smooth. She found his arms particularly fascinating, the strength beneath the wiry muscles, the bone and sinew and heat of them. Her fingertips traced the subtle bulge of muscle with renewed wonderment, brushing against his inner arm.

"Are you by any chance making a pass at me?" Clancy hadn't even moved. She had had no idea he was awake and she yanked her hand away with sudden embarrassment.

He didn't let it get far. "Because if you are, I'm all in favor of it," he said, catching her wrist and pulling her hand back. "Look at me, Red."

She couldn't bring herself to do it. Burying her face against his shoulder, she shook her head. He caught her under the chin, forcing her face upward. "That's better," he murmured, brushing the hair away from her bandaged forehead. She concentrated on some point past his shoulder, unable to meet his searching gaze. "How's the head this morning?"

"A little sore."

"How's the rest of you? Probably in the same condition."

That shocked her enough to look at him, to meet the tender amusement in his dark eyes. He kissed her then, a brief, still-hungry kiss before pulling away. "Enough of that. You need a little time to recover before we move on to advanced aerobatics. You find the candy bar while I make up the fire. A night like the last one makes a man hungry."

They shared the candy bar with solemn grace, and then, to Angela's amazement, Clancy brought her some bathing water to heat on the stove and then made himself scarce. She never would have thought he'd have that much sensitivity, but then, she was discovering a great many things about the man she'd been fool enough to fall in love with.

The Nescafé tasted even better an hour later when they shared the one tin cup Clancy had in his life-saving emergency pack. He'd burned the wrecked cot, and she'd watched the canvas and wood go into the old stove with mixed emotions from her spot in the corner, curled up under the blanket. Clancy's earlier good cheer had faded, leaving him thoughtful, almost brooding, and his mood infected Angela. She sat there, huddled against the lingering morning chill of the cabin, wondering when he was going to tell her this couldn't go on.

His words surprised her. "Don't make this flight, Angel," he said, turning from the stove and sitting cross-legged on the floor, too far away for her to touch.

"I have to."

He spent time searching for his crumpled pack of cigarettes, pulling them out and lighting two. He passed her one, his eyes not meeting her. "This run's a damn-fool thing," he said, finally. "There are some nasty cross winds as you fly over the gulf, the Atlantic's very unforgiving, and who the hell would want to fly from Newfoundland to Havana?"

"Newfoundland's the first stop for any transatlantic flight," she said calmly enough. "You know that as well as I do—you've flown more of them. From here most people will want to get to New York as fast as they possibly can. I intend to see how fast that is. And a goodly number of them will be interested in flying on to Havana or Chicago or

Florida. Hal picked Havana as his destination, and I'm following his route. I don't have the faintest idea why he chose Havana—"

"I do," Clancy said, stretching his long legs out in front of him, his booted feet almost touching the brass fender on the old iron stove. "He did it because of me."

"What are you talking about? He barely knew you."

"What makes you think that?"

"Because he never talked about you, and he'd tell me everything."

"Not quite everything, it seems. Ramsey and I used to be good friends. And rivals. For everything from poker games to the Bendix Trophy to women. I flew the Newfoundland-to-Cuba run on a dare. The best casinos are in Havana, the hottest night clubs, the prettiest women. The moment I did it, Hal decided he had to beat my time."

"Hal wasn't into anything that petty," she said flatly. "I don't believe you."

He tilted his head to look up at her. "Don't you?" he asked mildly enough.

Angela looked uncertain. "Why did he take so long to try it? We'd been working together for two years before he died. Why wait so long if he was simply out to beat you?"

"He'd tried it twice before. Didn't he tell you that?"

She nodded reluctantly. "I'd forgotten. So you mean he died all because of a stupid rivalry?"

Clancy shrugged. "I don't know why he died. I only know why he flew."

Silence reigned in the cabin for a while, but it had lost its comfortable quality. Clancy had sat up to stub his cigarette out on the stove when Angela finally spoke.

"That explains a lot of things," she said, her voice flat, hiding the pain slicing through her. "Is that why you came after me? Does this rivalry over flights and women extend even beyond the grave?"

He stared at her and she didn't know if her eyes were playing tricks on her or if he really turned pale. "Believe what you like," he said finally, rising and heading for the door.

She was aching for a denial, aching for a declaration of love. "Are you telling me that's not why you came to Chicago? Why you came to work for me?"

"I came to see Sparks. And, yes, I was interested in seeing the woman who'd finally managed to clip Hal's wings. And I needed work and a place for my plane. Just like I told you."

"I don't believe you."

"No," he said after a long moment, his expression bleak. "I don't imagine you do. I'm going to check just how much damage you inflicted on your plane. Get your things together while I'm gone. When I come back, I'm flying you back to Chicago and dumping you, and with any luck I'll never have to see you again."

He slammed the door behind him. She couldn't rid herself of the totally illogical suspicion that she'd hurt him deeply. Clancy wasn't a man who suffered from hurt feelings. He'd told her he loved her last night, but it was probably all part of his set patter for getting a reluctant woman into bed. She hadn't been reluctant and the memory of her behavior flooded her cheeks with shame.

She pulled herself to her feet and walked over to the door. The sun was glinting off Clancy's Fokker, and she stared at it, fighting off the hurt and misery that flooded her.

Suddenly she was running across the tundra, yanking the chocks away from the wheels and vaulting into the cockpit before her better judgment could take over. He'd filled the tanks—with her fuel, curse him—and the engine purred into life instantly.

He was going to kill her, she thought distantly as she taxied across the frozen earth. When he finally managed to run her to ground, he was going to strangle her with his bare hands, not just for stranding him in the half-frozen wastes of Newfoundland, but for daring to set her Philistine hands on his beloved plane. He didn't let anyone touch the controls of his Fokker, and he was already in a towering rage with her.

She half expected him to chase her down the wide expanse as she began to lift off, but there was no sign of him. She allowed herself a sudden panic that he might have run into trouble with her plane, fallen and hurt himself, and then she dismissed the notion. She'd never known anyone as adept at taking care of himself as Jack Clancy. He'd be just fine until Sparks and Will arrived with spare parts and more food.

The flight west passed with surprising speed. For the first few hours she was too entranced with the Fokker to brood, and then for the next few hours she was too caught up in brooding to be bored. She was flying over Toronto when she began to have very real misgivings about abandoning Clancy, and by the time she landed on the familiar runway at Hogan Air Transport she was half wishing she'd crashed rather than face Clancy's awesome rage.

At least she wouldn't have to do any such thing for at least twenty-four hours. She wasn't sure which would be worse—to send Sparks and Will back in the Fokker, thereby letting another alien pair of hands contaminate Clancy's beloved plane, or send them in the Percival. Probably the Fokker would be best—if she had any luck at all, he'd simply fly away, out of her life.

She managed a tricky landing on the darkened runway, wondering what Clancy would do if she'd damaged his precious baby. The place was deserted—Sparks was probably at Tony's, and Parsons would be holed up in his rooms again. She brought the plane as close to the hangar as she dared. She doubted she'd be strong enough to roll her into the hangar—the smaller Percival was almost more than she could manage alone, but at least it was a clear night. Not even a drop of rain would sully the beautiful red paint.

She unlocked the hangar, stepped inside and sat down by the radio set. The darkness and stillness all around her, the utter loneliness set in. Secure that no one would catch her, she did what she hadn't allowed herself to do during the endless, private hours of flight. She started crying.

Through her tears she heard it, and for a moment she was certain her ears were playing tricks on her. In the distance she could hear the sound of a plane, one that sounded uncannily like her Lockheed. But her Lockheed was nose-down in a swamp in Newfoundland, not anywhere near Chicago.

The plane came closer, closer, and Angela's insides knotted as her tears swiftly stopped. She knew the sound of her Wasp engine better than anyone. That was her plane circling the field, heading downward. And there could be no one on board but a very angry man.

She considered racing to the Packard and driving away, hiding from his awesome wrath. But her landing on the empty tarmac had been tricky enough for someone who knew it like the back of her hand. With the Fokker now taking up an important section of it, Clancy would need the lights. If she ran away now, she was risking his life.

She stood up, straightening her shoulders and lifting her head as she moved over to the landing lights. She threw the switches, then stepped out of the hangar and waited for judgment day.

She allowed her eyes an anxious moment to survey her beautiful blue bird. She was mud-splattered but undaunted. Clancy must have managed to patch her together in record time. And he'd managed to outfly Angela, coming in within minutes of her in a small plane with a single, less-powerful engine.

She leaned against the door of the hangar and waited for him, too proud to run away. He was out of the plane before the propeller had stopped spinning, and he didn't bother setting the blocks underneath the wheels. His first glance was for the Fokker, and she fully expected him to check it out before he dealt with her.

But that look was only a brief glance, ascertaining it was in one piece. And then his dark eyes focused on her from across the runway, and he started toward her, his big, strong body vibrating with menace.

HE WAS GOING TO KILL HER. He'd decided that quite calmly when he heard her take off in the *Angel*. He'd been tempted when she accused him of sleeping with her for the sake of an outgrown boyhood rivalry. He'd been almost certain of it when she'd given him that cold touch-me-not look. But when he heard his precious plane take off with her at the helm, he knew for certain he was going to strangle her.

He'd never let anyone touch his Fokker, not since he bought her off an old Dutchman in the Andes. It was a matter of superstition to him, almost as important as the tarnished silver cross he wore around his neck. All pilots, he knew, had superstitions, beliefs that kept them alive in the hairiest of circumstances, and it was suicide to tamper with them. Suicide for Miss Angela Hogan.

She was leaning against the metal siding of the hangar, waiting for him. His heart didn't skip a beat as he recognized the foolish bravery of her stance, his pulses didn't throb as he noticed her long legs, legs that had been wrapped around him less than twelve hours ago. He looked at her mouth, a mouth he'd kissed into hungry response. And he looked in her eyes, the eyes that drilled so coldly into him right before she'd stolen his plane, and he saw the traces of tears.

He stopped in front of her, his hands clenched in fists to keep from punching her. She glanced at those fists and winced faintly, but she didn't move, ready to take her punishment like a man. He asked the most important question first.

"Is she all right?"

Angela didn't pretend to misunderstand. "Of course she is. I know how to fly, Clancy. She rode like a dream."

"Like hell you know how to fly. I got an hour-later start and I'm here within minutes of you, in a damaged plane with less power. Explain that?" His voice was sharp, the words bitten off.

She shrugged. "I guess you're a better pilot than I am."

"Damned straight. What about you?"

She blinked at him, momentarily confused. "What about me?"

"Are you all right?" He couldn't keep himself from asking. She was pale, exhausted, the bandage dark against her forehead, and she looked on the verge of collapse. She wasn't going to collapse in his arms, nosiree. She was just lucky he hadn't decked her.

"Fine," she said, her voice a mere thread of sound. And she began to crumple.

He caught her before she fell, cursing under his breath as he hoisted her into his arms. For all her long legs, she didn't weigh much more than a bird. He told himself he should dump her back on the tarmac, but then, she really wasn't much of a burden. It wouldn't kill him to at least get her settled someplace comfortable. Loosen her clothing.

"Put me down, Clancy," she muttered, batting against him with weak, ineffectual hands as he carried her through the darkened hangar.

"Shut up, Red," he said, ignoring her. She felt deceptively frail, but he knew all too well the strength in her long limbs, the power in her razor-sharp tongue. She kept squirming, and finally he had enough of it, dropping her down on her feet and shoving her against the nearest wall.

He didn't know what he'd planned to do, but whatever it was, it vanished with the look in her eyes and the feel of her body. He pressed her against the wall and kissed her, a harsh, punishing sort of kiss, one of despair and goodbye, half expecting her to slap him, to push him away.

Instead she flung her arms around his neck and kissed him back, her desperation equalling his, her hands on his shirt, pulling it apart as he shoved her leather jacket off her shoulders and onto the floor. He'd reached the waistband of her pants when they both froze.

A moment later the hangar was flooded with light. Clancy immediately shoved her behind him, ignoring the fact that his shirt was half off. "What's going on?" Sparks demanded. "Is that you, Clancy?"

Thank God for Sparks's diminishing eyesight, Clancy thought weakly. "Yeah," he said, stalling for time as he felt Angela pull her disarrayed clothes back around her.

"Is Angie with you?"

"Yeah," Clancy said again, hoping Sparks wouldn't see that his belt was unbuckled.

"Where the hell have you two been?" Sparks exploded.

Angela stepped out from behind Clancy, and her voice sounded almost normal. "Newfoundland," she replied. "What's happened?"

"Oh, nothing. Sam Watson's taken his business from Charlie Olker and wants to sign a contract with you, but, hey, that shouldn't get in the way of you two having a little fun," Sparks said bitterly.

"What?" Angie shrieked. "He's Charlie's biggest customer. Not only that, he influences most of the other businesses in the area. If he signs with us, the others will."

"I've had a few phone calls," Sparks agreed wryly.

"But why? I thought he said he'd never hire a woman."

"I think he's relaxing his prejudices. For one thing, Olker's been overcharging him like crazy. For another, Robert Bellamy was caught by the FAA for flying drunk. Olker's on probation, Bellamy's grounded and people are grumbling like mad."

"I bet it's because of Clancy," she said, her voice giving nothing away.

"That might have something to do with it, but Sam Watson's no fool. He knows that no pilot's going to stay around forever, particularly someone with Clancy's reputation. Chances are Clancy'll be gone tomorrow, and Watson knows that. No, he's hiring you, honey. And we're going to make a go of it."

Clancy didn't move. For the first time in his life he wanted to smash his old friend into a pulp as he stood there calmly planning Angie's future and dismissing Clancy's part in it. "True enough," Clancy drawled. "As a matter of fact, I'll be out of here sooner than you think. Just long enough for Red to find another pilot, and then I'm gone."

"That suits me," Sparks said, the gloves off.

"I thought it might," Clancy drawled.

"What are you two talking about?" Angela demanded.

"You'll figure it out. Ask Sparks."

"I am," she said mutinously. "Right now."

Before Sparks could reply, another figure appeared in the hangar door, the familiar, stooped figure of Will Parsons. "Hells bells, what is this, a convention?" Clancy demanded.

"I was with Sparks. Am I the only one here who's got his priorities straight? I was checking the Lockheed for damage while you two were squabbling," he said in an aggrieved tone.

"How bad is she?" Angela immediately focused on the only controllable thing in a world gone mad.

"Nothing a little tender loving care won't fix. Who else is here?"

"Just us chickens," Clancy drawled. "Why?"

"I thought I saw someone lurking around the back of the hangar. Maybe I'll just go and check." Parsons turned around.

"Do that," Clancy suggested. "Why don't you take Angela home, Sparks? She's dead on her feet. I have a few things to take care of around here."

Sparks didn't need a second invitation. Like a perfect little gentleman he took Angela's arm and herded her over to the door. She went willingly enough, too weary to argue, to even look back at him when Clancy finally realized what was bothering him.

"Hey, Sparks," he called out. "You didn't spill any gas, did you?"

"Not recently. Why?"

"I thought I smelled some. Maybe it's my imagination."

Sparks paused, releasing Angela, and his busy eyebrows knotted in worry. "There shouldn't be any. Will and I have been working outside, and we've had the windows open. There shouldn't be anything left."

Angela suddenly stiffened, all her weariness vanishing. "I can smell it, too," she said sharply. "And it's not just a spill. I smell fire."

"Angie . . ." Sparks began, but she was already running across the nearly empty hangar, straight toward Clancy, a stunned expression on her face. A moment later, the west wall exploded in a sheet of flames.

## Chapter Eighteen

Clancy saw her running toward him, and he knew his first real moments of panic. He met her midway, spinning her around. "Get out of here, Red," he shouted.

Higher priorities suddenly reasserted themselves. "The planes!" she cried. "We've got to get the planes out."

Sparks was already on the move, sliding the hangar doors fully open to the night air. "Get out!" Clancy yelled again, but she was beyond listening, already behind the tail of the Percival and shoving. A second later Clancy joined her, then Sparks, and within moments the Percival was rolling out into the night, away from the inferno.

"Now the Avian," Angela said, starting back when Clancy grabbed her and yanked her away.

"Let it burn. It's not worth that much."

"The hell I will!" she screamed at him, tugging futilely.

"Then let Sparks and Parsons get it."

"I haven't seen Parsons," Sparks called as he dove back into the billowing smoke.

"I'm going after my plane," she shrieked, hitting at Clancy. "I won't let this happen, I won't—"

He silenced her quite effectively with a right cross to her stubborn little chin. She collapsed onto the tarmac, and he took just enough time to drag her farther away from the blazing hangar before heading after Sparks.

It was a damnably close call. The steel walls were buckling with the force of the heat, and Sparks was choking, on his knees, the smaller Avian almost at the hangar door. Clancy dragged his old friend out first, dumping him beside Angela's prone body, and then he went after the plane.

By the time he managed to roll her out onto the tarmac, the fire engines had arrived, along with half the sparsely populated neighborhood. Someone had wrapped a blanket around Angela, another person was checking on Sparks. It took Clancy a moment to realize it was Parsons crouched over Angela.

"Where the hell were you?" Clancy demanded, towering over them. Angela was still out but beginning to stir. Will was fussing over her like a mother lion.

"I don't like fires," he said flatly, glaring up at Clancy. Whether he liked them or not, he'd come a bit too close for comfort. Part of his beard was singed off and he'd lost his thick glasses in the fray. Clancy stared down into a face he'd hoped he wouldn't recognize and his anger hardened.

"Did you happen to start this one? Was that mysterious figure you saw some convenient scapegoat?"

"Why would I burn down the hangar?"

"Hell, don't ask me? Why would you take this job in the first place?"

With all the noise and commotion going on around them, there was a sudden silence between the two men. One of understanding and wariness. "You should be able to guess that."

"You think it was one of your old friends torching the place?" Clancy asked coolly.

"In a manner of speaking. It looked like Olker."

"Damn," Clancy muttered, moving away. After a brief conversation with the policeman he moved back just in time to see Angela's blue eyes flutter open groggily.

He squatted down beside her. Parsons had her half on his lap. If it had been anyone else, Clancy would have flattened him.

"What—what happened?" Angela murmured dazedly. "Is that you, Will?"

"It's me," he said, casting a warning glance up at Clancy. "The fire company's here and the blaze is under control. There's only so much damage you can do to a metal building, even one that's been torched, and it looks like they got to it fast enough."

"Torched? Someone did this deliberately?" She struggled to sit up, staring at the smoldering flames still licking the sides of the air hangar.

"Charlie Olker," Clancy said. "Or so Will thinks."

She shook her head, then groaned at the obvious pain. "But why...?"

"You beat him," Clancy said flatly. "My guess is he's a sore loser."

Her eyes focused on him for a moment, then narrowed. "You hit, me," she said. "You creep, you bully, you—"

"Shut your mouth, Red," he said dispassionately, "or I'll shut it for you."

To his amazement she did subside. "At least I've got insurance," she said in a feeble tone.

"That's the spirit." Clancy rose to his full height, afraid if he stayed closer he'd pull her into his arms and to hell with everyone watching. "Constance must have picked up the Packard while you were gone. I'll find a phone and ask her to come get you. You need a decent night's rest. You've got a lot of work ahead of you."

Parsons cleared his throat. "She's not home."

Angela stared up at him. "Where is she?"

Parsons didn't look any too happy. "She's gone to California."

"I must have gotten hit harder than I thought," Angela said, struggling to her feet.

"You heard me. She's left for California. She thinks she's going to become a movie star."

"That's crazy. She doesn't know anyone out there, she doesn't have any money...."

"Afraid you're wrong on both counts. She didn't go out alone. She went with your Cousin Clement."

Angela sat back down again, hard, on the tarmac, and Clancy could see the stricken expression on her face. "Sparks'll take you home," he said gently.

"I don't think Sparks is in any shape to take anyone anywhere," Parsons said, glancing over at the stretcher where they'd loaded his sturdy frame.

Angela struggled back to her feet and hurried to his side. "Sparks, are you all right?"

"Sure thing, honey," he managed to speak in a faint croak. "I just swallowed a bit too much smoke. I'll be fine."

"Let me come with you," she said, but the ambulance workers waved her away.

"We've already got one fireman down with smoke inhalation. Whatever they used to start this fire is a nasty one," a red-faced Irishman said. "You stay put, little missy. This one's a tough old buzzard. He'll be back on the streets in a day or two."

"Just the rest I needed," Sparks croaked, waving a weak hand at her before being carted off.

"I think I'm going crazy," she murmured brokenly. She turned to look at Clancy, and he could feel it, the tightening in his gut, the wrenching in his heart, the almost-overpowering urge to take her in his arms and tell her everything was going to be all right.

But he knew too well her night wasn't over yet. He had the suspicion that more unpleasant discoveries were yet to come, ones he couldn't shield her from.

When he didn't make any move toward her, she lifted her head as if to say, to hell with you, and instead turned her attention on the uniformed man approaching them.

"Captain Stark," she greeted him wearily.

The police officer kept his face averted from Parsons. "How are you doing, Angela?"

"As well as can be expected."

He patted her awkwardly on the shoulder, with the clumsy affection of an old family friend. "Well, we've got some good news. The fire chief says they've got the blaze under control, and the damage isn't nearly as bad as it seems. And we picked up Olker a few blocks away, running like crazy. Cheap son of a gun. If he'd hired a torch to do the job right, he might have gotten away with it."

Angela pushed her hair out of her face. "I can't say I'm not glad he's such a tightwad."

"One problem though, Angie," Stark continued, still not looking at Parsons. "He's singing like a bird. He's going to cause as much trouble as he can before he's put away."

Her face creased in confusion. "What kind of trouble could he cause me?"

"Yes, Captain," Parsons spoke up suddenly in his raspy, wrecked voice. "What kind of trouble could he cause?"

"The kind that I can't fix, old friend. You better get out of here and fast, before I have to put out a warrant." He turned away, focusing on Clancy. "You'll see Angie home safely?"

"If she'll let me."

"What the hell is going on here?" Angela's voice rose in a wail of despair. "And no, I won't go anywhere with you, Clancy, not if my life depended on it."

"One of my men will see you home, then."

"What are you talking about? What's Parsons done? Won't someone explain anything to me?"

"Good night, Angie," Captain Stark said gently. "We'll talk about this tomorrow."

She turned and directed all her anger at Clancy. "What's going on around here? You're behind this, aren't you?"

He raised his hands in a gesture of surrender. "Why don't you ask your mechanic?"

"I believe I'll do just that." She turned on him, that fierce expression on her face. "What's going on here? What have you done that Captain Stark could issue an arrest warrant? Why did he call you 'old friend'? For that matter, why did you know what Constance has done?"

Parsons's shoulders hunched in defeat. "The statute of limitations hasn't run out for flying in bootleg whiskey," he said flatly. "There's also a little matter of insurance fraud."

Angela held herself very still, peering into Parsons's unprotected face, looking, for the first time, past the beard, the scars, the gray hair and the ruined voice. And the expression on her face was so nakedly painful that Clancy wanted to turn away.

"Frank?" she said, her voice equally hoarse as she recognized her father for the first time.

He made no move toward her. "Yes," he said simply.

"Who died with Goldie? There were three bodies found in the boarding house. Goldie, Mrs. McCarthy and a man, supposedly you. Who was it? Did you kill someone and leave him there to take your place?"

Frank flinched. "I don't know who he was. Goldie always had her little...diversions. Constance knew about them, but you didn't. We figured you didn't need to know."

"Constance recognized you?"

"Yes."

She turned and stared at Clancy. "And you knew?"

"I guessed."

"And you didn't say anything?"

"It wasn't any of my business."

"No," she said after a long moment, "my life is none of your business." She turned back to stare at her father. "You heard Stark, you better get out of here if you don't want to land in the calaboose. You've got some back pay coming."

"I don't want your money, daughter."

"Don't call me that!" Her voice rose drastically, then she managed a tight smile. "Besides, I kept this place going with your blood money. You might at least benefit a bit from it."

"You don't owe me anything."

"You can say that again," she said fiercely. "Goodbye, Frank. I didn't get a chance to tell you that the first time around, while I was fool enough to mourn you. At least this time I won't even shed a tear. For either of you." And she turned and walked away, her back straight and slim.

The two men watched her go in sudden kinship. "You need a ride somewhere, Hogan?" Clancy asked finally. "I want to go check on Sparks at the hospital, but I could drop you at the train."

"The name's Parsons now," Angela's father said. "Might as well keep it that way. And I think I'll hang around here a bit longer."

"Why?"

"I don't want to leave until I make sure the Lockheed's in perfect shape. I know Angela well enough to know she's going to make that flight the moment she possibly can, and there's not another mechanic I trust as much as I trust myself. I figure I'd better make myself scarce by tomorrow morning, but I've got a few hours until then. I'm going to do what I can with her plane."

Clancy didn't move. "Need a hand?"

Parsons nodded. "I could always use one. We work well together, Clancy. If life had been a little kinder, maybe we could have been friends."

"Life isn't kind."

"No, it's not. Do you love my daughter, Clancy?"

"I don't believe in marriage."

"I didn't ask if you were planning on marrying her. I asked if you love her."

"Yes."

Parsons shook his head, but there was a glimmer of a smile in his damaged eyes. "Then maybe there's hope for her after all. Let's see how badly the tools were damaged."

"I think the power's out."

"Simple enough. Point the Fokker at the Lockheed and turn on the lights."

"And then my plane won't start."

"So you'll be stuck here. Best thing for both of you. Are you game?"

Clancy looked at the old man who'd caused so much trouble, and he thought of his daughter who was wreaking just as much havoc in his own life. "I'm game, old man," he said. "And I've got tools in the Fokker."

CONSTANCE HAD CLEARED everything out, all her clothes, her makeup and every interesting piece of jewelry Angela had ever owned. The place was a shambles—her departure must have been last minute—and the sink was full of dirty dishes. Angela moved through the place dispiritedly. It was after midnight, the end of an endless day, and still she couldn't cry.

The phone rang and she rushed to it, hoping someone would offer her some succor, some hope. Hoping, for some irrational reason, that it might be Clancy. But it was Clement's wife, Eleanor, haranguing Angela over her slut of a sister and her faithless cousin, and Angela set the phone back down in the cradle very quietly.

She ran a bath, practically falling into it. She smelled of smoke, she still had blood in her hair from her crash landing and her body still bore the imprint of Clancy's possession. She tried not to look at her reflection when she brushed her teeth, but she couldn't help it. Without the bandage, her forehead looked gashed but healing, her eyes huge and wounded. A small bruise adorned her chin where Clancy had knocked her out. At least she didn't have to look at the rest of her body. She didn't know whether her sore back came from flying twenty-some hours within the last forty-eight, from her rough landing or from lying on a pile of leather flight jackets with Clancy on top of her—and she didn't care. She found a couple of aspirin, swallowed them and crawled all alone into her empty bed in her empty house.

Her first thought when she awoke was that she hadn't slept long enough. It was early dawn—the sky was lightening past the window with its threadbare curtains, and birds were singing. Why shouldn't they sing? she thought, not moving. They didn't have a family who betrayed them, a man who didn't know what love was. They didn't even need a plane to fly. They could just spread their wings and soar. While she was earthbound and miserable.

She sat up, groggy, and stared at the mess around her. For the first time she noticed the note scribbled in Max Factor's Passion Fruit Red on the huge mirror. "Wish me luck, Sis," Constance had scrawled with her usual self-assurance. Not a word of regret, of apology. Of guilt.

Just like their mutual father. Angela had no idea why he'd taken the job she'd offered. She had to give him credit—he'd turned it down at first. He knew exactly who she was when she'd shown up in that shanty town, and it hadn't been AE's Lockheed adorning the wall of his shack. It had been hers.

He probably loved her in his own feckless way. But that wasn't good enough. Nor was Clancy's hit-or-miss affection. Love 'em and leave 'em was still his code. She knew perfectly well he would be gone when she arrived back at the hangar to survey the damage. And she knew she should count her blessings.

At least Constance hadn't taken the Packard when she'd stripped the house of everything valuable. The radio was gone, so Angela couldn't catch up with the news, but she decided it was just as well. With her luck, they would have played Bunny Berigan singing "I Can't Get Started." Or even worse, "Harbor Lights."

She moved aimlessly enough, running a comb very carefully through her hair, watching out for her tender scalp. All her clothes had been dumped on the floor, but she couldn't quite summon the energy to drag out the ironing board. She simply pulled on a sundress in deference to the burgeoning heat, a silly, feminine thing that she usually wouldn't be caught dead in. It was the only thing that didn't require ironing, and she was almost completely oblivious to the fact that it was outrageously flattering.

She arrived at the hospital by ten o'clock, determined to check on Sparks, only to be informed that he'd already been released.

"But he was just brought in a few hours ago," she insisted, incensed at such cavalier treatment.

"No, ma'am. He was admitted night before last with smoke inhalation. He was released yesterday afternoon."

"What day is this?" she demanded urgently.

"July 3, 1937. Are you all right, ma'am? Maybe you ought to be here yourself."

"I'm fine," she said dazedly. "I just lost a day."

All the better, she thought, driving toward the hangar. By now, Clancy and Will—no, Frank—would be well-and-truly gone. She'd never have to see them again, she could start to put her life back in order. And things would be easier without Constance around. Her sister was extravagant and her meager salary at Woolworths never covered even the basic necessities, much less things like the gasoline she used or the food she ate. One could live much more cheaply than two, Angela informed herself. And at least she wouldn't have to worry about her sister anymore. She already knew the worst had befallen her.

She was half-tempted to stop for a newspaper on her way to the hangar, then reconsidered it. It would only have bad news. Nothing good would have happened in the last few days since she'd taken off for Newfoundland so precipitously. Except that Amelia Earhart was due to finish her historic 'round-the-world trip, and right then Angela wasn't sure if she could summon up enough generosity of spirit to be happy for her. AE wasn't the sort to inspire jealousy, but Angela would have been envious of a saint like Eleanor Roosevelt in her current mood.

Sparks's roadster was parked outside the hangar. The steel walls were scorched but still standing, and in the heat of summer, the smell of smoke still hung heavy in the air. Two of the planes were out on the tarmac, the Percival and the Avian. Clancy's Fokker was gone, but that was nothing more than she expected, Angela told herself, squashing down the shaft of pain that threatened to engulf her.

The cavernous confines of the hangar were dark. Sparks was sitting in her office, sifting through damp papers, but he looked up with real relief when she appeared. "You're a sight for sore eyes," he said. "In more ways than one. How're you doing, kid?"

"Fine, I guess. How are you? I went to the hospital first thing but they told me they'd already kicked you out." She sank down in the chair opposite him, then jumped up, brushing the water from her sundress.

"Can't keep an old scoundrel like me down for long."

"Why is it so dark here?"

"Electricity's still out. They promised to get it up and running by this afternoon. Phone's working, though. You've already had a bunch of calls. You were right. Once people heard that Sam Watson was signing on with you, the others began following suit. Not that they had much choice, with Olker in jail."

"Exactly where he belongs," she said firmly.

"You got other messages. Some woman named Eleanor keeps calling and screeching. I usually hang up on her."

"That's probably our best bet."

"And someone named Langston Howard called and asked whether the job offer was still open. That wasn't who I think it was, was it?"

"He's a very good pilot."

"He's also colored."

"Tell you what, Sparks. You call up Sam Watson and tell him he's going to get the best damned air-freight service with the best damned pilots, and some of those pilots are going to be women, and some are going to be black, and some of them may even be Republicans. But they'll all be the best pilots there are, and if he's got any objections, he can stuff 'em."

Sparks chuckled. "I know Sam Watson well enough to say he won't care if the pilot's got polka dots, as long as he does the job. You sure like asking for trouble, don't you?"

"We need a new pilot, don't we?"

"Yes," said Sparks, "we need a new pilot."

"We need a new mechanic, too, don't we?"

Sparks nodded. "He's gone. Left late last night."

"I suppose you knew who he was, too?" she said wearily.

"We all guessed, Angie. We just figured you didn't want to see it."

"Maybe I didn't. Why'd he wait so long to leave? Captain Stark warned him he'd come after him with a warrant if he didn't disappear."

"He had something he wanted to finish."

"What's that?"

"He and Clancy spent the last thirty-six hours going over the Lockheed with a fine-tooth comb. He said for me to tell you she's as ready as she's ever going to be. You can make your flight, Angie. If you're still so set on it."

"He did that? For me?"

"They both did. Guess your dad thought he owed you."

"What about Clancy. What did he owe me?"

Sparks looked uncomfortable. "You'd know that better than me, kid. So what's it gonna be? You still going to make that flight?"

She glanced over at the Lockheed, still shrouded in shadows. "I don't know, Sparks. Sometimes I don't think I know my own mind at all. I'll have to think about it."

"You do that. For what it's worth, I don't want you to do it. We don't want to lose another woman pilot."

A sudden trickle of dread slid down her back bone. "What're you talking about?"

"Haven't you seen the papers? Listened to the radio?"

"Constance took the radio. What's happened?"

"Amelia Earhart went down yesterday. There's been no trace of her or Noonan anywhere. She's gone, Angie."

"She couldn't be! Haven't they got people searching . . . ?"

"Of course they have. And the papers are reporting every single false lead. But you and I know better. Every pilot knows better. AE's gone, Angie. I don't want to lose you, too."

She stumbled away from him, out into the hangar, the final blow in a series of crushing blows weighing down on her. She stared at her plane, at the larger, shadowy form behind it. And then her eyes began to focus in the darkness.

"What's that?"

Sparks had come up behind her. "The Fokker."

"What's it doing here?"

"You made an arrangement with Clancy—"

"Where's Clancy? I thought he was gone."

"Not yet. I imagine he's trying to get some shut-eye at Tony's. He's been up with your father, working on the Lockheed day and night. I don't think he's slept at all in the last forty-eight hours. He's— Where're you going, Angie?"

"We got enough fuel for the Lockheed?" she called without even looking back.

"The fire didn't touch the tanks, thank heavens. Why?"

"Gas up the Lockheed, Sparks," she said firmly. "I'm going flying."

## Chapter Nineteen

Tony's was as still and deserted as any bar at eleven in the morning. In the yard out back, Angela could hear the cheerful voices of Tony's large family, the splash of water as they washed the Hudson. She moved swiftly and silently up the rickety outside stairs. The last thing she wanted was Tony's and Rosa's smothering attention. She had too many things to do in too short a time.

His room was dark and still, only the sound of the ticking alarm clock and the distant sound of laughter marring the quiet. He'd pulled the shades, and she could see his still form smack in the middle of the double bed.

For a moment she panicked. What if he didn't want her? What if she didn't really want him? And then she resolutely shoved those misgivings from her mind. She couldn't afford to waver during the next few days. She had to set her mind on her goals and carry through with them. And Clancy was one of those goals, even though she couldn't even begin to think, to hope, to what extent.

She slipped off the sundress, leaving it in a pool on the living room floor. She took off her tap pants and camisole, her garter belt and stockings, even the ribbon that held her hair back. And she tiptoed over to the bed, lifted the cover and very carefully slid in beside his sleeping form. He was wearing rumpled linen boxer shorts and nothing else, and the silver cross lay across his chest, against the light covering of hair. She moved infinitesimally closer, not wanting to wake him up, only wanting to take some warmth, some comfort from him.

"Did anyone ever tell you," he said in a conversational voice, not moving, not even opening his eyes, "that it's the man who makes the advances?"

"No." Her voice was uncertain.

He turned his head to look at her. "Good. If they do, don't listen." And he pulled her into his arms.

By the time she put her sundress on again, it was late afternoon. Clancy lay in bed, the sheet draped haphazardly around him as he smoked a cigarette, and his expression was troubled.

"Give me a drag of that," she said, kneeling over him on the bed and reaching for it.

"That's a pretty dangerous position," he murmured.

"I like danger." She took a deep drag, then scampered off the bed again before he could grab her.

"I know you do." His voice was thoughtful, and she held her breath, waiting for the inevitable.

"You're going, aren't you?" he said in a flat voice.

She sat down on the faded slipper chair and began rolling one stocking up her long leg, checking to make sure the seam was straight. "Tonight. Sparks tells me the Lockheed's in mint condition, thanks to you and . . . my father."

"Thanks to us," he said morosely.

She hooked the stocking on her garter, then slid the other one on. Standing up, she stepped into her flat shoes, busying herself with the little feminine details she usually ignored. And then she looked across at him. "Don't ask me not to go," she said. "It's something I have to do. For Hal. For AE. And for me. I can't let it beat me as it beat them. I have to end beating it."

"What's 'it'?"

"Come on, Clancy, you're a pilot." Her voice was intense with emotion. "You know as well as I do. 'It' is fear, the elements, fate, life, if you will. All the things we battle just to survive. It's wresting victory out of the jaws of defeat. It's spitting in the eye of disaster. It's not giving in when something seems a little too dangerous, a little too scary, a little too different." She stopped, suddenly self-conscious.

"Well, you sure as hell don't shy away from things that are a little too different," he said finally. "I hear Langston's going to take up on your job offer."

"Someone has to take your place," she said calmly.

"That's right, someone does. All right, Angel. I won't tell you not to go. I won't even ask you. I'll just ask you one thing."

"What's that?"

"Be careful. If you crash in a plane I worked on, trying to break my record, then it'll look pretty bad for me. And you know how important my reputation is to me."

She just grinned at him. "That's all you care about, is it? Not whether I make it or not? Not whether I survive or not?"

"What do you think?"

"You won't be here when I get back, will you?"

"No," he said. "I've never made any secret of how I feel about being tied down. I'll never marry you, Red. You're better off without me."

"Am I?" Her voice was calm and steady.

"Yes." There wasn't the slightest bit of hesitation in his voice. "Good luck, Angel. I'll be seeing you."

She looked at him, sitting in the bed they'd just shared, watching her walk out of his life. She wasn't a woman who gave up on anything she wanted, be it an air-freight business, be it a record-breaking flight. She certainly wasn't going to give up when she'd found the only man she would ever love. "Yes, Clancy," she said, her voice definite. "You will."

HER LANDING IN NEWFOUNDLAND was perfect, judging the half-frozen turf to perfection. Sometime in the last three days someone had refilled the fuel barrels, and she knew she had one more thing to thank Clancy for. He may have hated like hell to have her make this trip, but he wasn't going to let that stop him from helping her any way he could.

She'd had the sense to bring a bed roll, and she slept surprisingly well in the cabin she'd shared with Clancy a few short days ago. She woke up early, before dawn, and had her tanks refueled and ready to go by sunrise. She took off just as the early-morning fog was lifting, soaring into the sky over the bitter blue North Atlantic, her nerves steady, her heart light.

This was her last great flight, and she knew it. And while that knowledge was bittersweet, it was also liberating. Never again would she face an endless, dangerous flight, trying to break someone else's record. Never again would she put her life on the line for something the world would probably find ultimately pointless. Only she knew how important it was.

Besides, it wasn't a solo flight. Hal was with her part of the way, pointing out dangers, keeping her alert. AE came along for the ride, with her usual no-nonsense good cheer. There were others, far too many others, who'd died over the last few years. She wasn't going to be one of them. And neither was Clancy.

She first heard the noise over Connecticut. She was following the coast, secure that if she did happen to go down, land might be close enough for a rescue, when the insidious little pinging sound invaded her imaginary conversation with the legendary Harriet Quimby, who'd died in the mud flats of Dorchester Bay almost twenty-five years ago. She immediately stopped her daydreaming, concentrating on the sound.

Why hadn't she learned more about the mechanics of a plane? She knew a fair amount, but nothing compared to fellow aviatrices like England's Amy Johnson or America's Jackie Cochrane. The time when she should have been learning how to take a Wasp engine apart and put it back together again had been spent shuffling paperwork, trying to keep her business alive, trying to keep enough money coming in to pay for fuel for her planes.

It sounded innocuous enough, that high-pitched little twang, but she simply couldn't be certain. The only thing she did know was that she wasn't going to stop short of the Teterboro Airport unless she crashed. That was her scheduled refueling stop, and that was where she was going. Her only acceptable alternative was the sea.

She didn't know what kind of mechanics Teterboro had, but she could only hope they'd know their stuff. It was a small New Jersey airport, but a great many people had used it, including AE for her landmark flight to Europe. Surely someone would be on hand who understood Wasp engines.

By now the newspapers would have been alerted to her flight, though whether they cared or not made no difference. She dropped down to ten thousand feet to see whether she could pick up any of the local radio stations, but all she got was static, and she didn't dare go lower. Not if her engine might decide to conk out and she had to glide to a dubious safety.

Teterboro was in sight, a small, well-marked landing strip with far too many towns surrounding it, when the smoke started pouring out of her engine. Angela took one look, used a word Clancy would have deplored and promptly began heading downward, ignoring the streams of smoke obscuring her vision.

She landed safely enough, rolling to a stop as the smoke continued to pour from the engine. By the time she'd unfastened her belt and jumped down from her plane, a white-suited mechanic already had his head stuck inside the engine.

"Do you think it's something major?" she asked the man, a note of desperation in her voice. "I'm already two hours ahead of the old record, and I'm not going to give up now."

"Just a faulty oil ring," the mechanic said, lifting his head and looking at her out of her father's eyes. The beard was gone, the hair was short and the obscuring glasses had vanished. "Go on in and talk to the reporters, use the can and then get back here. She'll be ready for you."

"How'd you know I was here?" she demanded.

"The papers have been full of nothing else."

"Frank . . ." she said, her voice hoarse with sudden emotion.

"Go on with you, now." He waved her away with a huge wrench. "We've both got work to do if you're going to trounce Clancy." And he stuck his head back in the engine compartment, forestalling further conversation.

The small airport was swarming with the press, from the papers, radio and newsreels. She took long enough to use the bathroom and wipe some of the grime off her face, then gave them five minutes, answering their shouted questions. It seemed the world needed her flight as much as she did. Amelia Earhart's loss was devastating—Angela was giving them new hope.

The engine cover was down. Frank was waiting by the door when she ran back across the tarmac, waving goodbye to the reporters.

"Everything's all set," he said, opening the door for her. "I put some coffee and sandwiches in there. There's talk of a storm around the Carolinas—keep an eye out and fly over it if you have to."

She stopped, looking into the face of the man who'd taught her to fly, who'd taught her to love planes, who'd taught her about duplicity and despair. "Isn't this a little dangerous for you? Aren't the police still on the lookout for you?"

"It's not the police I'm worried about. Capone's men have long memories, and no one gets away with stiffing their boss, even ten years after the fact."

She squashed down the sudden pang of fear. "Too bad you didn't realize that sooner. Maybe Goldie and Mrs. McCarthy would still be alive."

"You think I don't realize that? If I stood here and told you just how sorry I was you wouldn't get to Havana for three days. I can't make up for what I've done. I can't change it. All I can do is pick up the pieces and go on."

"Will I ever see you again?"

"Who knows? I'm going to disappear for a while, but things might cool off eventually. At least I was around long enough to help my daughter wow 'em. Go on and make me proud, Angie."

She nodded, starting into the plane, and then she jumped back out and flung her arms around her father, hugging him fiercely.

He was frailer than she'd realized, older and thinner. "I love you, Pops," she said, her voice raw.

"I love you too, daughter. Now go get 'em."

Her takeoff was smooth as silk, considering she was flying blind, her eyes filled with tears. She wiped them away as best she could with the leather sleeve of her flight jacket, not daring to look down at the hordes of reporters waving her goodbye, afraid she'd get one last glimpse of the man in the white coveralls, the man she'd probably never see again.

It wasn't until she reached a cruising altitude that her eyes cleared, her mind cleared and she started to set her mind back on course. And then she saw the cross.

It was hanging from the cabin light, off to one side, in the same position of honor it held when Clancy flew. She reached out for it with trembling hands, knowing even before she touched it that it was Clancy's, not a duplicate. Clancy's luck was with her. Nothing could stop her now.

Not the storms over the Carolinas, with gale-force winds buffeting her around. Not the iced-up wings as she climbed too high to try to avoid the weather. Not the flock of sea-gulls who committed suicide against her windscreen when she flew too low, obscuring her vision with feathers and blood and bone.

Not exhaustion, second thoughts, worries about her father and sister, who were following their own self-destructive paths. Not even thoughts about Clancy could slow her down.

By the time she set out over the Gulf, the weather was clear and beautiful, matching her mood. She let her heart do the flying, letting her brain rest, and as she flew she started singing. And it was only natural that she sang "I Can't Get Started."

She switched over into "The Man I Love," her voice low and torchy, more Libby Holman than Helen Morgan, and then she switched into "Ain't Misbehaving" for a few bars, ending with a *Snow White* medley. And then she lapsed into silence, letting the quiet, safe hum of her engine carry her along through the fleecy white clouds into the apricot sunset.

Cuba was sitting in the middle of the Caribbean, a green gem amidst the blue water. She was four and a half hours ahead of Clancy's record, but the knowledge brought her only passing satisfaction. For the last few hundred miles, all she could think of was finishing her flight and what she'd find when she landed.

At the end her plane set down at Havana with the grace and delicacy of a ballerina, rolling to a stop just short of the astonishing crowd that had gathered to cheer her arrival. She was practically pulled from the plane, hoisted on strangers' shoulders as the warm Cuban night settled around her and the cheers rang in her ears. It was all she could do to hold on to Clancy's cross as she was jostled this way and that, and by the time the police calmed the crowd down and extricated Angela from her over-enthusiastic admirers, she was feeling battered and bruised and at the point of tears.

She was bustled into a private waiting room, with the American ambassador and his wife and half the diplomatic staff there to greet her. "You'll be staying with us at the embassy, of course, my dear," the ambassador was saying. "The president has offered to put you up at the palace, but we thought you'd be happier with your own people. There's a small reception set for late tonight, and then a breakfast with some of the local bigwigs, a luncheon—"

"She's staying with me." Clancy's beloved voice broke through the ambassador's high-handed dictates.

Angela turned, the cross still clutched in her hand, relief washing over her. "Clancy," she breathed, as unaccustomed tears filled her eyes. "You're here."

"Where else would I be, Red? I knew you'd make it."

The ambassador's stout wife and three young diplomats were in her way. She plowed through them as if she were the *Normandie*, flinging herself into Clancy's waiting arms. "You flew without your cross," she said.

"I figured you needed it more than me. Come on, Red. Let's get out of here."

"But Miss Hogan . . ." the ambassador protested.

"Sorry," Clancy said, wrapping his arms around Angela and herding her out the door. "But my fiancée's not finished flying for the night."

She didn't know quite how Clancy managed it, but within moments they were outside, alone in the warm night, away from prying eyes and loud voices, the starry Cuban sky hanging over them like a velvet canopy.

"Did you mean what you said?" she asked.

"About what?"

"About me being your fiancée. I thought you said you wouldn't marry. That marriage and white picket fences and children weren't for you?"

"We can live at the hangar, and the kids can be pilots," he said easily.

"Who says I'm going to agree? I don't recall a proper proposal."

Clancy raised an eyebrow. "Don't tell me you're going to seduce me like you did yesterday and then fob off your responsibility? We're getting married, Red, as soon as I can find a preacher. There are churches on just about every corner in Havana—we'll just head for the nearest one."

"The ambassador probably could have arranged it."

"Yeah, but do you want to spend your wedding night surrounded by bureaucrats?"

"I want to spend my wedding night surrounded by you."

He kissed her then, hard, and then continued moving across the tarmac. "I'm going to fly DC-3s out of O'Hare Airport," he said in a conversational tone. "Langston's moving out with his wife and kids next week, and you were right about Sam Watson. He says as long as you fulfill the contract, he doesn't care if a cocker spaniel flies the planes."

She stopped short, her hand on his arm. "I don't trust this, Clancy."

"Don't trust what?"

"I don't trust being this happy. What if a war comes? What if you die?"

He stopped then, pulling her into his arms with surprising gentleness. "Listen, Red, if a war comes, I'll fight in it. Probably fly bombers and risk getting my butt shot off. But I'll come home to you. I know that deep in my heart, just as I knew I'd better be here waiting for you when you landed. Trust me, Angel. We're going to live happily ever after." And leaning down, he kissed her, a deep, passionate kiss that was a promise of a lifetime.

The night was clear and beautiful around them, and tomorrow would be a perfect day for flying. And Angela, twining her arms around his neck, believed that promise, as the warm Cuban night closed down around them, wrapping them in love and warmth and safety. The future was theirs.

# HARLEQUIN
## *American Romance*®

## ABOUT THE AUTHOR

Anne Stuart says that she has been making up stories since she was a toddler, and writing them down as soon as she learned how to do so. She's been published in many genres, including suspense, Regency, and gothics, as well as romance. Anne has also won numerous awards.

When asked how she came to write *Angels Wings*, Anne said that she chose the time period because, ''Despite the Depression and the oncoming war, the 1930s seemed to me to be a fascinating time, a microcosm of all that was good and bad about America, and I wanted to immerse my characters, and my readers, in that intense decade. From my earliest years I had two forms of much-needed escapism—romantic novels and old movies. For the first time I've been able to combine my love of both those forms in *Angels Wings* when I set out to write a 1930s adventure movie in the form of a novel. I only hope people enjoy reading it as much as I enjoyed writing it.''

Anne lives in Vermont with her husband and their son and daughter.

# ARE YOU A ROMANCE READER WITH OPINIONS?

Openings are currently available for participation in the 1990-1991 Romance Reader Panel. We are looking for new participants from all regions of the country and from all age ranges.

If selected, you will be polled once a month by mail to comment on new books you have recently purchased, and may occasionally be asked for more in-depth comments. Individual responses will remain confidential and all postage will be prepaid.

Regular purchasers of one favorite series, as well as those who sample a variety of lines each month, are needed, so fill out and return this application today for more detailed information.

1. Please indicate the romance series you purchase from regularly at retail outlets.

| Harlequin | Silhouette | |
|---|---|---|
| 1. ☐ Romance | 6. ☐ Romance | 10. ☐ Bantam Loveswept |
| 2. ☐ Presents | 7. ☐ Special Edition | 11. ☐ Other _____ |
| 3. ☐ American Romance | 8. ☐ Intimate Moments | |
| 4. ☐ Temptation | 9. ☐ Desire | |
| 5. ☐ Superromance | | |

2. Number of romance paperbacks you purchase new in an average month:

12.1 ☐ 1 to 4     .2 ☐ 5 to 10     .3 ☐ 11 to 15     .4 ☐ 16+

3. Do you currently buy romance     13.1 ☐ yes     .2 ☐ no
series through direct mail?

If yes, please indicate series: _____

                                          (14,15)     (16,17)

4. Date of birth: ____ / ____ / ____
              (Month)    (Day)    (Year)
              18,19      20,21     22,23

5. Please print:
Name: _____
Address: _____
City: _____ State: _____ Zip: _____
Telephone No. (optional): ( )

MAIL TO: Attention: Romance Reader Panel
               Consumer Opinion Center
               P.O. Box 1395
               Buffalo, NY 14240-9961

**Office Use Only**    ARDK

# Take 4 bestselling love stories FREE

## Plus get a FREE surprise gift!

# PASSPORT TO ROMANCE
# SWEEPSTAKES RULES

1. **HOW TO ENTER:** To enter, you must be the age of majority and complete the official entry form, or print your name, address, telephone number and age on a plain piece of paper and mail to: Passport to Romance, P.O. Box 9056, Buffalo, NY 14269-9056. No mechanically reproduced entries accepted.

2. All entries must be received by the CONTEST CLOSING DATE, DECEMBER 31, 1990 TO BE ELIGIBLE.

3. **THE PRIZES:** There will be ten (10) Grand Prizes awarded, each consisting of a choice of a trip for two people from the following list:
   i)   London, England (approximate retail value $5,050 U.S.)
   ii)  England, Wales and Scotland (approximate retail value $6,400 U.S.)
   iii) Carribean Cruise (approximate retail value $7,300 U.S.)
   iv)  Hawaii (approximate retail value $9,550 U.S.)
   v)   Greek Island Cruise in the Mediterranean (approximate retail value $12,250 U.S.)
   vi)  France (approximate retail value $7,300 U.S.)

4. Any winner may choose to receive any trip or a cash alternative prize of $5,000.00 U.S. in lieu of the trip.

5. **GENERAL RULES:** Odds of winning depend on number of entries received.

6. A random draw will be made by Nielsen Promotion Services, an independent judging organization, on January 29, 1991, in Buffalo, NY, at 11:30 a.m. from all eligible entries received on or before the Contest Closing Date.

7. Any Canadian entrants who are selected must correctly answer a time-limited, mathematical skill-testing question in order to win.

8. Full contest rules may be obtained by sending a stamped, self-addressed envelope to: "Passport to Romance Rules Request", P.O. Box 9998, Saint John, New Brunswick, Canada E2L 4N4.

9. Quebec residents may submit any litigation respecting the conduct and awarding of a prize in this contest to the Régie des loteries et courses du Québec.

10. Payment of taxes other than air and hotel taxes is the sole responsibility of the winner.

11. Void where prohibited by law.

## COUPON BOOKLET OFFER TERMS

To receive your Free travel-savings coupon booklets, complete the mail-in Offer Certificate on the preceeding page, including the necessary number of proofs-of-purchase, and mail to: Passport to Romance, P.O. Box 9057, Buffalo, NY 14269-9057. The coupon booklets include savings on travel-related products such as car rentals, hotels, cruises, flowers and restaurants. Some restrictions apply. The offer is available in the United States and Canada. Requests must be postmarked by January 25, 1991. Only proofs-of-purchase from specially marked "Passport to Romance" Harlequin® or Silhouette® books will be accepted. The offer certificate must accompany your request and may not be reproduced in any manner. Offer void where prohibited or restricted by law. LIMIT FOUR COUPON BOOKLETS PER NAME, FAMILY, GROUP, ORGANIZATION OR ADDRESS. Please allow up to 8 weeks after receipt of order for shipment. Enter quickly as quantities are limited. Unfulfilled mail-in offer requests will receive free Harlequin® or Silhouette® books (not previously available in retail stores), in quantities equal to the number of proofs-of-purchase required for Levels One to Four, as applicable.

# OFFICIAL SWEEPSTAKES ENTRY FORM

Complete and return this Entry Form immediately—the more Entry Forms you submit, the better your chances of winning!
- Entry Forms must be received by **December 31, 1990**
- A random draw will take place on **January 29, 1991**
- Trip must be taken by **December 31, 1991**

3-HAR-2-SW

YES, I want to win a PASSPORT TO ROMANCE vacation for two! I understand the prize includes round-trip air fare, accommodation and a daily spending allowance.

Name_____

Address_____

City_____ State _____ Zip_____

Telephone Number_____ Age_____

Return entries to: **PASSPORT TO ROMANCE**, P.O. Box 9056, Buffalo, NY 14269-9056

© 1990 Harlequin Enterprises Limited

## COUPON BOOKLET/OFFER CERTIFICATE

| Item | LEVEL ONE Booklet 1 | LEVEL TWO Booklet 1 & 2 | LEVEL THREE Booklet 1, 2 & 3 | LEVEL FOUR Booklet 1, 2, 3 & 4 |
|---|---|---|---|---|
| Booklet 1 = $100+ | $100+ | $100+ | $100+ | $100+ |
| Booklet 2 = $200+ | | $200+ | $200+ | $200+ |
| Booklet 3 = $300+ | | | $300+ | $300+ |
| Booklet 4 = $400+ | _____ | _____ | _____ | $400+ |
| Approximate Total Value of Savings | $100+ | $300+ | $600+ | $1,000+ |
| # of Proofs of Purchase Required | 4 | 6 | 12 | 18 |
| Check One | _____ | _____ | _____ | _____ |

Name_____

Address_____

City_____ State _____ Zip_____

Return Offer Certificates to: **PASSPORT TO ROMANCE**, P.O. Box 9057 Buffalo, NY 14269-9057

Requests must be postmarked by **January 25, 1991**

---

## ONE PROOF OF PURCHASE

3-HAR-2

To collect your free coupon booklet you must include the necessary number of proofs-of-purchase with a properly completed Offer Certificate

© 1990 Harlequin Enterprises Limited

See previous page for details